D0411649

Run Out The Guns

By the same author

PASSAGE TO JAMAICA

Run Out The Guns

Robert Challoner

CENTURY PUBLISHING
LONDON

First published in Great Britain in 1984 by
Century Publishing Co. Ltd,
Portland House, 12–13 Greek Street,
London W1V 5LE

ISBN 0 7126 0465 0

Printed in Great Britain by
St Edmundsbury Press, Bury St Edmunds, Suffolk
and bound by Butler & Tanner Ltd, Frome, Somerset

For my amphibious friend Peter Young

The ship is a Square-rigged Three-master. Here are the names of the sails and masts that provide her motive power:

1 Fore royal sail
2 Fore topgallant sail
3 Fore topsail
4 Foresail
5 Spritsails
6 Main royal sail
7 Main topgallant sail
8 Main topsail
9 Mainsail
10 Mizzen royal sail
11 Mizzen topgallant sail
12 Mizzen topsail
13 Mizzen sail
14 Fore topgallant mast
15 Fore topmast
16 Foremast
17 Main topgallant mast (v. Chap. 5)
18 Main topmast
19 Mainmast
20 Mizzen mast, with its topmast & topgallant mast

Facts and Figures about the ship
18 – 16 pounder cannons. 130 officers and men in the crew.

Dimensions: Length at gundeck, 110 feet.
Breadth: 28 feet.
Depth: 9 feet.
385 tons burden.

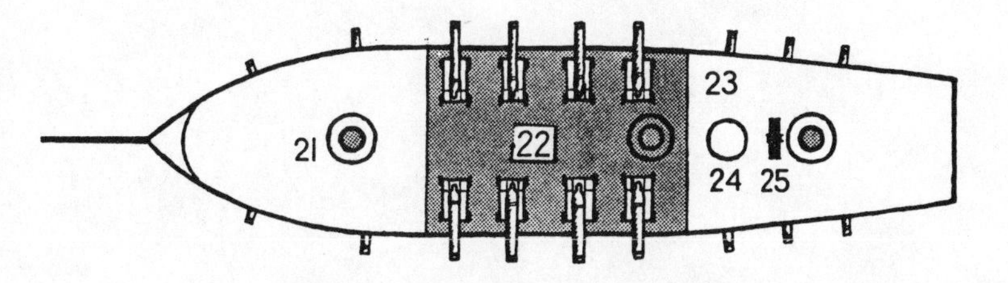

Decks: 21. Forecastle (fo'c's'le). 22. Gun deck (extends under fo'c's'le and quarterdeck). 23. Quarterdeck. 24. Capstan. 25. Wheel.

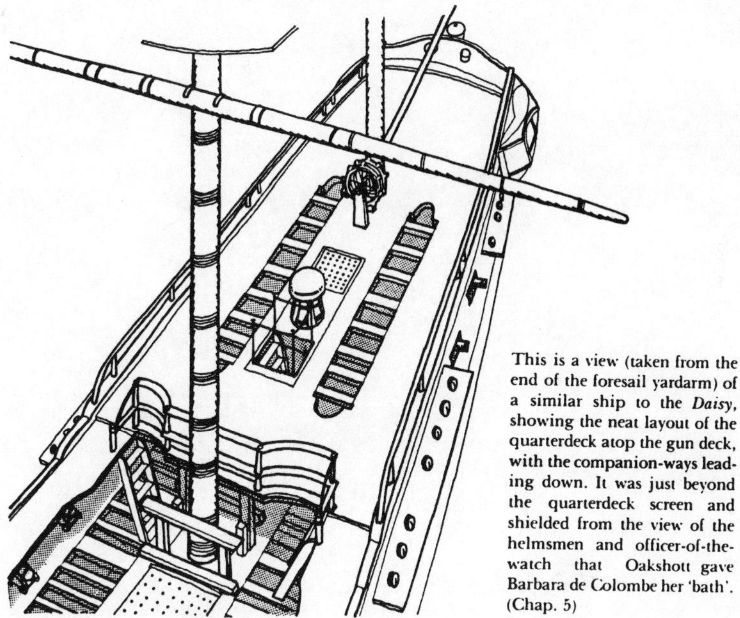

This is a view (taken from the end of the foresail yardarm) of a similar ship to the *Daisy*, showing the neat layout of the quarterdeck atop the gun deck, with the companion-ways leading down. It was just beyond the quarterdeck screen and shielded from the view of the helmsmen and officer-of-the-watch that Oakshott gave Barbara de Colombe her 'bath'. (Chap. 5)

'Heart of oak are our ships,
Heart of oak are our men,
We always are ready;
Steady, boys, steady!
We'll fight –
And we'll conquer again and again.'

David Garrick

Chapter One

RIDING ON A high tide of revolution, the French National Assembly offered assistance to any nation rising against its government, following this up by guillotining Louis XVI. Suspicious of French designs upon her Dutch allies, Britain threw out the French ambassador. A few days later, revolutionary France declared war on Britain and the United Provinces of the Netherlands. Apart from two short breaks, Europe was not to know peace till the gunsmoke cleared from the battlefield of Waterloo twenty-two years later.

In March of 1793, Charles Oakshott, who had been eking out a living as a lieutenant of six years' seniority on half-pay, and who, at his own expense, had spent a twelvemonth in the Low Countries adding to his professional stature by familiarising himself with the shoals and sandbanks of the Dutch and Flemish littoral, was returning to England upon a summons from the Board of Admiralty. The brig *Simon van Slingelandt* of Rotterdam, in which he was taking passage, had left the Hook on the previous night and sailed close-hauled through a brisk south-westerly which had kept her diverse collection of passengers in a greatly distressed state. Oakshott, who was sick only aboard large and slow-rolling ships in a beam sea, spent a serenely oblivious night wedged in a narrow bunk with the fumes of nigh on a whole bottle of geneva cosseting his brain to dreams of sunlit isles and complaisant women; and awoke in the dawn light to find that all motion had virtually ceased, and that, from the creaking of idle ropes, it was apparent that the brig was making poor headway in light airs – a fact that he was able to confirm when he went up on deck.

The wind – what there was of it – had backed to the south and was barely pushing the blunt-bowed brig on a broad reach. The slate grey waters of the German Ocean were overlaid by a creeping pall of mist that reduced visibility to little more than – Oakshott narrowed his eyes against the light and was aware that his head ached intolerably – five cables at most.

Simon van Slingelandt's captain was standing by his helmsman. He saw the tall, dark-haired figure in the boat cloak, and spat contemptuously to leeward. Oakshott had been more than a little drunk upon coming aboard the previous night, and had with difficulty been restrained from bringing two cheerful and equally inebriated dockyard strumpets with him. Captain Hendrik Kuyper, a strict Lutheran and a total abstainer, greatly disapproved of such goings-on.

'Good morning to you, sir,' called Oakshott.

'Humph!'

'Have we passed the Gabbards yet, sir?'

The mention of the two sand banks that stretch like fingers across the path of the unwary brought, if not a softening of Kuyper's attitude, a discernible heightening of his interest. A familiarity with the hazards of the German Ocean predisposed one to assume that the tall dark Englishman was of the nautical persuasion. He pointed out into the mist off the starboard quarter.

'Inner Gabbard – eight, ten miles,' he said gruffly.

'Then we should be sighting South Shipwash buoy any minute now,' said Oakshott.

The Dutchman opined that this was so. And there the conversation foundered. Oakshott went over and stood by the mizzen chains, supporting himself upon a ratline, closing his eyes and looking round inside his head. God, how much he must have drunk the night before! Not that he needed any excuse to get drunk, but it had been the blessed joy and release of being called back to service. *'You are requested and required to present yourself...'* There would be a *viva voce* examination before the Board for promotion to commander and a ship of his own. He might make admiral yet - provided the war lasted long enough.

Provided...

He must not think of that. He firmly shut out the vision of his brother's puffy, blotched countenance: the face of a man old and decrepit at forty-one - or was it forty-two? In any event, the creature could scarcely be expected to see five more summers. And that would spell the end of his naval career. No Admiral Lord Oakshott would ever lead his column against the Frogs; for him would be the grinding existence of upkeeping that miasma-haunted jumble of crumbling sandstone and pitted marble called home. He cursed quietly under his breath. *Noblesse oblige* be damned! To hell with the laws of entail and primogeniture!

No sign of that buoy yet. It could have gone adrift in the equinoctial gales. That surly Hollander should be taking soundings by now. A glance behind him showed that the captain had been prompted by the same notion. One man was up at the bowsprit with the lead and another was at the other mizzen chains with the end of the line. The bottle-shaped plug of lead was hurled out ahead of them, the line went abaft of the slowly-moving ship and was held taut and upright by the man at the chains, who called out something in his own language.

'What depth do you have, sir?' asked Oakshott.

'Nine fathoms,' growled Kuyper.

So they had crossed the ten fathom line. Oakshott peered out into the murk. Presuming that the Hollander was on course, they should be sighting the buoy that marked the southern tip of the long Shipwash Bank within minutes. If on course, he would prudently have made allowance to pass the marker within the present visibility distance of about half a mile. And that was cutting it a bit fine.

If the buoy was missing...

There came a shout from the masthead lookout. At first, Oakshott assumed that the fellow had sighted the buoy, and himself strained to pick it out. Then, by a gabble of excited orders, and the shriek of a bosun's pipe and the patter of bare feet mounting the companion-way to the deck, he was constrained to turn and look the way in which the fellow at the masthead was pointing, which was in the opposite direction - to southward.

Out of the drifting mist, with all plain sail spread to the following wind, and coming on at a spanking rate despite the exiguousness of that wind, was a big frigate. A thirty-two gunner at least. Even as Oakshott stared, another set of sails appeared beyond the first. And while he was juggling in his mind with the unfamiliar cut of headsails, the leading ship turned sharply to present her broadside - and revealed the tricolour of revolutionary France streaming at her mizzen peak.

A brief blossoming of lurid orange-red, a cloud of white gunsmoke, a thunderclap of sound, and a ball struck the water ahead of *Simon van Slingelandt's* bow, bounced twice and sank.

It was a signal for the Hollander to heave to. Nor was Captain Kuyper slow to appreciate the order and to carry it out. His crewmen were already swarming aloft to take in sail when he had brought the ship in irons; he was just about to give the command to his helmsman which would turn them into the wind, when he felt something hard being jabbed against his third waistcoat button. He met Oakshott's eyes. There was something about them - or so it seemed to the Dutchman - that was oddly unnerving, though for the life of him he could not fathom why.

'Turn downwind,' said the Englishman evenly. 'Run before 'em.'

In his hand, its muzzle pressed inconspicuously against the Dutchman's middle, so that it was all unnoticed by the helmsman at his side, was a small pocket-pistol with a brass cannon-barrel.

'You are mad!' breathed Kuyper.

'Not mad enough to want to spend the war in a Frog gaol,' responded the other. 'Nor should the prospect commend itself to you, mister. Turn her downwind, I say.' He reinforced his argument by giving Kuyper another sharp jab with his pistol.

Dutch obstinacy fought with a sailor's ingrained prudence. Kuyper had no way of telling if the pistol was primed, or indeed loaded; nor could he be sure that this strange Englishman would carry out his implied threat and kill him for disobedience. His instinct was to disobey and take the chance - but those unwavering, strange eyes looked to be chillingly in earnest.

He nodded brusquely to the helmsman and gave a gutteral command. The wheel was spun, the *Simon van Slingelandt* turned in her tracks with a creaking of cordage and a groaning of shifting yards, presenting her stubby stern to the two French frigates who were cruising in line half a mile distant.

'And now to see if they stand off and pound us,' said Oakshott, 'or whether they give chase. If the former, they'll damn well have to hurry, for we'll be out of sight in the mist within a couple of minutes.'

The Dutch captain narrowed his eyes dangerously and thrust out his lower lip. 'If we are hit, I shall instantly heave to,' he said. 'I am responsible for my ship and my passengers, and you may do your damnedest.'

Oakshott pocketed his pistol. 'That shall be a bargain between us, sir,' he responded gravely. 'While we stay unhit, we carry on. One hit and you may put up your helm and strike your colours. I see our friends are undecided as to what to do. Leastways, they have not turned to give pursuit, nor are their gunners nimble enough to give us a swift broadside. Ah! There they go! And what a miserable performance!'

The nearest frigate, which was by then all but lost from sight in the mist behind them, was suddenly obscured by smoke, and a ragged pattern of flashes revealed that she had fired a few of her guns in a hasty and ill-directed broadside. By the time the detonations reached the ears of those aboard the Hollander, both French ships had vanished from sight in the mist. Moments later, three splashes were kicked up in the water some fifty yards astern of the *Simon van Slingelandt*.

'I never saw such a display,' commented Oakshott. 'Well, one is told that the Frogs have chopped off the heads of most of their officers, which probably accounts for the state of their gunnery and is greatly to our advantage. 'Tis to be hoped that their seamanship is of a like order.'

'Officers or no, they will soon be upon us,' growled Kuyper. 'They will overtake us, one each side, and blow us out of the water at close range.'

'Sir, you have an uncommonly depressing turn of phrase,' said Oakshott. 'I bid you to leave the consideration of naval tactics to me and address yourself to determining how much water you retain under your keel.'

Their eyes met. Kuyper's, paler and less steady than those of his companion, widened in sudden alarm.

'The Shipwash Bank!' he exclaimed. 'You have headed us straight for the Shipwash Bank!'

'That is so,' admitted the Englishman. 'However, the appearance of the buoy ahead will give us ample warning of danger. Or, perhaps, we shall not have the pleasure of its acquaintance.'

'We – should have sighted it before now,' breathed the Dutchman.

'That had occurred to me, also,' murmured Oakshott. 'Might I suggest continuous soundings?'

Kuyper nodded vigorously; turned and shouted an order to the leadsmen, who still stood at their stations. Oakshott cast a glance astern and on each quarter, from whence, all too soon, the tall sails of the two Frenchmen must soon appear; there was nothing but the grey, oily-smooth water of the German Ocean and a pall of blanketing mist. He gave thanks for the mist.

The man in the chains shouted a numeral in Dutch.

'Depth?' asked Oakshott.

'Nine fathoms,' replied Kuyper.

'How much water do you draw?'

'Eight feet – a little more.'

Just over a fathom and a third, thought Oakshott. And the Frenchies drew perhaps twice as much, call it three.

The leadsman at the chains shouted again.

'Eight fathoms,' said Kuyper.

Almost immediately after: 'Seven and a half.'

The bottom was shoaling fast. *Simon van Slingelandt* was heading straight for the southernmost tip of the northward pointing finger of the sandbank. And so - presuming they were in pursuit - were the two enemy frigates.

'Five fathoms!'

'That settles it,' said Oakshott. 'The buoy has broken free, and, if the Frogs' navigation matches their gunnery and if they are not taking soundings, we have them, my friend - for even we will strike putty in less than a mile.'

His smile was not matched by the Dutchman, who was looking past the Englishman, back, over the taffrail.

'They are upon us!' he cried.

Oakshott murmured: 'For what we are about to receive...'

They came out of the swirling murk: sailing side by side, barely a cable's length apart - enough distance to envelop the *Simon van Slingelandt* in their two arms and destroy her with fire and flying metal. Moreover, the wind had freshened slightly and they were coming on fast, and the mist was clearing, so that it was possible to see men grouped in the foretops and the forecastles of both vessels.

'They have bow-chasers,' said Oakshott. 'Rather like our carronades: short-ranged and sixty pounds or more. How much water under us, mister?'

There was an edge of wild urgency in the Dutch captain's voice as he shouted an enquiry to the man at the mizzen chains and received an almost immediate response.

'Four and a half!' translated Kuyper.

'Damn this breeze,' said Oakshott. ''Tis clearing the mist, and the last thing we want is for the Frogs to sight the broken water atop the sandbank...'

His closing word was drowned by a deafening crash from astern, followed by a thunderous sound in the air, as by the passage of a flying object of tremendous bulk and force. There was a sharp thwakk above their heads, and a hole the size of a man's head appeared in the dead centre of the brig's fore-topsail. Oakshott, chancing to glance from there to the dark maw of the companion-way leading down into the passengers' quarters, saw a cluster of pale, frightened faces and staring eyes; men, women and children all, looking out at him. And his spirits suffered an anguished deflation.

'Captain, sir,' he said. 'I think we must now close our

bargain. You have been struck. The pistol remains in my pocket. Heave to, for the sake of innocent lives.'

But Dutch stubborness, which would have caused Hollanders to trade with the very Devil himself if they could have contrived ships to voyage through seas of fire, had taken complete command of Captain Hendrick Kuyper.

'We press on, sir!' declared he.

'As you will, sir!' responded Oakshott. 'And here cometh the second, unasked-for benison!'

Instants after, a sixty-odd pound ball of flying iron burst through the taffrail behind them in a shower of wood splinters and carried off the helmsman's head. Oakshott, who was standing close by, saw the wretched thing burst like a melon and vanish. The trunk stood for a few moments, pulsating thick blood from the stump of neck, then fell into the scuppers.

Oakshott took hold of the wheel, steadied it against the kick of the following sea; glanced at the captain.

'I await your orders, sir,' he said quietly. 'Do I put up the helm and heave to?'

The Dutchman's lower lip out-thrust, he replied: 'Continue your present course, sir.'

'Aye, aye.'

While Kuyper tipped the headless corpse over the side, Oakshott glanced back over his shoulder. The French were closing swiftly, with white water creaming under their sharp stems. He was elated to notice that neither ship appeared to be taking soundings, which indicated that their navigators had no notion that they were standing into danger. It seemed likely that they must know of the existence of the Shipwash Bank, but were anticipating the appearance of the south marker buoy. Well, so much the worse for them - if only the *Simon van Slingelandt* could stay afloat and unhurt for the next half mile or so.

'I would suggest you take no further soundings, sir,' he called to the Dutchman. 'It might alert the Frogs to their danger.'

Kuyper nodded, and shouted to the men at the lead and line.

The enemy bow-chaser did not speak again; the consorts were closing in for a quick kill, and the nearest vessel - the one coming up on the starboard quarter - had its long bowsprit almost in line with the brig's counter. From the distance of perhaps three cables, Oakshott could clearly see the men on the upper deck. He paid particular attention to those grouped at the quarterdeck - who must include the captain and some of his senior subordinates. All were hatless and there was no sign of anything remotely resembling a uniform. He was greatly heartened to see a line trailing in the water from the frigate's taffrail. Even more revealingly, there was a bundle of wood faggots hanging as a fender over the side by the waist. And nowhere a glint of polished brightwork.

'Not only done for their officers, but the bosun's mates and gunner's mates also,' he mused aloud.

But, even allowing for such evidence of slovenly seamanship and gunnery (surely the hit that took off that poor fellow's head was the merest fluke), they could scarcely miss with concerted broadsides at such close range. God, he thought, how much water beneath us now?

The frigate to starboard was half abreast by then, and its companion was three lengths astern to larboard. Oakshott met Kuyper's eye.

'Your last chance to strike colours, sir,' said the Englishman.

'Pray,' said the other.

'I am praying,' said Oakshott.

Ramming was out of the question, though the wild notion occurred to him. Given more headway and a livelier vessel, a quick turn might have taken unawares the fellow to starboard. But to put one's bowsprit over him, or, with luck, even to spring some of his planking, would only be to invite a cutlass-swinging boarding party. And what price the lives of the passengers then?

Surely they must be almost atop the sandbank by now!

'A sail!' shouted Captain Kuyper.

'She's a sixty-four!' cried Oakshott. 'And one of ours. By heaven - now we'll see a fine clatter!'

The newcomer came out of the mist on the Hollander's starboard bow, sailing close-hauled in deep water beyond the sandbank, her two rows of black gun ports plainly etched on her towering sides, sails straining, a white ensign curling from the jackstaff.

'The Frogs have seen her, too!' exclaimed Oakshott. 'They're going to turn and run. Ye gods, what would I not give for a loaded thirty-two pounder!'

The nearest frigate was making its turn. The sails were a-tremble, the yards beginning to swing; when suddenly, as if a giant hand had reached out and blocked the progress of the vessel, it stopped still in the water and lay there with sails and cordage flapping like a line of washing.

'She's aground!' shouted Oakshott, and was immediately embraced by the Dutch captain. 'She's hit putty!'

The second frigate, seeing her consort's plight, was swift to turn also. Masked by the *Simon van Slingelandt* from the sight of the oncoming sixty-four, her chances of escape seemed good.

'Let's get off this confounded bank before we strike too,' said Oakshott, spinning the wheel to lay the vessel on the larboard tack. 'How much water, mister?'

The answer soon came back: 'A fathom and a half!'

'We could get out and walk!' said Oakshott. 'That Frog must be well on. I pity those poor devils when that sixty-four opens up.'

The water around them was murky with mud. Already, the grounded frigate was a ghost shape in the enveloping mist astern. Of her consort and the British line-of-battle ship there was no sign. The man at the chains called out the depth of four fathoms, and seven soon after. They were safely off the narrow hump of the Shipwash. And then, from out of the murk behind them, came the rolling thunder of a thirty-two gun broadside.

'They'll not need to fire a second,' murmured Oakshott.

Nor did they.

That night, tied alongside the wall in Harwich, the

passengers insisted upon plying Oakshott with drink and presents, hailing him as their saviour. He, who knew better than anyone what might have happened below decks if even one of the Frenchmen's shots had come in, accepted their thanks with grave-faced civility, drank his fill, and kept his peace. Captain Hendrik Kuyper was so relieved to have escaped death or imprisonment that he was persuaded to down a bumper measure of schnapps, whereupon he embraced the embarrassed Oakshott. It was then it came upon him - what it was about the other's eyes that gave them such a mysterious and commanding quality...

'Hey, English,' he exclaimed, 'you have one blue eye and one brown eye!'

'They run in my family,' replied Oakshott. 'Have some more schnapps.'

Kuyper complied. Presently he said, with the button-holing cunning of the tipsy: 'That pistol of yours, it was really loaded, hein?'

'Yes,' said Oakshott.

'And you would have shot me if I had tried to surrender to the French, hein?'

'Yes.'

'I guessed as much. You are a hard man, English.' He hiccoughed, swayed, and sank slowly to the deck.

It was past two bells in the middle watch before the revellers had all gone to their bunks and hammocks. Oakshott went up on deck. The moon was full. By its light, he saw a tall ship rounding the tail of the jetty and shaping course into the mouth of the Stour. As he watched, the shrill of bosun's pipes came over the still, dark water and he thought he heard the splash of her bower anchor. The sails were quickly furled by unseen hands, disappearing like a handkerchief up the sleeve of a conjurer. A brassy bugle call sounded the 'secure'. Oakshott sighed.

It was certainly the sixty-four who had sent the broadside into the grounded French frigate - he recognised the cut of her bows. There would be rejoicing aboard her this night, he thought. Much in the way of larks in the midshipmen's gunroom, with late night feasting, illicit grog, and someone at the top of the companion-way ready to call *cave* in case the officer of the watch or one of his minions put in an appearance. Every man jack on that sixty-four would be reckoning his share of the prize money; for, to be sure, her broadside would have been aimed with no intent but to dismast the French frigate and encourage the regicide revolutionaries to haul down their colours. Like as not, the battleship had towed her prize off the sandbank and to a safe anchorage, with a prize crew aboard, outside Harwich, to await tomorrow's tide.

He fell to thinking of prize money, that by no means inconsiderable bonus afforded to a fighting sailor in wartime. Supposing he had a tremendous run of good fortune in securing, say, half a dozen valuable prizes in the next five years? As captain of his own vessel, he would be entitled to the lion's share of the proceeds. With, say, twenty thousand pounds, might one not re-roof Sennett and pay a bailiff to live in and administer the estate? His keenly arithmetical mind, more used to juggling with the azimuth of heavenly bodies and the rise and fall of tides, made a swift calculation of the outgoings and income related to his family's estate. There had been a deficit for as long as he had been alive (his grandfather, a noted rake and gambler of the '20s, had seen to that!); would even the sweetening of twenty thousand pounds long survive the depredations of a bailiff who was milking the account books? Such a pity about *noblesse oblige*. How singularly gratifying it would be, merely to turn one's back on the whole thing: let Sennett's roof fall in, let the tenants starve...

No sound from the sixty-four. Her riding lights and stern lanterns made wavy patterns in the dark water. He would have liked to have taken a boat and gone over to hear the news of the encounter; but it was late, and a long pull over there. He gave a sigh, pissed over the leeward side, and went below to his narrow bunk.

He hung up his clothes carefully, as he had always been taught, and laid his boots neatly side by side. Too tired and out of kilter to say his prayers, he flopped down upon the hard bunk and was enveloped by instant sleep.

*

Young Alexander Oakshott had fought for his king as cornet of horse at the battle of Marston Moor, and afterwards at Naseby, where an ill-placed musket ball had deprived him for ever of the full enjoyment that his marriage to one of the leading beauties of Caroline England - the ravishing, raven-haired Eulalia - should have entitled him - she with the disconcertingly arresting eyes that were always a puzzle on first encounter.

Recovering from his grievous wound, Alexander accompanied the Prince of Wales into exile, afterwards returning with him in triumph at the Restoration. He stood at his prince's elbow when they crowned him King Charles the Second. Eulalia stood at that freshly-anointed and libidinous monarch's other elbow - three months' pregnant.

For services rendered to the Crown by the Oakshotts, man and wife, in battlefield and boudoir, Alexander was made Marquess of Uffingham & Bow. The former half of the territorial designation related to the approximate part of the Vale of the White Horse from which the Oakshott family had derived, the latter to the district in the east end of London where Eulalia's forebears (she came of very humble stock; in truth, it was her outstanding beauty that had borne her up) had once peddled oysters in the streets.

The child was born with his mother's raven-dark hair and quickly established himself as also possessing Eulalia's eyes - both of exactly the same tone; but when puzzlement drew one to look closer, revealed themselves as being of different colour: one deep blue, the other a rich brown tending to hazel. It was an idiosyncrasy that was to make the infant heir - and some of his descendants, Charles Oakshott included - striking to men and disturbingly alluring to women.

The newly-created marquess accepted the boy as his own - for how could he do other? In any event, he was not a man to look a gift horse in the mouth, and for the rest of his relatively short life, threw himself into the building of what was to be the family seat: Sennett Palace, an ill-conceived mansion in the Baroque style, set on an ill-chosen site in swampy ground beneath the Lambourn downs and within sight of the eerie Iron Age horse carved by forgotten hands upon the chalk of the great hill. Even before Alexander's death (announced by the appearance of an apparition: that of a grey friar stalking the ruined nave of an ancient chapel alongside which Sennett had been erected), the central dome of the vast building had developed - in the phrase of Alexander's nautical descendant Charles Oakshott - a most decided list to starboard, and, by reason of swamp water, the wine cellars were rendered totally unusable for the fine vintages of wine the first marquess had brought back from exile in France.

The passing of nearly a century and a half - time which should have added an ennobling patina to the fabric of the mansion - further added to the decrepitude of Sennett. It is possible that, if a small fortune could have been spent upon the fabric in the early years of the 18th Century; on such things as providing a new roof, draining the surrounding land, even installing rudimentary sanitation, the slow shift to total collapse might have been arrested. Montgomery Arthur George, fourth Marquess of Uffingham & Bow and grandfather of sailor Charles Oakshott, put paid to any hope of that by gambling away all the liquid assets of the estate, and, when that was done, by mortgaging everything that was allowable under the terms of the entail, as well as populating the villages, hamlets and outlying farms with his black-haired bastards.

The sixth marquess, Jack, brother of Charles Oakshott, had inherited his grandfather's taste for dissolute living without succeeding to one iota of that cheerful rakehell's style and charm. Jack was a glutton upon whose palate the most subtle sauces went unregarded, a drunkard who could not distinguish good claret from rotgut, a lecher who made even tavern whores close their eyes and pine for a decent husband, half an acre and a cow.

It was to his brother's seat, his family home, that Lieutenant Lord Charles Oakshott, Royal Navy, directed his steps upon quitting the brig *Simon van Slingelandt* at Harwich. He arrived at Sennett in the moonlight, and thought he saw the ghostly horse on the chalk hillside throw back its head and lash its tail. Or it may have been the good geneva which he had brought back from Holland and with which he had been fortifying himself against his coming encounter with his brother and with Sennett, during the infinitely tedious staging from Harwich, via London.

'I saw the grey friar walking last week. I saw him thrice. Three nights in succession, from the window of my bedchamber. I saw him plain, as I see you, Charlie. You don't believe me, do you? It means death in the family, you know that, don't you? Yours, I shouldn't wonder, Charlie. Haha! Then that'll be the end of us. I'll be the sixth and last.'

The two brothers faced each other across the narrow width of the tremendously long refectory table which had, in more prosperous times for the Oakshotts, seen a hundred guests seated at one time, to dispose of feasts consisting of twenty courses with removes, and a different wine for every course.

Charles Oakshott picked at the pieces of cold, overcooked beef that formed the main burden of his present repast, and added a generous spoonful of mustard to mask the taste and smell of putrefaction. It was the very stink of Sennett, he decided, that so appalled him. And his brother - that bloated, lardy oaf seated opposite - he also stank. Once, as a twelve year-old midshipman, putting out on one of his first voyages, the ship he was in had passed one of the prison hulks moored by Deptford creek. The stink from them was the very same that gusted across the table from the creature in the filthy brocade dressing gown opposite. Jack never washed or dressed on rising; but merely shrugged that grease-plastered garment on over his night-shirt, clapped an outmoded bag-wig upon his nearly bald pate and sallied forth to greet the morn - or, more likely, the mid-afternoon. And yet, thought Charles, the fellow was greatly to be pitied and deserving of much compassion. The favourite of their father, Jack had been splendid and upright in youth, while he, Charles, disposed to be somewhat delicate and 'chesty', had inclined to his mother's influence. Both parents had been taken early; the fifth marquess by breaking his neck in the hunting field. Charles could never forget the afternoon they had brought Father home on a hurdle, and he with his broken neck all awry and staring sightlessly up at the wintry sky. By the end of the next half at Eton, the upright Jack, who had wet his bed on the night of Father's death and for long after, had become a fat and unpopular boy.

And Mother's end. He would not think of that...

'I fancy the grey friar may have had a gobbet of advance information about my mortality, but was ill-briefed in the particulars,' he said. 'I came uncommonly close to leaving you the last marquess t'other day, but the recording angel decided, in the event, to postpone my departure to the bosom of Abraham for a little while yet.'

The marquess displayed not the slightest interest in his brother's naval adventures; instead, he poured himself a bumper measure of wine, washed down a mouthful of food, belched loudly, and said: 'What did you in London, now? Did you visit any of the sporting clubs on your way through? I have heard tell that, at Mrs Fullbright's, there is *poses plastiques* with young fillies of the most superior pulchritude. Did you go to Mrs Fullbright's, Charlie? Did you see the fillies, mother-naked as they were, hey? Tell me swiftly, Charlie.'

'No, I did not,' said Oakshott. 'Mrs Fullbright's is too damned expensive for my pocket, as well you know. A woman must needs want me for what I am; I cannot persuade her to bed with bright gold.'

His brother pouted and looked self-pitying.

'Well, you are a lucky fellow, Charlie,' he said. 'Being blessed with youth and looks, while I, who have been dogged by ill-health since boyhood, am now what you see before you. Strumpets and serving-wenches are my lot.' He gave a sly glance from under his pouched eyelids. 'I've no handsome widow like you, to warm my bed o' nights, you cunning dog. I expect that you shall be seeing Mrs Chancellor while you're home, hey?'

'Like as not,' said Oakshott. 'I'm for London the day after tomorrow, so it's more likely that I shall see her when I return, while I'm awaiting the arrival of my new sea appointment.'

He wished to God that his brother would take his lewd, drooling mind off Irene Chancellor, the young widow of a boyhood friend, with whom he had had a sporadic and entirely satisfying relationship during his three interminably boring years on half-pay. Sometimes it occured to him that the reason he so disliked to hear her name on Jack's lips was because he was in love with Irene. The notion was unbearably depressing. He poured himself some more wine and pushed aside his half-eaten beef.

'Struthers has been watering the damned brandy again,' said the marquess, scarcely troubling to lower his voice as Sennett's elderly and incredibly dilapidated butler and Jack-of-all-work – shuffled over from the serving-table. 'The bastard is selling it to the parson, I'll be bound, and topping up the hogshead with Adam's ale. If I had proof, I'd throw him out.'

'Who would take his place?' asked Oakshott. 'And can you blame him if he robs you? The poor old wretch hasn't been paid in a twelvemonth.'

Struthers removed Oakshott's plate with a hand that trembled with ague.

'Will you be requiring anything further, Lord Charles?' he quavered. 'There is sago pudding and there is tipsy cake. There was syllabub, but the clouted cream as was laid atop it have turned sour, so I would not advise. Or there is a Stilton cheese.'

Oakshott indicated that he would have cheese.

'Leave the pudding dish upon the table before me,' said the marquess loudly, so that the old man would hear. 'Then up to the minstrels' gallery, and do you play us some airs. Sprightly airs, mind you, and none of your religiosity, your cantatas, fugues and the like. Start with "Roger de Coverley".'

'Yes, my lord,' said Struthers, and went to do his noble master's bidding: shuffling the vast length of the marbled hall to the Grinling Gibbons carved wooden screen at the far end, atop which was the minstrels' gallery and a vast pipe organ which had been imported from Westphalia by the second marquess. In past, happier years Oakshott had delighted to listen to his mother playing his favourite tunes, and had himself taken instruction upon the instrument from her. Only the palsied and unsure fingers of the old butler ever touched the yellowed keys now.

There was a pause while Struthers summoned one of the kitchen scullions to pump the bellows. Then, following a wheeze from those bellows, the opening bars of the famous old country dance, barely discernible even to the ear of faith, filled the vast space; rising to the shadowed ceiling, with its intricate, crumbling plasterwork and the vast mural representing the apotheosis of King Charles the Martyr, supported by his faithful captain the first marquess - a work of devotion whose effect had been gravely lessened by reason of the fourth marquess and his drunken friends shooting pistol balls up into it during one of their late-night revels in the '20s.

Charles Oakshott sat back in his chair, put his feet up on the table, chewed upon a hunk of exceedingly ripe and maggotty cheese and looked about him ruefully; at the signs of fast-approaching dissolution that were evident on all sides: the broken windows, some of them quite decently patched with squares of wood, others - more recently and vestigially - with brown paper; the dark streaks that marred the panelled walls, staining the buff leather coat which was displayed there, together with the back and breastplates, helmet and sword, that Alexander Oakshott had worn at Naseby (the older, darker stain upon the lappet of the coat came from the grievous wound that had deprived him, at one stroke, of his manhood and, indirectly, procured him a high peerage); and even discolouring Kneller's portrait of Eulalia Oakshott herself - the complaisant beauty who, from time to time, favoured some of her descendants with her raven-dark hair and the disturbing, two-coloured eyes (but not the present incumbent: under his shabby bag-wig, Jack was bald save for a few strands of mousy grey, and his rheumy eyes were both of washed-out blue).

The roof timbers were rotten and would collapse within

five years. Then down would come the painted ceiling, bringing with it the minstrels' gallery, pipe-organ and all.

'Roger de Coverley' was over and the musician was sketching his uncertain way through 'Sally in our Alley'. The unlovely voice of Jack, sixth Marquess of Uffingham & Bow was raised in song, a beat behind the organ and half a semitone flat:

> There is no lady in the land
> That's half so sweet as Sally;
> She is the darling of my heart,
> And lives in our alley...

Oh, my God, thought Oakshott, the maudlin fool was crying into the bargain, with the tears running unashamedly down his blue-veined and bloated cheeks. Another night of drink, gluttony and song lay before him. Such a night – and that not so far in the future – would be his last.

With a sigh, Oakshott rose, and, taking up one of the candelabra from the table, he bade goodnight to his brother. If the marquess heard, he gave no sign; but continued singing, eyes closed, tears flowing, and gobbets of sago pudding outlining the shape of his protruding paunch.

Oakshott's bedchamber was in the south wing, which was reached by way of a long curving corridor, one of a pair that flanked the main, central block of the mansion. Pools of stagnant water upon the marble floor betokened that the roof of the corridor was far gone. He fervently hoped that his bedchamber had so far escaped the depredations of weather and neglect. Ascending the staircase at the end of the corridor, he paused for a moment by the door of what had been his mother's room, then squared his shoulders and went on.

The sour smell of damp and decay that assailed his nostrils when he opened his own door confirmed his worst fears. The white plaster ceiling carried the tell-tale stains, and the once-splendid Persian rug in the centre of the room was speckled with black mildew. He crossed to the dressing-room and, opening the wardrobe, took out his full-dress uniform coat of a Royal Navy lieutenant. It felt damp to the touch and smelt vilely of mothballs, for which reason, without doubt, it had escaped the ministrations of that voracious insect. Well, if tomorrow was a fine day, he would hang it out and let the sunshine dry and sweeten it in time to wear up to London and appear before the Board.

Would they promote him commander and give him a ship of his own? He fervently hoped so. There were lieutenants a-plenty who had their own commands - of schooners, cutters, bomb-ketches and the like. The first-lieutenancy of a crack 74-gun ship-of-the-line had prevented him from enjoying the heady delights of being the master of his own vessel, however small; but he did not regret the tremendous experience of enjoying high responsibility in a fine ship under a fine captain. His only regret was for the three wasted years on the beach. Well - not entirely wasted; he now probably knew more about the coastline of the Low Countries than any officer in the navy.

Oakshott undressed and put on his nightshirt, which the chambermaid had laid out upon the bed. Gingerly slipping in between the sheets, he experienced the curiously sticky dampness of a bed that has been left unaired for months. Damn it, could they not have thought to put in a warming-pan?

Leaving one candle to burn itself out, he snuffed the rest and composed himself for sleep, letting his mind stray uneasily from the pleasurable contemplation of his possible ship command to the doleful prospect of his brother's early demise and what that would entail.

There was nothing else for it; against all likelihood and probability, Jack must be wifed and bedded before the Grim Reaper snatched him off, leaving Charlie Oakshott to be seventh marquess and presiding spectre at the dissolution of the Oakshott estate. That was the ticket: a wench must be found, be she as old and hideous as Old Nick's daughter - provided she was not too far gone to be brought to bed of an heir. And when drunkenness, gluttony and casual fornication had finally brought Jack to his marble mausoleum in the family chapel, the widow could run the estate in the name of the new, infant marquess. And, given even a modicum of wit and sense, she must certainly run it one hundred per cent more profitably than brother Jack.

What if - the very thought brought him upright in bed - what if a *rich* woman could be found? One who would bring a fortune to the marquisate.

No. Too much to hope for. Such themes are the stuff of fairy tales. No rich woman, be she ugly as a sow, would lay out good money to be Marchioness of Uffingham & Bow - not when it meant her being subjected to the repulsive embraces of poor old Jack. No - the woman in question would have to be both poor and hideous. Her only goods on offer: the quality of being female and of child-bearing age . . .

What was that? It was raining outside; he could hear it lashing against the shuttered windows. And something else: another sound was making slow counterpoint to those without: water was dripping down from the ceiling.

Oakshott climbed out of bed. By the candlelight, he discerned that there were two main patches of dampness in the ceiling just beyond the end of his bed; from each of them, in brief and regular intervals, sizable droplets of water were falling upon the parquet floor. Two puddles had already formed and joined together.

There was a pair of chamber pots in the night commode. Taking them out, he laid them on the floor under the drips, making the slight adjustments to their positions so that each succeeding drop fell precisely into the centre of the receptacle. Which done, he climbed back into bed.

He readdressed his thoughts to the pressing matter of finding a wife for his brother - for it was certain that Jack would never in this world find one for himself.

Drip - drip. One of the chamber pots was tuned to A sharp, the other to C flat.

Surely, somewhere, there was a potentially child-bearing woman so far gone in desperation at remaining a spinster all her life that she would even marry poor Jack and take upon herself the burden of the marquisate, a tumbledown mansion that let in rain, a couple of hundred hungry and mostly rebellious tenants, and a pile of debts.

He nagged at the problem, and all the time the drips continued.

A sharp, C flat. A sharp, C flat...

Chapter Two

ALL LONDON SPARKLED with the ever-new, ever-recurring whiff of Spring. The sun in the high blue sky above bustling Whitehall brightened every particle of dust that rose from the wheel-rutted street. Oakshott bought a bunch of aconites from a pretty young flower girl on the corner opposite the Admiralty; dropping the penny into the deep cleft of her ample bosom and tucked in the posy after it. Coaches, carriages, a flock of sheep, a whole tree trunk hauled upon creaking wheels by a team of oxen, moved in and out of the sunshine and shadow. It wanted twenty minutes to ten. Oakshott's appointment before the Board was at half past ten. Upon an impulse, he decided to kill the time in a nearby playhouse: one of the exceedingly genteel establishments that had sprung up in and around the Strand but had not yet taken upon themselves the title of 'Music Hall'. There one could take a drink, a bite to eat at table if one so chose, or merely promenade around and listen to singing and playing of variable quality. It suited Oakshott's mood: he was thirsty and in need of a temporary distraction. He chose a place that announced itself as 'Mogg's Diversions' - and by doing so changed the course of his whole life and career.

The auditorium was crowded before a large apron stage. At the rear of the chamber was a semi-circular counter, at which well upon a dozen wenches of decorous mien served the customers who were assembled round the promenade. Upon his entrance many appraising glances were turned upon the tall, striking-looking officer in the gold-laced coat, white nankeen breeches, silk stockings, cocked and cockaded hat of a naval lieutenant. With England newly at war, the Royal Navy - England's darling pride - was tremendously popular, for was it not the Navy and those far-off lines of storm-tossed ships that protected good Englishmen from the violent and bloodthirsty French revolutionaries, and their wives and daughters from vile ravishment? Oakshott went to the counter and ordered a glass of brandy; was somewhat put out when the young woman waived payment, and those about him raised their glasses to pledge, 'The King's ships and all who sail in them, sir!'

'Charlie Oakshott, as I live and breathe! Ahoy there, Charlie!' A voice from behind him. Oakshott turned, to see who it was who hailed him, and was immediately the target for a burly, blue-clad man who came hurtling pell-mell through the press; upsetting tankards and rummers to left and right, sending spilt ales and spirits a-shower like the fountains of Rome. Many were the angry imprecations thrown in his train - but all were instantly withdrawn when the speakers saw the size and the quality of the human juggernaut.

Oakshott was taken in a grip that would have choked the breath from out of an ox.

'Charlie, Charlie - how is it with you, old shipmate?'

Oakshott, presently released from the fearsome embrace, was able to respond to the other's greeting:

'Ned Daventry! Well, I'm blessed. And how are you, Ned?'

'As you see me, old fellow - full of life and brandy. And still a midshipman. Come over here and I'll introduce you to as fine and genteel a filly as you ever beheld.'

Oakshott followed his friend towards the ring of tables that described the inner line of the promenade, wondering, as he did so - and not for the first time - how it was that mere linen and broadcloth were able to contain the massive back and shoulders before him, and were not split asunder by the extension and contraction of the giant's muscles. Not for the first time he decided that Ned Daventry had missed his vocation by two or three score millenia, and that he should have lived in a cave, worn a bearskin and hunted sabre-toothed tigers with a stone axe.

'Miss Howarth, I have pleasure in presenting an old shipmate of mine...'

The lady whom Ned Daventry addressed was seated at table with a cup of coffee primly set before her. 'Prim' was the word that sprang to Oakshott's mind in first connection with the person in question: prim was her modest gown of sprigged cotton, high in the neck and long in the sleeve; prim and decorous to a degree was her glossy brown hair, drawn back into a modest chignon, with only a light embellishment of curls before and behind the ears, and briefly hinted at across the brow. Her eyes were grey, open and candid - yet, when they lit upon him, a certain cloud seemed to pass over their clarity, a hint of - what - defensiveness? Nevertheless, when she smiled and held out her hand to Oakshott, he was able to observe that she had, on the face of it, very little to be defensive about: possessing, as she did, a healthy country milkmaid's complexion and a set of white, unblemished teeth. Furthermore, the lifting of her arm also caused the slight raising, and revealing of, a remarkably fine bosom.

'Miss Howarth, Charlie Oakshott is a walking paradox, since he combines the roles of brother to a marquess with that of lieutenant - and both with elegance and expertise. Old friend, Miss Howarth is a singer of remarkable purity of tone as would put a skylark to shame and a sweetness of musical colouration as would cause a nightingale to hide his head under his wing for envy.'

Miss Howarth's defensive air was crossed by a slight smile at Ned Daventry's extravagance, revealing that beneath the prim exterior there dwelt a sense of humour.

'Do you sing here, ma'am?' asked Oakshott, when they were seated, all three.

'I am so obliged, Lord Charles,' she replied, and the defensive look came upon her again. 'My father, the Venerable Archdeacon of Granchester, must turn in his grave to think that I should be reduced to such a state as to sing in public where drink is being purveyed - but with an ailing, widowed mother and three hungry sisters to provide for, Lord Charles, what can a body do – a weak woman – in this day and age?'

That takes care of the defensive air, thought Oakshott. The old story of an impoverished daughter of a cleric, with curtains at the windows and a hunk of mice-riddled cheese in the pantry. And she knows her way around. Gave me my correct title. She's an interesting little thing...

His reverie was interrupted by Ned Daventry: 'Potman, more brandy for my friend and me.' And to his companion-in-arms: 'Charlie, I'm before the Board today,' he said. 'And this time I hope to sail through to my lieutenancy on a sea of strong spirits.'

'As good a way as any,' said Oakshott.

'And you're summoned too, hey? For a command, I don't doubt. It would be more than a coincidence that you'd be around Whitehall on the day that the Promotion Board is sitting, Charlie.'

Oakshott shrugged. 'A command – it's to be hoped, Ned.'

'Then I wish you well, Charlie,' responded his friend. 'For none deserves it better. I tell you, Miss Howarth, ma'am, no one in the Navy more deserves advancement more than my old shipmate Charlie Oakshott.' He hiccoughed.

'I'm sure you are right, sir,' responded Miss Howarth primly.

Ned Daventry was not the oldest midshipman in the navy, but it must have been a close-run thing. Seventeen successive appearances before the Board to undergo *viva voce* examination for lieutenant had resulted only in unremitting failure. A good, practical seaman and as brave as a lion, Ned suffered from a cardinal fault that would forever bar his advancement: in the realm of navigation by spherical trigonometry he was both literally and metaphorically all at sea. And yet, thought Oakshott, watching his old shipmate over the rim of his brandy glass, what a splendid fellow he was: a tower of strength when the guns sounded off, a cool head on a lee shore, a staunch arm to pull away from the rocks.

They downed their drinks and Oakshott called for another

round. They fell to talking of old times, old ships, old faces: of the ship's master, long since dead in a gun action off Finisterre, who would masthead a midshipman for an unguarded thought; of nights ashore in Portsmouth, Tobago and St Kitts; of the never-ending feud that existed between midshipmen and dockyard mateys; of storms long blown-out and half-forgotten landfalls.

Miss Howarth watched and listened with a certain absorbed interest, occasionally sipping at her coffee, and no doubt remarking to herself of the frequency with which the two officers called upon the potman to replenish their glasses.

Presently, she rose. 'Gentlemen, I must leave you,' she announced. 'The singing is about to commence, and I'm for the first rendition.' She held out her hand. 'It has been a pleasure to make your acquaintance, Lord Charles. Mr Daventry, good day to you, sir. I trust that you two gentlemen will be successful in your enterprises today.'

They both thanked her. She inclined her head gracefully to them both, and took her leave.

'A nice lass,' said Ned Daventry. 'Much come down in the world. And a person misses more what is lost than what he or she has never had.'

'Very true,' replied Oakshott. 'Oh, how very, very true. Hi, fellow - more brandy here!'

A four piece ensemble presently struck up the seafaring favourite *Tom Bowling*, and on to the stage came Miss Howarth, now dressed in the semblance of Britannia, carrying a trident, with a Grecian helmet set upon her soft brown mane and a chiton over-draped with the Union Flag.

> Here, a sheer hulk, lies poor Tom Bowling,
> The darling of our crew;
> No more he'll hear the tempest howling,
> For death has broached him to...

It was a small voice, but very true as to pitch. Oakshott and Daventry joined in the last words of the refrain and became most sentimental.

Assisted by the brandy, it was but a step from the

sentimental to the maudlin, and Oakshott was led to unburden himself of his fears for the future, and tell how his brother's early death would certainly put an end, for him, to the naval life that had been the pleasant burden of their discourse. To all this, Daventry made a comment that made Oakshott chuckle with amusement, in the doing of which he swallowed a mouthful of brandy - part of his seventh glass - the wrong way. By the time the heavy hand of his old shipmate had pounded his back sufficiently to restore him, Oakshott had come to the conclusion that he was more than slightly drunk - and that they were both a quarter of an hour late for the Navy Board.

Oakshott and Daventry had but a short walk to the Admiralty, but the latter nearly terminated his unpromising naval career under the wheels of a passing brewers' dray, and was only stopped short by his companion's hand upon his arm. Side by side, they then negotiated the many lines of traffic and emerged, dusty and laughing, through the fine Adam screen and into the cobbled courtyard of the Navy's holy of holies.

'That was a damned amusing thing you said to me back there,' said Oakshott, 'though for the life of me, do you know, I can't remember what it was.'

'Damned if I can, either,' responded the other. 'Charlie, old friend, I think we've ditched ourselves this time. I didn't give a fig for my own chances, but I should be might sorry to see you lose a chance for a command.'

'We'll see, we'll see,' said Oakshott. 'The game may not be lost yet.'

Up the high-pillared portico's steps they went, walking with the over-careful steps of the inebriated; into the entrance hall, which was bustling like a hive of overturned bees. Harassed clerks rushed to and fro bearing buff-coloured folders and sheaves of paper done up in pink tape. And the noble line of the main staircase, under the glass dome, was described by a queue of midshipmen, who stood, two by two, from the bottom step to the top.

There was a clerk, more harassed-looking than most, who, upon seeing Oakshott, rushed over to him.

'Is it Lieutenant Jones, Trelawney, or Oakshott?' he demanded, peering at the black-haired man over the top of his spectacles. 'We have received unconfirmed information that Mr Jones has been drowned. You are late, of course, but the Board has not yet commenced proceedings since two of the members have still not arrived. I suppose the town is very crowded with military traffic. Did you say your name?'

'Oakshott - and I can give you no information upon the fate of Mr Jones.'

The clerk peered short-sightedly at Oakshott, and his nose twitched. 'Hmm. Pray attend outside the Board Room on the first floor. You will be summoned in alphabetical order. And you, sir' - he glanced flatly at Daventry, taking in his advanced age, the high flush of his complexion, threadbare cuffs, and the rest - 'will take your place at the end of the queue with the other - er - young gentlemen, who will be summoned after the lieutenants.'

'Good luck, Charlie,' said Daventry, and they shook hands.

'We'll have another drink when it's over,' said Oakshott. 'By the length of this queue, you'll be well sober before your turn comes. Good luck.'

'Here - take these.'

Oakshott glanced down at what his friend had left lying in his palm.

'What are they?'

'Cloves. The Chinese mandarins are obliged to chew 'em before they're allowed to address their emperor. Do likewise, for I shouldn't wonder if your breath couldn't be touched-off with a slow-match.'

'Thanks, Ned.'

He mounted the stairs. Yes, he was really quite - possibly fatally - drunk, and would need to watch his step; to be careful - yet not too obviously careful. He bit upon one of the cloves. If only he could remember the damnably odd thing that Ned Daventry had said back there.

Another clerk fussed at the top of the stair.

'Jones, Trelawney, or ...?'

'Oakshott.'

'Please wait by the double doors over there, Lieutenant. You will be called in alphabetical order, and, since Mr Jones is reputed to be ...'

'... drowned, I shall be first. I quite understand.'

The man's eyebrows were raised in surprise.

Lieutenant Trelawney presented himself soon after. The meeting of old shipmates in a tavern had not delayed that serious-faced young man, but the state of the traffic in the bustling city in its state of war preparedness. He told Oakshott how he had been stuck for over an hour behind a convoy of artillery in Piccadilly and had finally been obliged to pay off his hackney cab and walk.

He also said: 'I'm informed that Pell's on the Board this week, in which case we are in for a stormy passage. Do you know him?'

'We have a passing acquaintance,' said Oakshott. 'I was a mid in *Theseus* when he was first lieutenant.'

'Well, I don't need to say any more.'

'You do not,' responded Oakshott. 'Damme, it's hot in here. Why doesn't someone open a window?'

As when a wheeling goshawk silences a field of cawing rooks, the appearance of a tall and cadaverous figure in the gold-laced, full-dress coat of a post captain crossing the entrance hall brought a sudden and awesome stillness to the 'young gentlemen' lining the stair rail. Those who were seated and trying to winnow a last, desperate fragment of knowledge from Robertson's *Elements of Navigation* or Maskelyne's *The British Mariner's Guide* sprang hastily to their feet. As the fearsome apparition mounted the steps, each and every one came to attention and touched a forelock. The gold-laced captain's washed-out blue eyes examined every countenance, as if seeking a victim. Set in a chalk-white face, a slash of a mouth bared a set of yellowed teeth like lichened tombstones. This was Captain Abel Pell, RN, sometime first lieutenant of *Theseus* and presently one of the most cordially detested commanding officers in the service. Pell had learned his trade – as had the great navigator Cook before him – in the east coast colliers, had passed from there to the lower deck of the Navy, and won his way to the quarter-deck by valour and merit not untainted with ruthlessness. Like so many officers who had, as the phrase went, 'come up through the hawse-hole', Captain Pell had a marked aversion to anything that smacked of privilege and preferment – and even in the late eighteenth century there was plenty of both around in the Navy.

'Stand by to receive a raking shot *en passant*,' murmured Lieutenant Trelawney.

Oakshott bit on the last of his cloves, swallowed the gritty fragments and attempted to assume an expression that suggested relaxed alertness.

Pell came towards them, pale eyes flickering to and fro. They swam over Trelawney; dismissed him. They met Oakshott's gaze, moved on, returned.

The pointing finger of the claw-like hand was directed straight to Oakshott's chest.

'*Theseus* – what name?' The voice was like a whisper emerging from the chill depths of a mausoleum.

'Oakshott, sir. Foretop division.'

'Oakshott.' The sepulchral voice mouthed the word, chewed upon it, spat it out in contempt: 'Oakshott, eh?'

Captain Pell entered the Board Room, and the double doors were shut behind him.

Trelawney exhaled loudly. 'By God, I think he remembers you,' he said.

'By God, I think he does,' said Oakshott.

The fussy clerk, who had accompanied the newcomer into the room, presently emerged.

'One member of the examining board has still not arrived, gentlemen,' he said, 'but the admiral opines that the proceedings should commence without him or they will not be terminated within the day.' He nodded to Oakshott. 'Pray go straight in, Lieutenant.'

'Good luck,' murmured Trelawney.

'Thank you.'

Taking a deep breath, Oakshott tapped upon the door, and entered a dark oak-panelled room where four officers were facing him across a table with a fine, tooled leather top. There was a vacant seat to the right of the central figure. They sat with their backs to three tall windows that looked out to a line of grey stone wall surmounted by a strip of dazzling blue sky.

'Be seated, Lieutenant - er - Oakshott.' The speaker was in full-dress admiral's coat, and Oakshott recognised him instantly as Sir Richard Cartwright, Rear-Admiral of the Red, a veteran of the American Revolution, who had distinguished himself during that conflict in a single ship action against a rebel privateer, a feat which had won him his admiral's rank, a fine sword from the Patriotic Fund, and the unique privilege of becoming the subject of a popular ballad entitled '*Black Dick's Revenge*'. The shock of black hair and beetling eyebrows were flecked with white now, and the jutting jaw that had been limned upon countless cheap prints and hung in every tavern tap-room in the land was now softened with the plumpness of self-indulgence; but the voice that had addressed Oakshott still possessed the deep-throated timbre of fifteen years before, with which, in the words of the song, he had cried:

Mark you, Master Gunner.
Rake them through from stern to bow!

Two of the others were senior captains unknown to Oakshott. All wore the new-fangled epaulettes. And then there was Pell.

In a corner, out of Oakshott's range of vision, a long-cased clock gave forth a loud and stately tick. A rustle of papers, the admiral cleared his throat, and began:

'Gentlemen, this officer is to be considered as to his suitability for a sea command. A copy of his service record is before each of you. As you will observe, he was placed upon half-pay in late 'eighty-nine. Before we commence a *viva voce* examination into his present professional competence, are there any questions of a general nature that you may wish to address to the candidate? Pray feel free to be as frank and searching as you choose. The responsibility of command of one of His Majesty's ships in time of war, however small that ship, cannot be lightly given. Captain Pell?'

Pell was on the admiral's left. From where Oakshott was sitting, the sunlight from the window beyond shone through the man's thin, unpowdered hair, making it as insubstantial as a halo and giving his head a skull-like appearance.

'Yes, sir, I have a question to put to – *Lord* Charles.' The sepulchral cadences of Pell's voice closed in an undoubted snarl as he pronounced Oakshott's courtesy title.

'Pray proceed, Captain,' boomed the admiral.

Oakshott gathered together his resources for the ordeal of assimilating Pell's question, and of assembling – after not too long a pause – a concise and satisfactory reply, unmarred by any slurring of the speech that might betray his condition – yet without the over-careful manner of address which, in itself, is one of the worst of self-betrayals.

The question – when it came – was blessedly bland and permitted of an instant reply that would give him the opportunity of a moment or so to compose a more particular reponse:

'How have you employed yourself during your three years on half-pay?'

'Variously, sir.'

'Variously? Humph!' The skull-face grinned to show the two rows of gravestones. 'And, no doubt, among the various – employments – you spent a very great deal of time enjoying the roundelay of smart society, hey?'

'I do not mix much in smart society, sir,' said Oakshott.

'Come, come, Lord Charles, do not gull me so,' grated Pell. 'No taking of the waters at Bath, no visits to Italy and the like, to sketch from the antique pictures and statues, no fox-hunting in the Shires?'

The swine is trying to rouse me to an indiscretion, thought Oakshott, for he has probably gleaned that I have had one over the eight. Well, he shall not catch Charlie so easily . . .

'Sir,' he said, 'I do not ride to hounds, for I have to confess to you that I do not greatly like fox-hunters. As to drawing from the antique, I should tell you that a ruled pencil line upon a chart is the sum total of my artistic ability.' Best not give the swine my opinion of damned Bath, he thought, for flippancy would be the worst self-betrayal of all. And what was that tremendously amusing remark of old Ned Daventry's that had tickled my fancy so much back there?

The admiral fidgeted in his chair. Himself the beneficiary of early advancement in the service, he knew full well the motive behind Pell's venomous insinuations and had only borne them thus far because of his junior colleague's undisputed professional stature. He now decided to interrupt:

'With the greatest respect, Captain Pell, I do not think this line of questioning greatly advances us,' he said. 'Instead of speculation, might one not allow Oakshott to tell us in his own words of the various employments - the most relevant employments - with which he has occupied himself during his three years on half-pay? Oakshott...?'

'Sir, I have spent the last twelvemonth in the Low Countries,' said Oakshott. 'For the purpose of learning the pilotage of their river estuaries and inlets, notably the East and West Schelde, the distributaries of the Rhine...'

'From the poop deck or stern gallery of a fine yacht, I shouldn't wonder!' The interjection came from Captain Pell. 'Worked by a paid skipper and crew, while the owner and his friends took fine wines and baked meats while regarding the passing scene.'

The man's animosity, so blatant, so shameless, caused his colleagues on the Board to drop their gazes in embarrassment, to shuffle their papers and examine their fingernails. It was Black Dick who broke the silence that followed Pell's remark:

'Well, Oakshott?' said he.

'I took berth in a coaster plying out of Vlissingen, sir,' replied Oakshott quietly. My God, he thought, the old death's-head nearly got under my guard then.

'Cabin passenger!' sneered Pell.

Oakshott thought of his life aboard that coaster: the miserable five guilders a month that her frequently drunken master had paid him to do all his donkey work, stand watch in the worst of the weather - and all because, with all his faults, the Dutchman knew more about the hazards of the littoral than any man alive. He said nothing.

The admiral cleared his throat diplomatically. 'Well, we shall be glad to learn of your experiences in that particular quarter, Oakshott,' he said. 'There are not many officers in the Navy who have had the opportunity to study closely that particular part of the European coastline which, with the war now upon us, will likely play a signal part in our strategies.'

Black Jack was lending his weight to counterbalance Pell's assault upon Oakshott, as gentleman to gentleman; but the man who had come up through the hawse-hole had shots a-plenty left in his locker.

'I would suggest, Admiral,' he said, and he licked his bloodless lips, 'that Oakshott should not be examined upon the pilotage of the Low Countries, expert though he be in that quarter. Or so he leads us to believe.'

'Why so, Captain?' demanded Black Dick, raising a beetled eyebrow. 'Will it not be an excellent opportunity to gauge the extent of the candidate's professional knowledge of that particular area?'

All eyes were upon Pell. The other two captains, who had thus far taken no part in the proceedings, gazed upon their cadaverous colleague with wary awe - such was Pell's reputation and the grudging respect it commanded among his peers.

Captain Pell's washed-out blue eyes never left Oakshott's eyes as he said: 'With respect, Admiral, I would advise against it. The candidate has told us this and he has told us that. We are left with the impression that he has filled in a year of his half-pay in extending his knowledge. No doubt he wishes to display that knowledge, aware as he is that we officers of the Board possess no more and no less familiarity with the area in question than any British captain who has had occasion, from time to time, to take his ship into a port of the Low Countries.'

'I do not follow your line of argument, Captain,' said the admiral - while looking like a man who had followed it exceedingly well, was anticipating the conclusion, and fervently hoping that it would not be expressed in so many words.

Oakshott continued to hold Pell's gaze, wishing, meanwhile, that he had never had the impulse to venture into Mogg's Diversions.

'I am arguing, sir,' said Pell, in his sepulchral hiss, 'that if we question the candidate upon the navigation and pilotage of this area which he lays loose claim to be an expert in, we give him the opportunity to fill out any deficiencies in his knowledge by the exercising of his imagination - secure as he is in the conviction that none of the Board here assembled may contradict him, or find him in fault, on matters of detail. In short, sir, we shall not be gauging the candidate's professional knowledge, but his capacity for - romancing.'

It had been said - as nearly as made no odds. Oakshott was accused of being a potential liar and cheat. He looked to the admiral for some support against the accusation: Black Dick Cartwright had none to offer; comfortable self-indulgence and a blandly successful professional career had quite overlaid the legendary fire-eater of the popular ballad - if that fire-eater had, indeed, ever existed. The eyes that looked to Pell from under the fierce brows were clouded with indecision, telling of a mind that was seeking for a compromise. The other two captains, who were both junior to Pell, had returned to the careful examination of their fingernails. For the tenth time, Oakshott inwardly cursed himself for having destroyed his defences with brandy: to be other than terse, brief, matter-of-fact, must be to betray his condition to the rest of the Board - a condition of which, he was now convinced, Pell was well aware.

The admiral cleared his throat and said: 'What then do you propose, Captain Pell?'

Pell's thin lips parted in a skull's grin of triumph.

'Might I suggest that the candidate is examined upon his knowledge of the entrance to the English Channel, sir?' he said.

There was a distinct relaxing of the tension within the room. The admiral sat back in his chair and looked bland. The two junior captains nodded to each other. The multifarious problems concerned with the safe progress of a ship making a good landfall and passage of the Channel - one of the most hazardous stretches of water in the world -

were among the most written about, most discussed, topics of navigation. There were standard rules, precepts, laid down and accepted by all captains and masters. The Royal Navy - supreme professionals - knew and accepted them unquestioningly. The members of the Board knew them by rote, and none better than Captain Abel Pell, who was arguably the navy's finest navigator since Captain Cook.

Lieutenant Lord Charles Oakshott knew, and could recite them, as well as any... when sober!

The washed-out blue eyes burned out of the skull face, the graveyard teeth were bared at him. The man who had clawed his way without preferment or privilege up out of the hawse-hole was all set to sit and watch Oakshott destroy his professional career out of his own halting, stumbling, drunken mouth. And all for resentment at a hollow title, and a conviction that it had brought in its train the preferment and privilege denied to the Pells of this world.

(Ye gods! If only he knew, thought Oakshott. Father, before he died, had done the best he could - rest his soul; but, lacking either fortune or connections, the marquisate of Uffingham & Bow, despite the sonorous title, could scarcely advance even a humble midshipman. There had been representations made, early in Oakshott's naval career, to Cousin Hubert, who had been at that time very big in Bristol, the Slave Trade, with a rotten borough in his pocket and a reputed ear at Court - representations concerning little Charlie's early promotion to lieutenant. Whether Uncle Hubert's influence could have stretched that far, or no, had never been put to the test, for almost immediately after, the Bristol nabob's world - social, financial, and in the very literal sense - had fallen apart. Cousin Hubert put a pistol ball in his brain, and little Charlie remained a midshipman till he was past nineteen.)

Oakshott was dragged from his gloomy recollections by Pell's graveyard croak:

'You are approaching the entrance to the Channel on a sou'-westerly wind under bad visibility, on dead reckoning. Name your hazards, and the measures you will take to avoid them.'

The admiral and the other two captains sat back in their

seats, folded their arms and looked smugly at the candidate. Pell's question was a classic. Any competent officer in the service could have answered it without hesitation, without stumbling over a single detail.

Oakshott drew a deep breath, and began:

'Mindful that, by dead reckoning, I may be far off course, I take constant soundings and keep sharp look-out.'

Pell nodded - almost benevolently. 'Yes. And...?'

So far, so good. He was more sober than he had thought. Why, then, could he not remember the next part?

There was a long silence.

'Pray continue, Lieutenant,' murmured the admiral, not unkindly.

'Aaaah...' Oakshott was probing his brain, which seemed to have turned into a place of empty corridors and abandoned rooms.

'Concerning the hazards to north and south,' prompted Black Dick - a prompting that won him a savage sidelong glance from Pell. 'And considering the state of the wind...'

A door opened in Oakshott's brain. Inside, he discerned a familiar ambiance.

'The wind, being sou'-westerly,' he said, 'is fair, of course; but, as is the nature of things in the Channel, may well fly to the northward, which, if I find myself to be standing too far to the French coast when I reach soundings, will put me on a dead lee shore.'

'And so, what precautions will you now take?' This from Pell.

The door of memory was closing again; he fought to assemble the well-learned, classic answer.

'I...'

'Yes?' Pell leaned forward across the table, his thin, white hands toying with the knot of his sword, which lay across the tooled leather. 'You appear to hesitate, *Lord* Charles.'

'Concerning your latitude, Oakshott,' said the admiral, 'will you not, perhaps, stand to the northward?' Another prompting, as from one gentleman to another - and another glare from Pell.

'Yes! I will stand to - inherit...'

'Inherit? Did you say... *inherit*?'

Now they were all looking at him as if he had gone mad. The word had slipped out from one of the empty rooms in his brain. The inheritance. His inheritance - when poor Jack shuffled off this mortal coil and departed to Abraham's bosom. The unwanted inheritance. Unless - and that was the nub of it: the remembrance had come to him on the instant of replying to the question: he had recalled damned odd thing that Ned Daventry had said back there, and, forgetful of the company he was in, gave a chuckle which he had the presence of mind to turn into a not very convincing coughing fit. He groped in his coat-tail pocket for his handkerchief. The members of the Board stared at him with expressions varying from astonishment to - in Pell's case - malice triumphant.

At that moment, the door opened, and a slight figure in captain's uniform was issued in by a clerk.

'Admiral, my most sincere apologies.' The newcomer advanced to the table, and accepted Black Dick's proffered hand. 'I much regret my lateness.'

'Pray do not concern yourself, my dear fellow,' responded Black Dick warmly. 'It was thoroughly disobliging of me to summon you all the way from Chatham while in the course of working up your new ship. How fares *Agamemnon*?'

'Exceedingly well, sir,' replied the other, who had by that time taken the vacant place on the admiral's right, and met Oakshott's eye. A slight smile was playing on the corners of his full, exceedingly mobile lips.

Oakshott, for whom the interruption had been an undeserved blessing, had by then quenched the paroxysm of mirth with the gloomy thought that he had almost certainly dashed his chances of promotion and a command. He replaced his handkerchief and waited for his destruction, as a patient ox attends the slaughterer's pole-axe.

Gesturing towards the victim in the chair before them, the admiral said: 'We are at present examining this officer regarding his suitability for command.'

'So the clerk apprised me, sir,' replied the newcomer. 'I trust that these proceedings are a mere formality, and that

Lord Charles will be given his ship without delay, and the concomitant promotion.'

The admiral stared at the speaker. The rest of the Board stared at the speaker. Oakshott also.

'Why do you say that, my dear fellow?' asked Black Dick.

For answer, the new arrival rose to his feet, rounded the table, and advanced upon Oakshott, hand extended. Oakshott, bemused, stood up.

'Lord Charles, I am exceedingly happy to make your acquaintance. My ship, it was, that came upon the French frigate you so skilfully enticed upon the Shipwash. My name is Nelson.'

Numbly, Oakshott took the proffered hand. Captain Nelson's eyes were dark blue verging on grey - like the waters of the German Ocean that washed England's eastern shore. His prominent nose twitched at the nostrils - perhaps catching the reek of brandy, lightly masked with cloves, upon Oakshott's breath.

'Pray will you be so good as to explain what this is all about, my dear Nelson,' said the admiral.

Then - unbelievably - Oakshott was listening to the account of his exploit, as told to Nelson by the captain of the Dutch brig, when he had quizzed the Hollander on the morning after Oakshott's departure for home. Captain Kuyper had laid it on mightily thick, with much dwelling upon the Englishman's cool handling of the brig under heavy fire, his simple and audacious plan to entrap the French. In the telling, it sounded vastly unlike the sequence of events as Oakshott recalled them; but it had a marked effect upon the members of the Board - particularly upon Captain Pell, who was glaring at his intended victim with the look of an angler who, after having played a trout with consummate skill to the very lip of his landing net, sees the fish escape from his hook and go streaking away to freedom.

Then they had all risen and were shaking hands with the hero.

Oakshott found his voice. To Nelson, he said: 'I trust, sir, that your prize was brought safely to harbour.'

The other shook his head. 'Regrettably not, Lord Charles,'

he said. 'Our broadside carried away her mizzen entirely, together with her main topgallant, whereupon the Frenchies hauled down their colours. I had just called away a boat to land a boarding party, when - would you credit it for the devil's own luck? - she broke free of the sandbank and was away, re-hoisting the confounded tricolour as she went. There was no catching her; even without mizzen and main topgallant, she was able to show a clean pair of heels to my *Agamemnon,* notwithstanding that she's the finest sixty-four as ever came out of Buckler's Hard and the best sailer in the fleet.'

There was much general talk - professional talk - about the superior sailing qualities of French-built ships, particularly of their extremely fast frigates; and interspersed with comments upon the perfidy of an enemy who would cut and run after having struck his colours. Oakshott found himself being gathered up in the conversation between his superiors - almost as if they regarded him as an equal (all excepting Pell, who continued to treat him to black looks). All spoke knowledgeably, but none more so than Captain Nelson. Oakshott had heard of Nelson: he was reputed to be something of a stormy petrel, marked for high command, a captain of some considerable seniority, since he had achieved that rank at the exceedingly early age of twenty - though whether through his own merits, or because of influence (his uncle, as Oakshott recalled, had been Suckling, a former Comptroller of the Navy Board), one had no way of telling.

The various alarms and excursions seemed to have quite dispelled the alcohol from his brain. Nelson was talking to him, now, and shaking his hand.

'Congratulations,' said he. 'You will get your ship, and I trust she brings you fame. We may meet again, and if it be at sea, I shall know that *Agamemnon* is in good company. The best of fortune go with you. Farewell - Commander.'

He was a commander! And now they were all shaking him by the hand, congratulating him; even Pell - though that cadaverous spectre at the feast of his triumph proffered his cold and clammy hand with no more accompaniment than a sniff of displeasure.

Oakshott left the Board Room walking ten feet in air; met the anxious face of Lieutenant Trelawney, who was next to be summoned, and whose trepidation was in no way lessened by the obvious success that was written all over his brother officer's countenance.

The young gentlemen on the stairs looked up from their navigation books at his passing; all save Ned Daventry - last in the line and not like to be called much before the late afternoon - who was fast asleep, a seraphic smile upon his homely, bovine face.

Out in the sudden sunlight of the Admiralty courtyard, Oakshott was struck by a fear that a resolve newly formed in his mind might have been thwarted by time's passing: it was close upon half past eleven and perhaps he was too late. He took his life in his hands in the crossing of Whitehall; leaping from under the wheels of a passing phaeton, elbowing his way past a herd of cows, ducking beneath the stomach of a slow-moving shire dray-horse.

Darting up the Strand, he came to the doors of Mogg's Diversions and elbowed his way in. The musical entertainment had ceased, but the establishment was even more crowded than before, with the midday *flâneurs* and dandies strolling the promenade in search of a fair cheek and a roving eye - nor did they need to look far, for the ladies of the town had arrived in some profusion.

Oakshott looked anxiously about him. She whom he sought was not seated at the table that they had shared together with Ned Daventry. He was too late, he told himself. She had gone - no doubt glad, having finished her turn of singing, to shake the dust of Mogg's Diversions from her prim, dainty heels.

But - no...

He sighted her some distance away, seated with two other ladies who had the looks of singers or actresses. She met his eye and inclined her head with the grace that had so commended her to his taste.

Oakshott, his mind still upon the amusing response that Ned Daventry had made to his plaintive declaration that a wife simply must be found for his dolefully unattractive brother, could only conclude – at that precise moment of encountering Miss Howarth for the second time – that his old shipmate's lightly-made suggestion had really been an utterance of the Delphic Sybil placed into his drunken mouth, all unsuspected.

He approached her table...

Yes, distinctly wholesome, with child-bearing hips and ample means to suckle a whole new breed of Oakshotts. And, thanks to her upbringing, she had the style to wear a coronet. Nothing like religion and genteel poverty to bring out the best in a good woman. There remained the task of introducing her to the notion, of course; but that would be like falling out of a hammock compared to steering her through her first encounter with poor old Jack.

She was smiling at him.

'Hello again, Lord Charles,' she said. 'How went your enterprise?'

'Very satisfactorily, ma'am,' he replied.

'And Mr Daventry – he is not with you?'

'He is still awaiting to appear, ma'am,' said Oakshott. 'The notion of returning here was entirely mine. I had feared to find you gone.'

'Oh, I am to sing again at noon, sir. Will you take a seat? May I introduce you to these ladies?...'

Introductions having been briefly made, Oakshott declined to take a seat, but, bending low over Miss Howarth, he murmured: 'Ma'am,is there somewhere we can go and talk quietly? I have a proposition – a rather singular proposition – to put to you.'

It says much for the fascination of the tall, dark man with the oddly alluring eyes that the Archdeacon's daughter acquiesced to the suggestion of a *tête-á-tête* almost without hesitation.

Chapter Three

THE BANNS OF MARRIAGE having been called on three successive Sundays in the private chapel of Sennett Palace, Jack Oakshott, sixth Marquess of Uffingham & Bow, was joined in holy matrimony on the Monday following with Miss Harriet Howarth, spinster.

Miss Howarth, her natural modesty at odds with her pressing need to make better provision for her mother and sisters than could be obtained from singing in Mogg's Diversions, had been with some difficulty persuaded by Charles Oakshott to visit Sennett, meet Sennett's incumbent, and see for herself.

Sennett (she having no architectural knowledge and, the weather being fine at the time, unaware of the leaking quality of its roofs) enchanted her, being everything that her fundamentally snobbish little heart had yearned for ever since the demise of her father had led to their expulsion from the modest, but elegant, Queen Anne house in the cathedral precinct. As to her putative intended: Oakshott had taken his brother firmly in hand; a visit to London to procure a new wig and a ready-made coat in the French style, together with accessories such as silk stockings, breeches, pumps, shirts and plain stocks and a decent-looking hat, greatly improved Jack's appearance. In fact, as his brother was the first to concede, the sixth Marquess, bathed and shaved, dressed up and pomaded, cut not a bad figure at all. Rather more than merely mature, perhaps - but maturity adds a certain distinction when coupled with high rank. And, well cleaned up, the essential Oakshott good looks gleamed fitfully through the wreckage of thirty years of debauchery and gluttony.

Jack, all dolled up and forcibly kept off the bottle for the whole of the twenty-four hours preceding the encounter, scored a palpable hit with Miss Howarth, who, considering her pressing needs and having regard for the prospect of a dizzy elevation to the higher ranks of the peerage, was less than inclined to look a gift horse in the mouth. She privately intimated to Charles Oakshott that, should the Marquess formally propose marriage, the offer would merit serious consideration.

Jack, it was, who raised all the objections...

'I won't say the wench ain't comely,' he conceded. 'But she has a prim and prissy, a sort of purse-mouthed look about her that I always associate with religiosity and a backwardness in bed. In short, Charlie, I am greatly obliged to you for your trouble, but she simply ain't to my taste.'

'I am aware of your taste in womanflesh, Jack,' responded his brother, 'but this is not the seventeenth century, and marquesses are not marrying whores this season. Better to marry than to burn, Jack - for burn you will, soon or late, with the fires of the pox, unless you quit tumbling every doxie in Berkshire and London, and settle for a good woman. And you have said yourself that Miss Howarth is comely...'

In the end, it was lust that trapped Jack Oakshott. The firm rebuffing of a fumbling attempt on his part to anticipate some of the peripheral delights of the marriage bed only served to fan the flame of his desire. While Miss Howarth readjusted her bodice, he blurted out his proposal - and was accepted. Accordingly, as aforesaid, upon a fair Monday morning in the Year of Our Lord 1793, he took to himself, for better or for worse, for richer or for poorer, in sickness or in health, the late Archdeacon's daughter.

Commander Lord Charles Oakshott, Royal Navy, in a new gold-laced dress coat, stood up as best man for his brother. In the tail-pocket of the selfsame coat reposed a letter from My Lords of the Admiralty requesting and requiring Cdr Ld Chas Oakshott, RN to repair to Portsmouth forthwith, there to assume command of HM Sloop-of-War *Daisy*, 18-guns. It had fortuitously arrived that very morning. That - and the brandies that Oakshott had imbibed with breakfast - accounted for the feeling of high euphoria which caused him to look upon the proceedings with such geniality.

The bride's relations were represented by the widowed mother and the sisters - all tricked out in new clothes for the occasion. Also present were a bevy of aunts, great-aunts, nieces and nephews - all of them agog, and suitably impressed by the eminence to which their Harriet had raised herself.

The local rector and chaplain to Sennett Palace, whose living was in the gift of the marquess, performed the ceremony and delivered the two and three-quarter hour long sermon afterwards: a protracted speech that began, in all good faith, and illuminated by suitable texts, as a dissertation upon the virtues of holy matrimony, and drifted almost imperceptibly into a homily upon the virtues of the snaffle bit and the advantages of keeping the hounds well whipped in when drawing a covert. The Rev Mr Clarence Hardcourt-ffinch was a hunting parson of the classic mould, and a three-bottle man of repute.

The quite astonishingly lovely bride had marched up the aisle upon Ned Daventry's well-muscled arm, past the crested resting places of five Marquesses of Uffingham & Bow, their seven Marchionesses, and the numerous fruits of their noble loins; under the tattered banners that Oakshotts had borne in the Civil Wars and subsequent conflicts; skirting the crocks that had been laid out to catch the drips of rain-water which had penetrated the crumbling leads of the chapel roof the night before. Ned was in a brand new lieutenant's coat, having, against all expectation and likelihood, passed his examination before the Board - a chance so unexpected and unlikely as quite to upset Ned's equilibrium and deprive him of the solace of being very nearly the most senior midshipman in the Royal Navy, in exchange for becoming one of the most junior (and oldest) lieutenants.

The two and three-quarter hour long sermon having ended, and Charles Oakshott and many others having awakened, the bride proceeded down the aisle upon her husband's arm out into the sunlight, to receive the plaudits of the couple of hundred mostly hungry and rebellious tenants, who, thanks to having been generously breakfasted at their lord's expense upon fat bacon, chitterlings, pigs' cheek, baked potatoes, parsnips, turnips and curly kale – all washed down with cider, strong ale, with small beer for the children and infirm – were in the mood to give loud huzzahs for the marquess and his lady-wife. Dipping his licentious gaze towards his new bride's bosom and other charms, Jack Oakshott, Marquess of Uffingham & Bow, decided that he had, after all, made a good match: one that was popular with his family, his tenants, and, by Jupiter, what a pair of bubs she had upon her!

Amid the huzzahs and the throwing of much rice and flower petals, the marquess and his new bride were driven off to their nuptial bed that awaited them in the south wing of their mouldering seat. Their wedding coach was none other than that in which the previous incumbent but one (the rakehell marquess) had had made to take him to the coronation of King George II. It was of fine wood, and cunningly carved and gilded in the Baroque manner, with naked nymphs, satyrs, and putti painted upon the door panels. Disastrously worm-eaten and its springs long since gone, it was questionable if it could have crossed the yard that separated the south wing entrance to the palace from the chapel porch, let alone returned there, had not the two pairs of matched greys that drew the conveyance been so senile and gentle that they were only with difficulty whipped up into a slow walk.

'My dear Charles. How are you?'

Oakshott turned to face the speaker, of whose presence he had, from time to time and when awake, been uncomfortably aware during the marriage ceremony. Tall, nearly as tall as he. Blonde as he was contrastingly sable. Green eyes that complimented his particoloured ones. Irene Chancellor – even when she had been married to his boyhood friend – had always possessed the power to move him in a curious way.

He bowed over her hand.

'I thank you, Irene, I am well,' he said. 'I need scarcely ask of yourself, since your good health is splendidly writ all upon you.'

There was not an ounce of coquetry in her, to respond to his gallantry; she merely looked at him from under unbelievably long lashes, and with a gaze as steady and candid as could be, and said: 'Charles, you have been home in England a month and more, yet you have not once visited me, nor even sent me a line. Have I, perhaps, in some way offended you?'

'Madam, you have not,' replied Oakshott.

'Why, then, have you neglected me so?'

Oakshott spread his hands. 'Irene, I will not dissemble. The truth is, I have been greatly concerned with a great crisis of my life.'

'Touching upon what matter, pray?' demanded Irene Chancellor.

'Upon two connected matters: the first being my prospects in the Navy and the second being that of my brother Jack's wedding, bedding, and siring of an heir, to relieve me of the intolerable burden of the succession.'

With her fan, she tapped the gleaming new facings of his full-dress coat.

'As to the first, I see, and have heard, that your future prospects are assured, Charles, and that we must now call you "Commander" - for which I offer my congratulations. As to the second' - she directed her fan towards the ramshackle coronation coach and matched greys, which by then, and with much travail, had managed to cross the yard - 'that matter has also been brought, if not to final fruition, at least within the scope of conception.'

'Happily, that is so,' admitted Oakshott.

'You will, then, call upon me soon?'

'That I will, ma'am.'

'Today - for tea.'

'Ma'am, as you know, I am not one for tea.'

'Ah, I had quite forgot.' She touched her satin cheek with a forefinger, and the green eyes looked thoughtful. 'And -

would you credit it? – I cannot ask you to supper, for there is not so much as a mutton chop in the house.'

He was very close to her, so that he caught the soft odour of her body, which was compounded of musk and violets. Oakshott swallowed hard.

'Then, Irene, I shall be obliged to go supperless,' he said huskily. 'At what hour shall I present myself?'

The green eyes met his – squarely.

'Be in no great hurry, sir,' she said. 'Take your supper. Take wine and brandy – not too much brandy – and call upon me at some suitable and convenient hour. Shall we say – midnight?'

He bent over her hand. 'Midnight, as ever is,' said he.

Portsmouth struck Oakshott as being like an overturned beehive. He had taken shank's pony from the posting inn to the dockyard, hiring a lad with a barrow to follow at his heels with his sea-chest and other traps. The streets teemed with traffic, the pavements with seamen of all sorts, hawkers and beggars, doxies, bawds, spavined children with hands outthrust for coppers. Everywhere was the smell of humanity, of stale fish, tobacco, beer, onions, and rum. Narrowing his eyes against the glare, Oakshott peered out across the harbour. From the Hard to Haslar, from Southsea to Cosham, bristled a forest of masts and spars; the assembled might of Albion's seafaring sons gathered to go to war. Not far from where he stood and paused to give the lad with the barrow time to draw breath, a three-decker bearing the pennant of an admiral of the Blue was being warped alongside. His professional eye roved over her towering sides and rigging, searching for a flaw to her magnificence. The marines drawn up on the forecastle were graded according to size, tallest for'ard; she having entered harbour with aid of headsails and mizzen, topmen were swarming the yards and furling all plain sail. The instant her bow kissed – ever so gently – the protective bundles of faggots against the quay, jib and flying jib were taken in as neatly as roller blinds. Among the be-cocked and braided officers upon her quarterdeck there was one who deliberately raised a telescope to his eye and treated Oakshott to a brief inspection. The latter had just noticed that - all unobserved by the preening peacocks on the quarterdeck - a line of sailors' none-too-clean small clothes was hanging out to dry in the shadow of the heads; he raised his hat to the three-decker's ensign and went on his way, smiling.

'*Daisy*? Be there any o' you what knows a sloop name o' *Daisy*?' The bum-boat man whom Oakshott approached enquired of his mates. Someone opined that the *Daisy* was over close by the Haslar shore, and treated Oakshott to an all-over look of speculation, so that the latter was half inclined to ask if the fellow was familiar with the vessel and her crew; but restrained his eager curiosity. The lad with the barrow having been paid off, and the bum-boat man having been given his two shillings fare in advance (for even braided commanders were known to bilk on settling their score), Oakshott, his sea-chest and traps were rowed across the scummy waters of Portsmouth harbour, with seagulls swooping and screaming about his head and his heart fit to burst with pride and joy at his first command.

Past anchored frigates, lean and deadly as lurchers; betwixt two lines of mixed sixty-fours and seventy-fours, moored bow to stern; and beyond, where smaller fry lay clustered alongside, three and four to a buoy. Somewhere among them must lie his own *Daisy*. He scanned their sterns for the magic name - but saw it not. And any one of them would have suited him admirably, for all were in prime condition as to paintwork, cordage, and general smartness of appearance.

Beyond the buoys were a line of piles close inshore, used for colliers, herring boats, harbour craft and the like. At the end of a line of such humble vessels, close by Haslar pier, was a small, full-rigged ship with a string of - he made a swift count - nine gun ports along her side. A grimy white ensign drooped forlornly from her mizzen peak. Oakshott knew upon the instant, and with a sudden lowering of the spirits and sinking of the heart, that he was gazing upon his new command - a fact that was confirmed a few moments later when, having drawn closer, he was able to discern, in faded gold-leaf letters upon her counter, the legend *Daisy*.

The vessel next in line along the piles was a herring boat and stank vilely. The *Daisy* sloop had a different stink: fainter, yet more unpleasant and pervasive. It put Oakshott in mind of the prison hulks, or of his own brother's unwashed state.

''Ere we be, mister,' said the boatman, sculling the craft close by the sloop's accommodation ladder. 'And as ill-kempt a tub as I ever did see, s'welp me if she ain't.'

'Shut your damned mouth!' snapped Oakshott, and was immediately sorry.

Two steps up, both hands on the gunwale capping, and he was standing in the waist of his new command. Below, the gundeck; and the quarterdeck to his right, with main capstan, mizzen, and wheel beyond. The stink welled up from below. There was not a soul about: no bosun's mates, no officer of the watch, nobody.

'Ahoy!' shouted Oakshott.

No response.

He swung himself down the companion-way on to the gundeck; peered into the gloom aft. At that moment, a screen door opened and a figure in shirt and breeches lurched out.

'Who the devil is it?' demanded the apparition.

'Who is in present charge of this ship?' countered Oakshott calmly.

'Why, the first lieutenant,' said the other. 'And who may you...?'

'And where is the first lieutenant?'

'Ashore. At least, he was ashore when I got my head down.'

'And the remainder of the crew - do they also have their heads down?'

'Tis a make-do-and-mend afternoon.'

'I see,' said Oakshott. 'A make-do-and-mend afternoon.' He glanced down at his feet, and was disgusted to see a pile of food scraps lying there.

The man whom he was addressing, having come closer, revealed himself to be a fellow in his early twenties. The shirt he wore, though none too clean, was of good cambric, and the breeches were decent nankeen. Presumably an officer. His sleep-bleared eyes having become accustomed to the glaring sunlight beyond the shadows of the quarterdeck-head, he was able to discern that the silhouetted figure who had been interrogating him so closely wore the braid of a Commander, RN. His manner immediately ceased to be surly and became truculently defensive.

'The first lieutenant, it was, who ordered a general make-and-mend - sir,' he said. Not that 'tis any of your damned business, whoever you may be, he implied.

'Then be so good as to summon a couple of hands to bring down my chest and traps,' said Oakshott. 'Then show me to my day cabin.'

'Your - your day cabin?' Not only bemused by sleep, the fellow was half drunk.

'I am your captain,' said Oakshott quietly.

In such a manner did the heir presumptive to the marquisate of Uffingham & Bow come to his new command.

The officer introduced himself as Lieutenant Stevens, senior officer aboard after the absent first lieutenant. He affected this introduction in the day cabin aft, which had a three-light window looking out at the bows of the herring boat astern, a pile of dirty clothing littering the let-down cot, a table bearing the broken remains of a meat pie, a half-filled jug of beer, and a map of Portsmouth harbour spread out like a tablecloth and bespattered with beer and gravy. The compartment reeked of decayed food, tobacco and feet.

'And this is Mr Quinch the master, sir. And this is Midshipman Shacklock. The rest of the officers are ashore.'

Stevens had put on his coat. The others were also fully dressed, with the appearance of those who had only recently achieved that state - indeed, the lappet of the midshipman's breeches was half-unfastened. He, a lad of thirteen or fourteen, struck Oakshott as something of a handful, with the half-idiot, half-sly look which young gentlemen of his age employ as protective colouring in fraught circumstances. Quinch the warrant officer seemed a decent sort of fellow and clearly overawed by his new captain. Of the three, only he appeared to be at all conscious of the cabin's appalling state: from time to time, his worried, pouched spaniel's eyes wandered towards the table, and from there to the cot, thence to the unemptied chamber pot in a corner.

Oakshott felt disinclined to shake hands with the trio at that particular moment; contented himself by nodding stiffly at each presentation. He then sat down at the table, pushing aside the dish containing the remains of the meat pie.

'Mr Stevens,' he said mildly, 'I should be obliged if you would bring me the ship's log. Also if you would inform me as soon as the first lieutenant - er - Mr ...?'

'Mr Hodges, sir.'

'If you would be so good as to inform me as soon as Mr Hodges repairs aboard.'

'Yes, sir. Will that be all?' Stevens looked down at the meat pie, then at his captain; seemed about to laugh, but settled for an expression of flat contempt.

'That will be all, thank you,' responded Oakshott.

'Aye, aye, sir.' Stevens touched his forelock, turned about, and strode out of the cabin with the tall, loping master and the diminutive, grinning midshipman in his wake.

'Ah - Mr Shacklock - a moment, if you will.'

'Yes sir?' The youth spun round at his captain's voice, the grin vanishing like a rabbit up a conjurer's sleeve, to be replaced by the sly idiot look.

'Be so good, Mr Shacklock,' said Oakshott, 'as to tell off a boy to come and square off my cabin somewhat, will you, please?'

'Aye, aye, sir.'

'Where are you from, Mr Shacklock?'

'From, sir?' The idiot look was intensified.

'From which part of the country do you hail, Mr Shacklock?' said Oakshott patiently.

'Falmouth, sir.'

'Falmouth - ah!'

'Yes sir.'

'You are a Cornishman?'

'A what, sir?'

Oakshott very deliberately thought of a number - twenty-three - determined its cube root, and divided it by seven, before he replied:

'A Cornishman, Mr Shacklock,' he said. 'One who is born, bred, raised - indeed, mayhap, whose forebears have been born, bred and raised within the duchy from time immemorial. Are you one such, Mr Shacklock?'

'We be Devon folk, sir,' replied the midshipman - and the unmistakable west country burr that had prompted Oakshott to quizz the youth as to his antecedents broadened richly. 'My father, he was a Plymouth man, and my grandad before. The family moved to Falmouth afore I was born. My father, he's a lawyer, sir.'

'A lawyer - ah.' A lawyer's son, thought Oakshott, and a younger son, without doubt. How many younger sons of the professional classes - offsprings of lawyers, parsons, physicians and the like - debarred from lack of funds from following their fathers' footsteps and those of their older brothers, were sent to be officers? Upon such an unpromising source, as also upon the younger sons of the nobility, did all England, the Navy in particular, now rely in her hour of need. Well, let her not rely in vain - even upon such an unpromising-looking source as the youth who stood before him.

'Yes sir,' said Shacklock, for no reason in particular.

'You may go, Mr Shacklock,' said Oakshott. 'And mind you tell off a boy.'

'Aye, aye, sir.' The animation that had briefly touched the youth's unaccommodating countenance when he had spoken of his antecedents had given away again to that of calculated stupidity.

The boy was long in coming. Before he arrived, Stevens had brought the ship's log and Oakshott was well into it. The ship's boy - officers' servant in times of quiet and powder monkey when the guns roared, for which he was paid the princely sum of six shillings and eight pence a month - turned out to be a vastly more engaging youth than the recently departed Mr Midshipman Shacklock, and who, without a word or gesture and without disturbing his captain at his labours, set to and made some considerable inroads upon squaring off the appalling state of the day cabin: emptying the slops and the remains of the meat pie out of the stern window; quietly sweeping up the teak-boarded deck, bundling the soiled clothing into a pillow-case, and silently stealing away when all was done.

Oakshott never once looked up from his concentrated attention upon the volume before him: the written record of everything that had occurred in and around HM Sloop-of-War *Daisy* since she had been taken, along with many others such, from moorings in a remote part of Gosport creek where she had lain since the conclusion of the American Revolution ten years previously, and put into commission for the new war. She had been recommissioned three months before, with Lieutenant Percy Hodges, RN, as first lieutenant, acting captain, and half the complement of 130 crew. Her new career had not been ardous as to distance run: she had merely been towed from Gosport creek to her present berth off Haslar pier. Considering her appearance, thought Oakshott ruefully, it was not surprising that the authorities ashore had tucked her so well out of sight of the good citizens of Portsmouth town, for she was not an object to arouse much confidence in the populace.

Despite *Daisy's* slender contribution to the overthrow of the wicked French, life aboard her in the first three months of her commissioning, as recorded in her log-book, had been lively to the extreme - as Oakshott read with mounting concern and astonishment.

The last page having been turned, bringing the account almost up to date (Hodges, who had penned the main body of the text - in a particularly varied handwriting that permitted a rich field of speculation - had not made the entries for that day, nor the previous day). Oakshott took a scrap of paper and made an abstract of the crimes and misdemeanours committed aboard during the three months and of the punishments doled out for the same. The cold figures, the flat recitation of the facts, made astonishing reading.

On the first day of the recommissioning, and while the ship was still in Gosport creek, Alfred Cummings, able seaman, Norris John Burke, able seaman, and Cyril Cooper, shipwright's mate, had been found guilty of slackness and summarily sentenced to twenty lashes of the cat-o'-nine tails apiece. That had been only the first thread in a pattern of crime and punishment which had become inextricably woven into the warp and weft of life aboard the ship. The tale was repetitive almost to the point of monotony: Hubert Timmins, ship's boy - silent insolence - twenty lashes; five others on the following day - slow to obey orders of a superior - thirty lashes; slackness; lateness; silent insolence; skulking below deck; more silent insolence; and no other punishment save the lash, all in multiples of ten, up to the number of fifty. One entry, only, broke the pattern: John Sugg, able seaman, for striking a superior rating, had been sent ashore for court-martial a week previously and had been imprisoned.

Oakshott totted up the doleful sum, and calculated that, of the sixty-odd ratings who made up *Daisy's* half-complement, there could scarcely have been a handful who did not carry the weals of the cat upon their backs. And many had been punished several times over.

Laying aside the log-book, he crossed to his sea-chest, took out a finely-carved walnut case, in whose cushioned interior nestled a pair of decanters containing port wine and brandy respectively, together with two crystal glasses. He poured himself a generous measure of the spirit, rolled the glass between his hand to warm and release the delicate vapours; took a deep and steady draught.

Replenishing his measure, he went out of the cabin, out into the dying sunlight of the summer's eve. There was a small group of seamen huddled on the fo'c's'le. Their heads turned as one at the sound of his tread - and immediately looked away. Before Oakshott had climbed the companionway to the quarterdeck, the men had made themselves scarce below. He was alone on the upper deck.

The rosy light of evening did little to soften *Daisy's* neglected charms, though the jaunty rake of her masts and the fine spread of her yards told of a proud past and - perhaps - a not unpromising future. But the rail upon which Oakshott rested his hand was rickety to the touch, the scuppers were jammed with accumulated filth, and there were uncoiled ropes' ends everywhere - more like a chandler's shop than a ship-of-war. Oakshott sighted, reached up and took hold of a ratline in the mizzen mast rigging - one of the hand and footholds upon which men's lives depended. It was half rotted through; one sharp tug and it parted in his grasp.

From away across the water, the brassy notes of a bugle sketched out the Retreat. It was taken up by others, and by shrill bosuns' pipes from all round the assembled fleet. A belated clatter of footfalls, and Midshipman Shacklock raced up the companion-way, hat askew and buckling on his dirk. A seaman followed him. At the sight of his new captain, the youth's sly eyes flashed terror. He clumsily saluted Oakshott.

'S-sunset, sir,' he stammered.

'Make it so, Mr Shacklock,' responded Oakshott.

The midshipman nodded to his seaman companion, who, placing the bosun's pipe to his lips, essayed a hopeful attempt at the prescribed call to accompany the lowering of the ensign at sunset. Shacklock himself performed the lowering - after an embarrassing delay in untying the knot that secured the ends of the ensign halyard to the taffrail - almost certain proof that the knot was of long standing, indicating that the *Daisy* had carried her ensign through the night for long since.

Oakshott saluted the scrap of filthy red, white and blue bunting that represented all England's hopes against a cruel and implacable enemy, and went below. There, he poured himself another brandy, and thought of Irene Chancellor for a long while.

Three hours later, well after midnight, the first lieutenant came back aboard.

Lt Hodges, considering the state in which he had lived in the captain's day cabin, and considering the state in which he had for so long allowed the ship to remain - was himself remarkably well turned out, in an undress coat that was innocent of the slightest speck of lint (no mean feat with navy blue broadcloth), stark white linen, highly-polished Hessian boots. Standing before Oakshott, (who remained seated behind the table), with hat tucked under one arm and sword hilt lightly supported at the level of his lower rib, one foot advanced like a dancing master, head erect, he looked every inch the gallant naval officer personified in the patriotic broadsheets, darling of every maiden and envy of gentlemen in England now a-bed.

'Welcome aboard, sir,' said he.

Oakshott thought of the broken ratline, and merely nodded.

The fellow was about his own age, and handsome with it, in a florid, heavily-jowled, blue-chinned way. His mouth was small, the lips curly and soft-looking. His hair was jet-black and unpowdered, worn in a long queue. But it was his eyes which commanded Oakshott's interest - and attention; they were of the palest blue imaginable, and they were never still. Upon entering the cabin, they had seen - and clearly noted - that some effort had been made to tidy the compartment; next, they had observed the opened drinks' container, the half-empty decanter of brandy and the glass at Oakshott's elbow. Oakshott, they had observed, was in shirtsleeves, with his stock unfastened. All this they had seen - and surely that was a contemptuous sneer upon those girlishly-chiselled red lips?

He thinks I am a slack dresser, thought Oakshott. And that I'm drunk in the bargain, I shouldn't wonder.

He pushed the decanter and glass across the table.

'Help yourself, Mr Hodges,' he said.

A slight wariness of manner slipped from the first lieutenant, but the sneer remained - allied to a confident jauntiness. He poured himself an uncivilly large measure of brandy and raised his glass in salute.

'To you, sir - and to your new command,' he said smoothly.

'I thank you,' murmured Oakshott.

'She's a fine sailer, I am informed, sir,' said Hodges. 'French-built, you know. Taken in the last war. They can build ships that go like the devil to windward can the Frogs. Mind you, there's much to be done to her till we have her shipshape and Bristol-fashion. 'Tis a long-term policy. Yes, a long-term policy.'

A damned long-term policy indeed, thought Oakshott. Damn-all done in three months. He said nothing.

Hodges drained his glass. The pale eyes flickered momentarily over the decanter.

'It'll not be easy, though,' he said. 'Only half a crew they gave me. The battleships have the pick of the men. Not that there's any quality about. Sweepings of the seaports, most of 'em pressed. Idle, mutinous swabs. Only one thing they respect – and that's the cat!'

Oakshott tapped the decanter.

'Help yourself to another, and tell me more about the crew, Mr Hodges,' he said quietly.

'Thank you, sir,' said the other, and did so. 'Er – do you mind if I sit down, pray?'

Oakshott gestured towards a stool, which the first lieutenant took and placed by the table, opposite his commanding officer. He smiled suavely over the rim of the glass.

'The toast is the same, sir,' he said.

Oakshott inclined his head. 'I thank you, Mr Hodges. Pray continue your extremely interesting dissertation.'

The small, rosy mouth was pursed in a sudden anger, and the pale eyes flared wide.

'Scum of the earth!' he hissed. 'My first intent has been to break them. No use attempting anything till that was done. I've flogged 'em all, men and boys both.' He licked his lips, moist as they already were. 'Men and boys both. They jump to it now when I call all hands. Have no fear on that score. You can leave them to me and rest easy in your mind.' His manner changed again, the storm of fury fading as suddenly as it had begun. The gaze that roved over the man seated opposite – taking in the travel-crumpled shirt, the loose ends of the neck-stock, the ruffled hair, the empty glass at

Oakshott's elbow – was now frankly patronising. 'I take it you, also, have been out on half-pay?' he asked.

Oakshott nodded. 'Three years.'

''Tis a long time, a cruel long time,' said Hodges, and the rosy mouth pursed again. 'I have had four years on the beach, damn' the Admiralty. But times have changed. Now, it's "Bravo, gallant Jack Tar!" There'll be pickings in plenty for us, Captain mine, just as soon as I've broken the spirits of that mutinous rabble up for'ard and put this ship in order. Oh, yes, Captain mine, we'll all be rich on prize money before the year is out, see if we ain't!'

'That will be very – acceptable,' said Oakshott flatly.

The other beamed at him. 'Sir, I like you,' he said. 'You, sir, are a gentleman who's been much put upon, I can see that plain. Three years on the beach on half-pay has left its mark on you. Now, with me it was different. Percy Hodges, now he isn't the sort to starve in the midst of plenty – I say, this is remarkably fine brandy, do you mind if . . .?'

'Please help yourself,' said Oakshott.

The other readily obeyed, spilling the spirit as he poured. 'Ha, I could make your hair curl with the tales of how I've made ends meet these past four years, Captain mine,' he said. 'Percy Hodges ain't one to starve. Ha! There are ways and means. Ways and means.' The pale eyes took on a sudden cunning. 'Since we're to be working so closely together, you and I, I may tell you that there's ways and means, even aboard this ship, wherein a man may more than make ends meet. And I am not speaking of prize money now. Ha!' He quaffed deeply of Oakshott's brandy.

This is the truth of it, thought Oakshott. Condemned out of his own mouth, his tongue loosened by a few bumpers of spirit. The mystery of a man who will flog an entire crew and then order a make-and-mend day aboard a ship as filthy as a pigsty. A man who himself has lived in the most utter squalor, but who steps ashore as if he'd just walked out of a naval tailor's emporium.

The truth of the first lieutenant of the *Daisy*: he was insane!

*

Oakshott rid himself of the man an hour later: watched him stagger unsteadily to a cot that had been made up for him in the wardroom. He then sent for the purser, and, finding that there was no such person aboard, settled for the purser's mate; who arrived, sleepy-eyed and fearful. Ten minutes over the supply books - plus a keen questioning of the wretched purser's mate - elicited the fact that Hodges' boast about 'making ends meet' in *Daisy* had been nothing less than a systematic - and extremely clumsy - defrauding of the ship's funds and victuals, a pursuit in which the purser's mate had been the unwilling accomplice, upon threat of the cat-o'-nine tails.

Oakshott slept on his findings, rising at six in the morning to douse himself, naked, under the deck pump; then to gird himself in full-dress uniform coat, hat, sword, telescope. Which done, he sent a message for Hodges to attend him immediately. Hodges was not soon in coming, and presented, when he did, a vastly different picture from the gallant officer of the night before: stock hastily tied, hair tousled, unshaven, stockings wrinkled. The pale eyes, red rimmed now, came to rest upon the supply books lying significantly open on the table. They flashed to meet Oakshott's, questioningly, defiantly. Oakshott realised, with something of a shock, that it was the first time that Hodges had looked him squarely in the eyes.

'Well?' demanded Oakshott, who was standing behind the table, his hat on, telescope held like a field-marshal's baton. 'What is your defence?'

'I don't know what you mean?' came the reply.

Remember he's insane, Oakshott told himself...

'I will put it plain,' he said aloud. 'You have two options. If you choose, I will send these books, with the evidence of your fraud, to the admiral commanding Portsmouth...'

'I deny it!' cried Hodges wildly. 'I demand a court-martial, to clear my name!'

'Or,' said Oakshott, 'you will pack your traps immediately and leave this ship. I will furnish you with a letter to the admiral, suggesting that you be given an indefinite furlough, on full pay, because of illness brought upon you in the King's service. And we will forget about the supply books. Consider the options. The choice is yours.'

A moment's pause, and Hodges said: 'Forget - about the supply books.'

'So be it,' said Oakshott. 'You may go. Be off the ship by eight bells. That gives you an hour and a half.'

The pale eyes swam away from him, the tongue licked at the too moist, too rosy lips. As if upon an impulse Hodges extended his palm. 'Will you shake my hand, sir?' he asked 'The hand of a man who has been greatly maligned in his time.'

Oakshott turned his back and looked out of the stern windows, to where the seagulls were swooping and screaming about the herring boat astern.

'Good day to you, Mr Hodges,' he said wearily.

Chapter Four

WORD OF HIS doings must already have spread round the ship. The ship's boy of the previous evening brought him a mug of steaming coffee shortly after, all unbidden. The lad found his captain in full-dress uniform, writing at the table; a gobbet of news that he would take back to his cronies grouped about that souce of all shipboard speculation, the galley fire. Oakshott glanced up from his writing, grunted his thanks and instructed the boy to ask Lieutenant Stevens to attend him.

The senior lieutenant, for all the earliness of the hour, was swift to put in his appearance, dressed, shaved, with the attentive air of a man who has spent more time than is comfortable in a haze of speculation, but devoutly hopes that he is shortly to be led into the light of truth.

'Er - good morning, sir,' he said.

'Good morning to you,' replied Oakshott, folding the sheet of paper upon which he had been writing, addressing its face in his slanting, italic scrawl, and holding it out to the other man. 'Be so good as to give this into Mr Hodges' keeping when he goes ashore.'

'The - the first lieutenant is going ashore, sir?' asked Stevens.

'You are no doubt aware that his traps are being packed?'

Stevens was a pale-skinned young man who coloured easily. 'Er - I had been informed, sir. May I enquire if Mr Hodges is absenting himself for long?'

'Mr Hodges is absenting himself permanently,' said

Oakshott. 'You, Mr Stevens, are appointed acting first lieutenant as from this hour. My congratulations.'

'I - I thank you, sir. This is a tremendous surprise.' Pleasure and awe were writ in equal proportions upon the young man's countenance as he gazed down upon his captain: a figure who seemed, to him, to have grown immeasurably in stature since the previous eve, when, as a taciturn and seemingly irresolute newcomer, Oakshott had scarcely found words to complain about the state of his quarters.

Oakshott nodded. 'Now, to business, Mr Stevens. I will not dwell upon the condition of the ship, nor insult your intelligence by particularising upon its awfulness. Suffice it to say that it will be cleaned and made sweet from stem to stern, from main royal to keel. The running rigging will be renewed, and much of the standing rigging also. It is possible that some, or all, of the sails will have to be repaired, perhaps replaced. The ship must also be completely revictualled and provided with powder and shot for protracted cruising. Once that is done, we will address ourselves to the question of completing our complement of crew. Now - how long will you need for the task of turning *Daisy* into a ship that can sail and fight?'

'Shall we say a month, sir?' said Stevens, the light of resolve and enthusiasm burning in his eyes. 'And I will try to improve upon that by a week. Three weeks at the most. Yes.'

The black-haired man cocked an eye towards him. 'Mr Stevens, today is Tuesday, so I believe,' said Oakshott.

'That it is, sir,' confirmed the other.

'I give you till sunset on Thursday to complete the work, Mr Stevens,' said the captain of the *Daisy*.

Oakshott deliberately kept to his cabin that day, as much to enrich the crew's speculations about their new captain as to wade through the ship's books with the purser's mate and review the inventory of charts and navigational instruments with the master.

Stevens, when he had recovered from his shock and dismay

at the time limit set upon his labours, had responded with the inspired stoicism of a man who has nothing to lose and everything to gain; had suggested that lower deck be cleared for the captain to address the crew; a proposal which Oakshott had declined: let Stevens himself speak to the men, he had said, he was confident that Stevens would do it uncommonly well. The new acting first lieutenant had marched out of the day cabin with his shoulders squared and his heart and resolution high.

The following day, shortly after colours had been hoisted, Oakshott showed himself on deck, and was quietly pleased with what he saw. The teak planking had been holystoned from bow to stern and gleamed whitely under the haze of wetness that was evaporating under the morning sun. The lower shrouds of mainmast and mizzen had already been re-rove with new ratlines, and the work was proceeding from the tops. A score of men were seated round a sail that had been partly unrolled upon the widest expanse of the gundeck. Palms and needles in hands, they were patching and re-roping the spread of tough canvas. All eyes slid sideways at the captain's approach, and swiftly returned to their task. When Oakshott had passed, one of them began to whistle a lively air. Nothing sullen and hangdog there. And he was glad to see that, like a symbol of the new regime aboard the sloop, a brand new white ensign fluttered bravely from the mizzen peak. And the prison-hulk stink had quite gone.

Stevens was pacing the quarter deck with Quinch. He and the master touched their hats when Oakshott mounted up there.

'Good morning, sir,' said Stevens. 'I have to report that the work proceeds according to plan. I await the arrival of victualling stores in the forenoon. We ammunition ship in the dogs.'

'Thank you, Mr Stevens,' said Oakshott. 'Are there any men for punishment today?'

Their eyes met.

'No men for punishment, sir,' said Stevens with a touch of pride.

'Very good,' said Oakshott mildly. 'Will you please inform the officers that I should be honoured by their company at dinner tomorrow night.' He paused, and added: 'In celebration of the successful refit.'

'Aye, aye, sir,' said Stevens. 'And with much pleasure.'

Oakshott nodded and went down the companion-way, leaving them.

When he was out of earshot, Quinch said: 'You'll mark how he leaves you no scope for failure? You'll have a successful refit - them was his very words.'

'He's a rum 'un, and no mistake,' said Stevens. 'Full of surprises. Any other captain would have taken the opportunity to harangue the men. Considering that he'd just got that mad bastard Hodges off their backs, they'd have cheered him to an echo. But he left it to me. He's certainly not seeking to be Popular Jack.'

'He'll stand watching,' said Quinch. 'I've a mind he's plenty more surprises up his sleeve, that one. Number One, do you mind if I take the jolly boat ashore to pick up fresh charts?'

By noon, a brimming lighter had been unloaded of victualling stores: barrels of 'hard tack', the hard-baked ships' biscuit which was the staple bread substitute at sea; casks of 'junk' - the salt meat that was frequently of such an age and consistency as to be capable of being carved into snuffboxes and such knick-knacks, and to take a high polish with an interesting grain; casks of lime-juice, against scurvy, hogsheads of dark Jamaica rum for daily issue, mixed two to one with water as grog. In the evening watches, racks of 16-pound round shot were hoisted over the side, together with grape, faggot, bar and chain - projectiles with which to blast rigging, spars and sails, as well as the bodies of men. Down into the felt-lined magazine below the sloop's waterline were lowered three tons of black powder in cask - enough explosive to blow the *Daisy* and all aboard her into fragments if so much as a spark got among it. It was dark before all hands were secured to rest. Oakshott heard the bosun's call while at a solitary dinner in his stern cabin and was well-satisfied.

That night, a storm broke over Portsmouth, with jagged flashes of lightning that lit the Solent as brightly as day, and struck the mainmast of a three-decker, causing a serious fire among the sails and cordage that only the torrential rain was able to douse. That night, also, a party of sailors returning from shore in a cutter were drowned to a man when their craft was swamped by a freak wave off Southsea, where their limp corpses washed up on the morrow's flood.

The thunder and lightning ceased with the dawn; not so the teeming downpour of rain. Lower deck was cleared, as ever, aboard the *Daisy*, officers and men grouped in oilskins, while hands were told off for their day's labours. All through the morning watch, and the afternoon, men worked in the rigging, high above the streaming decks; while others hung over the ship's side in bosun's chairs, patching worn planking, recaulking seams. The rain ceased towards the end of the first dog watch, enabling them to put on the last lick of brave ochre paint that banded the black sides at the level of the gun ports.

At eight bells of the last dog watch, when the bell of the dockyard clock was striking seven o'clock, and a rainbow hung over the wide harbour from Cosham to Southsea, Stevens tapped on the door of his captain's day cabin and admitted himself at the call.

Oakshott was waiting in full-dress, sword, telescope and all.

'Ship refitted and ready for inspection, sir.'

'Pray precede me, Mr Stevens.'

'Aye, aye, sir.'

Stevens leading, they stepped out from under the break of the quarterdeck, into the evening sunlight. The crew was drawn up in the waist and on the fo'c's'le, in two ranks facing outboard, the officers of their quarters to the fore. All were in their best slops, the officers in full dress, every man close-shaven, save only for the ship's carpenter, who sported a beard that overflowed his brawny chest.

Oakshott paused before the mainmast; looked upwards

and all about him. Masts and spars, newly painted; freshly-tarred rigging. The decks snowy-white, with scuppers cleared of filth and carefully limned in red – a reminder of their grim function in the horrors of battle. Well aware that every eye in the ship was covertly upon him, and every heart beating faster, every breath held in suspense, he made much of his inspection; not neglecting to run his hand along a new length of rail that had been let in, with the air of a man who appreciates a finely-grained piece of elm; fingering a particularly grand Turk's head knot with which some diligent tar had, beyond all call of duty, embellished a rope's end; cocking an eye at the neatly-racked roundshot. Not saying a word of approbation or disparagement, knowing all the while that every ear was strained to catch either.

The tour of inspection ended where it had begun: by the mainmast. Stevens touched his hat in salute to his captain, his face expressionless, but his eyes betraying anxiety.

'Permission to carry on, sir?'

'The refit, Mr Stevens . . .'

'Sir?'

'Up to standard, Mr Stevens.'

'Thank you, sir.' The acting first lieutenant's face turned a bright pink.

Pause.

'Splice the mainbrace, Number One.'

'Aye, aye, sir!'

The mainbrace having been spliced: a double issue of grog having been doled out to every man aboard the ship, officers included, Oakshott also – he took his in full view of the grinning crew, standing by the issue cask; pledging King, Country, the Navy, and HM Sloop-of-War *Daisy* – the crew fell to to a supper of fresh meat, potatoes and Soft Tommy, that is to say shore-baked fresh bread. Aft, in the candlelit day cabin, Oakshott presided over white napery and gleaming silver, supplied from his own sea chest. Stevens sat on his right, the master on his left, lieutenants to the number of four disposed in seniority down the table, with three midshipmen beyond, the most junior midshipman facing Oakshott from the far end.

Stevens said Grace. Soup was brought in by ship's boys, two of them, scrubbed and barefoot. Conversation fell to generalities, with no mention of the business that the *Daisy* and her crew had been about during the previous hectic three days. Oakshott joined in the talk, interposing an occasional remark and giving straight reply to questions addressed to him; and all the time studying the faces, speech and bearing of his guests. Quinch the warrant officer excepted, all were clearly of gentle birth: sons of minor aristocracy, the landed gentry and the professional classes. Well, they would be the material from which he would forge a weapon against the French. Some changes might have to be made. Stevens had so far measured up to the demands made upon him, but suffered from having been under the malevolent influence of the insane Hodges, and might have to be replaced. A surgeon would be needed, and another mid to act as master's mate would not come amiss. And if only he could secure Ned Daventry, who, like a breath of fresh air from outside, would stiffen the wardroom and be his sheet anchor. It was worth trying. He would float the idea to the admiral commanding on the morrow.

Meanwhile, there was the question of completing the ship's complement. No use relying on the shore people to send him a draft; their first consideration was to man the battleships and sent them off to blockade the enemy ports, in conformity with the Navy's strategy. The maids of all work - frigates, sloops and the like - would have to make what shift they could, or rely upon their own press gangs. He, Oakshott, had no objection to pressed men, provided they were genuine seamen. Which brought him to the question of women: he supposed that, the refit over, Stevens would request permission to allow the local doxies aboard. No prude, Oakshott did not approve of women aboard warships - they were always a source of strife; given a handful of complaisant whores a vessel swiftly became like a farmyard full of strutting bantam cocks, each ready to tear his rivals to shreds at the drop of a feather. Best for them to receive orders to sail before the question of women arose...

Stevens was addressing him. Stevens had imbibed quite a lot of claret, which, taken in conjunction with a double tot of dark Jamaica rum, had quite changed the normally unforthcoming acting number one.

'As I was saying, sir, concerning young Charteris...' His normally pale countenance was fairly ruddy.

'My apologies, Mr Stevens, I have not been attending,' said Oakshott. 'Charteris?'

'The junior mid,' said Stevens, nodding down the table, to the boy furthest from Oakshott, 'has requested leave to visit his people in Norfolk. His father has just died. They are the Thetford Charterises, you know, sir. I told the lad that I was sure you would give his request favourable consideration.'

'Did you so, Mr Stevens?' said Oakshott. 'Did you so?'

Mr Midshipman Charteris looked to be about thirteen or fourteen, with butter yellow hair worn very smoothly across a somewhat narrow brow, and pansy-dark eyes fringed with girlish lashes; a well set up youth with good, powerful shoulders. As Oakshott watched, the lad raised his eyelashes and flashed a glance towards the acting first lieutenant - a glance both enigmatic and curiously familiar. Ho-hum, thought Oakshott.

'Shall I ask Charteris to attend you formally, sir?' asked Stevens.

'That will not be necessary,' replied Oakshott. 'I will hear his request immediately after dinner and give him my answer.' He poured himself another bumper of claret and passed the decanter to his neighbour. 'I should like you to be present on the occasion, Mr Stevens.'

'Aye, aye, sir,' murmured the other, helping himself to the wine.

Soup and fish were followed by a very excellent hindquarter of beef which had been obtained for Oakshott by the good offices of a Portsmouth butcher and poulterer, at considerable expense. This massive joint, upon which the officers of the *Daisy* cut and came again till there was nought left but the great bones and enough scrap meat and gristle to feed the ship's three cats, was succeeded by a noble Stilton cheese well doused in Port wine of a notable vintage.

Throughout, Oakshott ate in silence, with his private thoughts.

The ship's boys having cleared away the last of the remains and retired, leaving the officers with their port, brandy and claret, Oakshott tapped the table for quiet.

Addressing the epicene Mr Midshipman Charteris, in the time-honoured manner, as junior officer and vice-president of the dinner, he declared:

'Mr Vice - the King!'

To which the other replied: 'Gentlemen - the King!'

'The King!' responded all. The toast, as dictated by custom and the lowness of the deckhead beams, which caused Oakshott and all near six feet in height to walk with a stoop, was drunk seated. A buzz of talk ensued, while pipes were lit, pouches of favoured tobacco being passed from hand to hand. Oakshott, who abhorred the Virginian weed, took the opportunity to rise from the table and casually open one of the stern windows.

There followed more general talk, mostly about the prospects of the war, of politics, some veiled hints about the delights of womankind - all indications that the rigid convention against matters political, professional and sexual being discussed round a dinner table had, through over indulgence in wines and spirits, given way. Oakshott, after the decent interval of half an hour or so, cut it all short by rising to his feet.

'Gentlemen, we all have a long day ahead,' he said. 'I thank you for your stimulating company and wish you a sound night's sleep. Good night to you all.'

All rose obediently, some, by their looks, showing that they would have wished the celebrations to have been more protracted; but their captain's firm, yet mild, expression precluded any argument. Mumbling their thanks, they took their leave, one by one, the most junior last.

'Mr Charteris, remain behind if you will,' said Oakshott, when the midshipman of the butter-yellow hair nodded farewell to him. 'I understand you have something to ask me.'

Charteris blushed becomingly, flashed a glance to Stevens, and remained where he was.

'Well, Mr Charteris?' prompted Oakshott.

'As I informed you, sir...' began Stevens, but silenced himself at a sidelong flash of his captain's eye.

'Sir, I...' began Charteris, who was quite clearly wishing that he were elsewhere.

Oakshott turned his back on both of them; looked out of the stern windows, at the lights of the herring boat, to the lights of the fleet beyond, the lights on the distant hillsides.

'Tomorrow, Mr Charteris,' he said, 'tomorrow, I shall make a signal to the admiral commanding that this ship is in all respects save one ready for war. The sole reservation is the matter of crew. And I do not doubt but that we shall be left to settle that matter ourselves in the usual manner. All this must be known to you, yet you choose this occasion to make a request that you, an officer, must know to be - inopportune.'

'Sir, I am sorry,' said Charteris.

Oakshott spun round.

'Mr Charteris, I am sorry to hear of the death of your father. Your mother, she is still alive, I trust? You have other family?'

At the note of unexpected kindness in his captain's voice, the boy's nether lip trembled treacherously. 'Yes, sir,' said he. 'I have my mother and three sisters.'

'I will write to your mother and offer my condolences upon her sad loss,' said Oakshott.

'Thank - thank you, sir,' whispered the midshipman, eyes glazed with sudden tears.

Oakshott snuffed the nearest candelabrum upon the table, shielding the lad's shame. He crossed to the window and threw all three lights wide open.

'This damnable tobacco smoke!' he exclaimed. 'Attend to me now, Mr Charteris. There are two precepts that an officer must keep before him always. One, he must never make a request that cannot be granted. Two, he must never give an order that cannot be obeyed. A moment's thought upon your part' - he cast a cold glance towards Stevens - 'upon anyone's part, would have prevented you from transgressing against the first precept. Do you understand?'

'Y-yes, sir,' faltered Charteris. 'I-I see that now, sir.'

'I am glad to hear it,' said Oakshott.

'Only, sir...'

'Only what, Mr Charteris?' said Oakshott. 'Do you, perhaps, have reservations?'

'Sir, I understand the first precept and how it must be avoided,' said Charteris. 'But as to the second - why, sir, surely an officer's order must always be obeyed, sir.'

Oakshott smiled down at him benignly. 'So it must, Mr Charteris, so it must,' he said. 'Example - you have come alongside an enemy ship. The grappling irons are across and holding fast. There is a gap of eight - ten - feet between you. The enemy are lining the rails, waiting for you, pistols primed and ready, cutlasses out-thrust. You give the order - "Board!" Whereupon, Mr Charteris, you, yourself, leap across the gap and are the first to be killed, which is your inestimable privilege as an officer. And be assured that your order will be obeyed. Do you understand?'

'Yes, sir,' said Charteris.

Oakshott made his signal on the morrow, it was soon acknowledged by his masters ashore and the *Daisy* was ordered to proceed forthwith to Dartmouth, there to await further orders. The truth was that, Portsmouth being filled to overflowing with ships of all descriptions, and a large force of Mediterranean-bound battleships expected on the next tide, every available berth - even the lowly line of piles inhabited by the *Daisy*, the herring boats, the colliers and the rest - was at a premium.

Accordingly, shortly before noon, the *Daisy* cast off and was carried on the ebb out of harbour, making sail as she proceeded; bosuns' pipes shrilling wild salutes to every King's ship in sight (for there was none in all of Portsmouth harbour above the size of a schooner or a cutter whose captain was not senior to Oakshott). Off Ryde, they sighted the incoming fleet - four sixty-fours and a 100-gunner -

rounding Selsey Bill to larboard, far off, in line ahead. Midshipman Shacklock was at the signal book, singing out their names as his colleague Charteris read off their distinguishing flags. Second in line was Nelson's *Agamemnon*. The *Daisy* made a good passage with a favourable wind and tide, her scant crew keeping watch and watch about, and glided into the high-walled and wooded entrance to Dartmouth on the following morning.

The best bower splashed into the limpid blue water. There was no other Navy ship present; only a handful of fishing boats; that and whitewashed cottages rising on high above the western shore, so close that, surely, a small boy could have thrown a pebble down upon the *Daisy's* holystoned deck.

'Pipe hands to breakfast,' said Stevens.

'Aye, aye, sir.'

Oakshott paused in his pacing of the quarterdeck.

'Mr Stevens,' he said, 'why are the church bells playing on a Saturday?'

'Perhaps it is a funeral, sir,' hazarded the acting first lieutenant.

'Altogether too noisy and cheerful-sounding for a funeral,' said Oakshott. 'What is that crowd of people yonder there, heading for the church?'

Stevens raised his telescope.

'Sir, I think it is a wedding party,' he said. 'Yes, I see them plain. The bride a-front, on the arm of a portly party who must be her sire, and half a hundred guests in tow. The groom, I don't doubt, is waiting at the altar.' He lowered his glass and met Oakshott's eye.

'We have a magistrate's warrant, duly signed and dated?' demanded Oakshott.

'That we have, sir,' attested Stevens.

'Valid for this day's date – all shipshape?'

'Yes, sir.'

'Belay the pipe for hands to breakfast, Mr Stevens,' said Oakshott. 'And call away all boats for a shore party.'

'Aye, aye, sir,' said Stevens.

'Mr Stevens...'

'Sir?'

'No violence, mind. It would not - considering the circumstances - be seemly. But, one thing...'

'Sir?'

'A church is like a tavern. It has a back door as well as a front. Mark that you set good watch upon the vestry door, Mr Stevens, or some of your best clients may show you a clean pair of heels out the back. Do not hoist your colours and strike till after the ceremony is over. And only genuine seamen, Mr Stevens. There is no room on a small ship for passengers.'

'Aye, aye, sir.'

All hands were called, and the ship's boats lowered. Into them descended a dozen of the brawniest fellows aboard, all armed with cudgels, with cutlasses belted about them. A lieutenant and two midshipmen went also, with Stevens in overall charge. Oakshott watched them go. The water was very still. The twin herringbone pattern of the two boats spread the width of the anchorage. Not a soul watched from ashore - surely, everyone in the little fishing town must have been up at the church - as the press-gang descended upon peaceful Dartmouth. The boats were made fast, the men formed up on the jetty, and marched off into the narrow streets and were lost from Oakshott's sight. He sighed and went below.

An hour or more passed before there came a message from the officer of the day that the boats were returning. Oakshott went up on deck, in time to see the larger craft, the cutter, coming alongside. It was greatly down in the water, having added to its burden to the number of - he made a quick reckoning - eight. Eight men in homespun wedding finery, some with flowers in their buttonholes, all sullen and scowling. Two of them wore bruises on their faces. One lay unconscious across a thwart.

Stevens was in the cutter's stern sheets; he was the first aboard, saluting Oakshott briskly and looking mightily pleased with himself.

'It went well, sir,' he said. 'Twenty able-bodied seamen in all. Another boat load will see them all offshore.'

'What about - him?' Oakshott nodded towards the unconscious man who was being hoisted inboard by his arms.

'Caught him sneaking out of the vestry door, sir,' said Stevens. 'The bosun's mate brought him down at the run and he hit his head on a gravestone. He'll be as right as a trivet in an hour or so.'

The cutter having been emptied and the pressed men having been ordered below - an order which they obeyed sullenly but quickly as the bosun's mates wielded their starters - the boat turned back to shore, and its smaller consort, the jolly boat, took its place alongside at the steps. It carried six pressed men, of the similar type and appearance to the previous boatload: honest Devon fishermen who would as lief have served time in the prison hulks as be condemned to fight for King and Country aboard a Navy ship. Oakshott was reminded of Dr Johnson's oft-quoted remark: 'life aboard ship is worse than life in gaol, with the additional danger of drowning' - to which the great lexicographer might have added: 'and, in the case of a King's ship, the extreme danger of having one's head blown off'.

Six Devon fishermen.

And there was a woman!

The bride. There was no mistaking her: plump and pretty in her tawdry wedding finery, her face streaked with tears, eyes red and swollen. Midshipman Charteris - for he it was in charge of the jolly boat - looked shamefaced when he climbed aboard, and was roundly addressed by the first lieutenant.

'Mr Charteris, what in the hell do you mean by bringing the wench offshore! She'll have to be taken back, and we're not running a trot-boat service for half Devon!'

Oakshott listened to the exchange, but did not interfere. The six men were ushered aboard. And the bride came with them.

'Get that woman back in the boat and take her ashore!' ordered Stevens.

Oakshott turned his back on the affair and went to the quarterdeck, where he dismissed the whole thing from his mind and, scanning the sky to southward, made a reckoning of how long it would take them to make Plymouth on a broad reach.

At Plymouth would come the testing time; there he would receive his first war orders on his first command, orders that might make or break him. Fail in the test and he might just as well return to Sennett, for nothing would save him, not even Nelson's patronage – not with a hundred officers waiting to step into his boots, to earn glory and prize money, a sword of honour from the Patriotic Fund and...

'Sir...'

Oakshott turned. It was the young bride. At close quarters, he could see the raw loveliness behind the dabs of paint and khol that she had inexpertly applied for the great occasion. She could not have been more than nineteen.

'Ma'am?' Oakshott touched the brim of his hat. He had a fair guess at what was coming.

'My lad, sir. My Ned. We was only married but a half an hour ago. You'll not be taking him, sir. You be a brave gentleman and a captain, and there must be charity in your heart for a poor young couple who've just been wed and never bedded.'

Oh, my God, thought Oakshott. The pretty little thing hasn't even been tupped by her man. By what exigencies do we crew our ships!

'Ma'am,' he said, 'your husband has been pressed with the due force of the law, by a warrant from a magistrate which is enforceable this day. And that's an end to it, ma'am. I am sorry for your circumstances, but you will appreciate that no exceptions can be made for anyone, no matter what his circumstances. I bid you a good day, ma'am.' He touched his hat again, turned upon his heel and looked out over the taffrail to the blue sea that curled and broke white water beyond the harbour entrance.

Yes, definitely, one must succeed – and succeed mightily – in one's first task, be what it may. And, meanwhile, what is happening at Sennett? Has poor Jackie got his little songstress with child yet?

'Sir...'

Her hand was searching out his wrist. He turned and looked down at her with his disconcerting eyes.

'Dear lady, it's no use,' he said gently. 'No exceptions can be made.'

Through her tears, she tried to smile at him. To his horror, she forced a certain coquetry. Her shapely, plump fingers were touching the strings that maintained her amply-filled bodice.

'You be kind to me and my Ned, sir,' she whispered, 'and I be kind to you, that I promise.'

'Good God, ma'am,' said Oakshott, 'do yourself up, I beg you. There's nothing can be changed, I tell you. Your Ned is a seaman and must now fight for his king.'

She drew a sharp intake of breath. 'Sir, my Ned's no seaman!' she cried. 'He's - he's a barber!'

'A barber?' Oakshott looked at her askance. She really was a pretty little thing. And to think that she should offer - and on her wedding day and still unbedded...

He called for the officer of the day to have the bridegroom brought on deck. This was done. Ned whatever his name sported a bruise over one eye that told he had not succumbed to the press gang without a fight. He was a big fellow, solid as an ox, with shoulders that could pull on a rope's end with the strength of three.

'Your lady wife tells me that you are no seaman, but a barber,' said Oakshott. 'Show me your hands.'

At this, the young bride gave a cry, pressed the knuckles of a hand to her mouth. Was silent.

'Your hands, fellow,' repeated Oakshott, in the same flat, calm voice as before. 'Show them.'

The man Ned showed his hands. Scrubbed and bleached they were for the great occasion of his life, the fingernails cut back to the quick; but all this attention could not hide the betraying signs of his trade: the ingrained blackness that comes from lifelong, daily contact with tarred rigging, the hundred small scars that a seaman inherits in his hard occupation.

The man continued to hold out the hands. The woman - girl - began to sob. Oakshott was silent for a while.

And then: 'Yes, you are a barber right enough,' said the

captain of the *Daisy*. 'I perceive from the smooth state of your hands that you have never done more than shorn a lock and drawn a tooth in all your working life. You may go.'

A great release was shown in the fellow's washed-blue eyes, and the young bride made as if to embrace Oakshott, but was restrained by the officer of the watch, one Lieutenant Jobling, who had been regarding the exchange with some wonder.

'Call away the jolly boat to put them both ashore, Mr Jobling,' said Oakshott.

'Aye, aye, sir.' The response was immediate: not even the raising of an eyebrow, such was the unquestioned authority of a Navy captain, no matter now bizarre the circumstances.

'Oh, captain, sir, you be a true saint and a gentleman!' cried the young bride, who had not yet bethought herself to lace up her bodice - somewhat to the interest of young Jobling.

'It is a pleasure to accommodate you in some measure, ma'am,' responded Oakshott.

'Sir, I do be most truly grateful,' said the man Ned.

Oakshott fixed him with a steady glance. 'Do you know the hour, fellow?' he asked quietly.

'Why, yes, sir,' replied the other, glancing across the harbour to the church clock that told it plain. 'It be eleven o' clock of the morning, sir.'

'Ebb tide is at six, fellow,' said Oakshott. 'Take your bride, whose protestations have softened my resolve somewhat, and my blessing go with you both.'

He pointed upwards. 'You know what that is?'

The other knew well enough. 'Why, that be the mizzen peak, sir,' he replied, puzzled.

Oakshott nodded. 'A good guess, Master Barber,' he said. 'And now you mark this well: if you are not back aboard this ship before we sail on the tide at six, you will be sought out by the shore authorities, and you will be found and brought to this ship in Plymouth. And I will hang you from that mizzen peak. Get you gone. Your time is short.'

★

HM Sloop-of-War *Daisy* sailed on the ebb tide from Dartmouth that evening between the humped slopes of Berry Head and the Start, past Battery point and Dartmouth castle bristling with cannon and alive with blue-coated gunners waving from the ramparts. Oakshott laid course for the south-west and found it good. He then went below for a dinner of tasty fish burgoo and a light wine from Germany. And was incidently gratified to notice that Tom the bridegroom - his full name being Tom Mudge - was there in the waist, hauling upon the main sheets.

Towards sunset, the wind failed and Oakshott, mindful that they were upon a lee shore, stood off into the Channel. It was mid-morning of the following day, due to the fickle weather, before they skirted Eddystone rocks and made into Plymouth. Once alongside the wall in Devonport naval dockyard, he put on his full dress coat, hat, sword, and repaired to the office of the commander-in-chief.

That august personage not condescending to receive a junior commander of a mere sloop-of-war, the task was delegated to a Navy secretary who introduced himself as Manthorpe, and who occupied a chamber only slightly larger than Oakshott's stern cabin in the *Daisy* and smelt of stale ink.

'Commander Oakshott,' said this personage, when the latter was seated on a hard-backed chair before him, 'you are for Toulon.'

'Toulon, you say?'

'Toulon, sir - which is on the Mediterranean coast of France, east of Marseilles.'

Oakshott nodded, knowing very well the location of the French port and naval base.

'For what reason, sir, am I to go to Toulon?' he asked.

Manthorpe brightened considerably. He was a dried-up little mannikin, but with a sprightly eye that put Oakshott in mind of the Exmoor pony called Bimbo who had been the pride and joy of his boyhood.

'I will apprise you of the situation, Commander,' he said, 'if you will bear with my tedium in some patience.'

'Pray go ahead,' responded Oakshott, amused.

'Well, then,' said the other, 'we have the situation where the troops of the French National Covention - as it calls itself - have taken Marseilles but are halted before Toulon by royalist forces still faithful to their allegiance. The latter have applied to the British for their help.'

'The devil they have,' said Oakshott. 'So Britain, who is now at war with France, is to take sides in a French civil war.'

'Succinctly put, Commander,' replied Manthorpe with the patronising and slightly surprised air of someone who has all unexpectedly found himself the owner of a talking dog. 'That is precisely the position. And a situation greatly to Britain's advantage, since the denial of Toulon to the revolutionary forces must greatly strengthen the Royal Navy's position in the western Mediterranean.'

Oakshott nodded. 'That is good reasoning, sir. And what part is the *Daisy* to play in this enterprise?'

'Ah, a most important part, Commander,' replied Manthorpe. 'You will be the vanguard of the expeditionary force which will be leaving Plymouth next week, as soon as the soldiers are loaded aboard the transports and as soon as Commodore Pell deems that he has assembled a sufficient fleet.'

Oakshott sat upright as if his backside had come in contact with a nail. 'Pell - did you say *Pell*?' he demanded. 'And did you say -Commodore Pell?'

The other nodded. 'Pell is appointed commodore of the inshore squadron of the Toulon expedition under Admiral Lord Hood.'

'God help us all!' breathed Oakshott.

The other's eyes twinkled. 'That is the opinion of many,' said he.

'Not that Pell isn't a good seaman,' said Oakshott. 'Don't take me amiss - there's none better. But there are ways of doing things, Mr Manthorpe, and Pell simply has not learned that you catch more flies with molasses than with vinegar.'

Manthorpe spread his hands and smiled agreement. 'That has always been the general opinion in Devonport, Commander. However, happily for you, and detached from the inshore squadron as you will be for some time, it is likely that you will not encounter Pell till you have made your mark.'

'I devoutly hope so,' said Oakshott. 'What then is my task, Mr Manthorpe?'

The admiralty secretary put on a pair of steel-rimmed spectacles and took up a paper. 'Your orders are to proceed to Toulon with all dispatch, bearing aboard with you the royalist French general who is to assume command of the garrison. You will then remain in or near the port, as circumstances dictate, giving what aid you are able till the main fleet arrives.'

'That sounds a nice, wide brief,' said Oakshott.

'Plenty of opportunity to make your name, Commander,' replied the other. He gazed at his companion with a certain wistful envy. 'Are you well known to Captain Nelson, sir?'

'Why do you ask, Mr Manthorpe?'

'He it was who proposed you for the task, sir,' said Manthorpe. 'He most particularly asked that you should be given it, for I have minutes of a meeting that was held in Portsmouth last week.'

'Well, God bless him,' said Oakshott, gratified.

'You have a good friend there, Commander,' said Manthorpe, 'for I tell you that Nelson will go far, and will be remembered when the Pells of this Navy are long forgotten.'

'I'm sure you are right,' said Oakshott.

'Well, now, as to details,' said Manthorpe. 'Your passenger is styled General the Marquis de Colombe. I have not made the noble gentleman's acquaintance, but I am instructed that he has been advised to repair aboard the *Daisy* at his earliest convenience, along with his baggage.' Here the clerk paused, and, peering over the rim of his spectacles, watched the progress of a fly that took to the air from the lid of his roll-topped desk, circumnavigated the little office and alighted on the oil lamp that was suspended from the dingy ceiling. 'As regards his baggage, Commander – if I may be permitted the vulgarity – the marquis has with him a lady, who will accompany him to Toulon.'

'A *lady*?' Oakshott was aghast at the thought of a female

sailing aboard a tiny sloop-of-war with a hundred and thirty deprived seamen gawping on. 'It's not possible. Can this lady not travel with the fleet, in a battleship. Pell's, for instance?'

The other shook his head. 'The lady, who is the Marquise de Colombe and married to the general's brother so I am given to understand, has had a special dispensation to accompany her brother-in-law. Ours not to question the dictates of authority, Commander.'

'Quite,' agreed Oakshott. 'But - a woman! And I shall have to give my cabin up to her, of course, and sleep in a hammock slung in the flat.'

Manthorpe clucked sympathetically, and said: 'There is another gobbet of information I may pass your way, Commander. The lady, as I am told, is not a Frenchwoman by birth, but a colonial - or, rather, a former colonial.'

Oakshott stared at him. 'You don't mean...?'

Manthorpe nodded. 'A Yankee, Commander. Not only are you to be engaged in a civil war betwixt your country's enemies, but you must accommodate one of - that lot!'

Oakshott had made application of the admiral commanding Portsmouth for Ned Daventry to be appointed to the *Daisy*, but predictably nothing had come of it; in all likelihood the request had been placed on file, there to gather dust to the millenium. So he resigned himself to making shift with the officers he had, who were all competent - particularly the master - and adopted the handy philosophy that one must make bricks with whatever straw lies to hand: as with the possible offspring of a vicar's daughter for the marquisate of Uffingham & Bow, so with the officers of the *Daisy*.

In Plymouth, they took aboard stores, both ordnance and victuals. Among the latter came a crate of live chickens that was set up near the heads, together with a cage of live rabbits as would have sent a Devon tinner loopy.

And on the third day came aboard General the Marquis de Colombe and his sister-in-law the Marquise.

It transpired in this way: Oakshott, who had spent the

night working on his course to the Mediterranean with the master, and who had imbibed a tolerable amount of brandy while doing so, was having a post luncheon nap in his cot when the officer of the watch burst in with less ceremony than usual and announced the arrival of the newcomers. Oakshott, correct as ever to the niceties of protocol, slipped his stockinged feet into his best boots, shrugged on his full-dress coat, ran his fingers through his black thatch, clapped on his hat and went up on deck.

There was a child on the upper deck - Oakshott's first opinion - but more correctly, a youth of about sixteen or seventeen, clad in the white regimentals of the defunct French monarchy, well laced with gold braid, a cocked hat with a cockade a mile high, and a powdered bag wig of the sort that had gone out of fashion in English society around the time of the American Revolution. He was also, in Oakshott's instant summation - and Oakshott knew men, though deficient in some reckonings of women - a thoroughgoing little prig. This was immediately evidenced by his first remark to the captain of the *Daisy*, delivered in a high pitched voice, but in very tolerable and well-accented English:

'Are you in command of this little vessel? I had thought that I should be transported to Toulon in a craft that was of sufficient importance to be in keeping with my dignity as General Officer Commanding Toulon, Designate.' He actually announced his military title with capital letters.

Oakshott steeled himself to salute General the Marquis de Colombe as his senior officer in the present enterprise, while resisting the impulse to boot the lad's backside.

'Monsieur le Marquis,' he said, 'I have not been consulted as to your transportation, but have merely accepted my orders as given. You are welcome aboard the *Daisy*, and I shall deem it my duty - and indeed my pleasure - to transport you and the lady to Toulon with despatch, and with as much comfort as my exiguous circumstances provide.'

The child - youth - remembered his manners and the woman at his elbow.

'My dear Barbara,' he said, 'may I present the captain of the *Daisy*, whose name is?...'

'Oakshott,' supplied the latter. And bowed over the woman's presented hand. She was tall, almost as tall as he, with a shock of blonde hair which owed nothing to powder, an admirable bosom, deep blue eyes with an off-putting directness which reminded Oakshott of Irene Chancellor.

'Delighted to make your acquaintaince, Captain Oakshott,' said she, in the accent of the English west country that the ex-colonials had seemed to have adopted and amended to their own taste.

'Commander Oakshott, ma'am,' responded he, and thought: damned to the American Revolution, here is one revolutionary against whom I would warm my feet any night you choose. 'Would you like to step this way, and I will show you what accommodation I can offer - which isn't much.'

The boy general and the beautiful American following after, Oakshott led the way to his stern cabin, which the powder monkey had, upon the arrival of the two distinguished passengers, contrived to tidy up somewhat. The detritus of luncheon had been thrown out, Oakshott's dirty small clothes shoved out of sight, the chamber pot emptied. All in all, it did not look too bad, thought Oakshott, and he must mark that young lad for advancement.

'The cot lets down from the bulkhead and makes quite a tolerable bed,' said Oakshott. 'I think that the lady will find it quite comfortable.'

'Impossible!' declared de Colombe. 'If, as I understand it, this is the largest compartment in the ship, it must be mine. I shall need this table here for my maps and my notebooks.' He looked at Oakshott down his long and aristocratic nose - no mean feat considering that he was a head shorter than the captain of the *Daisy*. 'At all times, you must remember, Commander, that I am a general officer of the French Royal Army and that I have a campaign to fight, a battle to win.'

'Yes,' said Oakshott. There did not seem much else to add.

The marquise was accommodated by the simple expedient of turfing Stevens out of his quarter cabin, which was the grand name for a doorless hovel on the larboard quarter about the size of a largish coffin, with a let-down cot and nothing else. A sailcloth curtain was contrived over the entrance to provide a modicum of privacy for the fair occupant. Her baggage, which was considerable, was stowed in the stern flat along with the boy general's gear. This left Oakshott just enough room to stand and undress before hauling himself up into the hammock that was to be slung athwart-ships across the flat. Stevens was consigned to the wardroom, there to sling a hammock along with the rest of the officers.

Oakshott decided to take a firm line over meals, and this system he commenced by inviting his two passengers to dine with him at table in his stern cabin - an offer that de Colombe could scarcely refuse. Accordingly, the boy general's gear was cleared from the table and Oakshott's best napery and plate laid out.

The trappings of generalship, as evidenced by the pile of maps, notebooks, coloured crayons, little flags stuck on pins, and - unbelievably - a considerable number of toy soldiers greatly intrigued Oakshott and he was inclined, during dinner, to quiz de Colombe as to how he had achieved such military eminence so early in his career. The latter answered up quite unselfconsciously. It was the old story of influence, preferment, purchase - a system commonly exercised in the force of the British Crown though not to the degree of making a general with an active command out of a raw youth. De Colombe frankly admitted that he had never heard a shot fired in anger, but that his mother had been a Lady of the Bedchamber to Queen Marie Antoinette, that one of his ancestors had died in the arms of King Louis the Ninth on a crusade (so very many aristocratic French families claimed this distinction; it is a wonder that the saintly monarch had any time for fighting), that his father had perished on the Paris guillotine the day following the execution of the late monarch - and that he, Armand, Marquis de Colombe, was going to save Toulon. Oakshott thought he detected the fair American in the act of smothering a yawn.

The ebb began at two bells of the first watch, and the *Daisy* slipped past Drake's Island in a glorious summer's eve, with seagulls screeching and wheeling about her and folks waving from the Hoe. Clear of the headland, they laid course for Cape Finisterre and the start of the enterprise. Oakshott, standing on his quarterdeck with the boy general by his side, had distinct qualms about the outcome, but tempered them with the thought that de Colombe's appointment might well be purely of a political nature, and that older and wiser heads would direct the course of fighting at Toulon, leaving the lad to play with his maps and his toy soldiers.

His sense of foreboding had been greatly exacerbated by a letter delivered aboard the ship almost immediately before departure. It was from his new sister-in-law, the Marchioness of Uffingham & Bow, cleric's daughter and sometime *chanteuse* Harriet Howarth. She betrayed, in her prim grammar and careful handwriting, an assiduous education painfully earned. And the missive had the prime literary virtues of brevity and drama:

> Dear Charles,
> I declare that I am quite put out. Your brother proves to be quite intolerable to a woman of sensibility.
>
> Last night, when after pleading a headache I declined to accompany him to his bedchamber, he chased me round the table in the great hall - in full view of Struthers!
>
> The truth is, I have come to find him quite revolting. By the time you come home from sea, you will almost certainly find me gone - back from whence I came.
>
> Charles, with the greatest esteem,
> I remain,
> Harriet Uffingham & Bow

The dark pall of Uffingham & Bow and the rotting miasma of Sennett Palace lay heavily over Oakshott that evening, as he saw the lights of the south Devon coast fading astern. He lingered topsides till the end of the watch, contemplating his estate, revolving upon the task ahead of him. The delivery of the two passengers presented no problems save those of discomfort - that and the hazard that he might be impelled to boot the boy general up the arse.

More inspiring by far was his wide brief to offer what assistance he was able to the Toulon garrison. This might include a bombardment of shore, the sending of a landing party, even the landing of guns to support the defence. It was an exciting prospect. By eight bells Oakshott had cheered up considerably.

He went below. The stern flat, illuminated by a single lantern, presented an unappetising prospect, with his hammock swinging forlornly over the piled up traps of his two passengers. Blessedly that powder monkey had thought to lay out a bottle of brandy and a glass; he really would have to advance that lad.

Oakshott poured himself a bumper, took a deep sip, and undressed himself, which done, he swung himself into his hammock, brandy and all.

His gaze fell upon the bolt of sailcloth that sheltered the fair American from the eyes of the lustful sailory. She who had scarcely spoken a word throughout dinner - hardly surprising, since her brother-in-law had carried the burden of the conversation almost entirely.

Yet, thought Oakshott, as he drained his glass and laid it by the pillow behind his head, her eyes carried infinite promise; the fair ex-Colonial was more than a decorative appendage to an ancient aristocratic family of France.

Two bells rang out. The *Daisy* dipped before the edge of an Atlantic swell.

Oakshott fell asleep.

Chapter Five

WITH A FAIR wind and a calm sea the *Daisy* made good two hundred and forty miles in the first day after rounding Ushant, going, in Oakshott's colourful phrase, as recorded in the ship's log: 'At a spanking fine pace at her best point of sail'. On the eve of the second day out, and well into the Bay of Biscay, the wind shifted and with it the fine weather. By dusk, the sloop-of-war was sailing full and by and rolling like a whale in wet grass, as the saying goes.

Oakshott dined with the de Colombes that evening, in his own stern cabin, with the boy general's toys stowed in a corner. They ate the last of the fresh beef, cabbage and roast potatoes, and a bottle of very tolerable red wine of the Rhineland, which does not travel well because the Germans do not grow much red grape and prefer to keep it for themselves.

His relationship with the couple had not greatly improved, even after de Colombe had elicited, by indirect questioning, that – to his intense relief – the man with whom he had to share table was also of aristocratic birth. Though relieved, he was not greatly impressed, since in pre-Revolution days, all French officers had to be of noble blood and when he learned – again by indirect questioning – that the Marquisate of Uffingham & Bow dated only from the previous century he closed the subject and sulked into his syllabub.

The beautiful American remained taciturn, and greatly intrigued the captain of the *Daisy* by so doing. He tried to draw her out by quizzing her about life and times in the former colony of America, but she would have nothing of his conversation, answered only by yes and no and pushed her food around her plate as if willing it to go away. It occurred to Oakshott, then, that she might be feeling seasick. It was a condition from which he seldom suffered and he found difficulty in understanding why it should happen so frequently to others.

In the event, the fair American declined the syllabub and, asking to be excused, quitted the cabin. After joining de Colombe in a brandy and listening to that untried boy telling how he was going to drive the revolutionaries away from Toulon, out of Marseilles, out of the Midi, and eventually bring them to book in Paris, Oakshott, seizing upon a suitable break in this oration to make the excuse of having to attend to the navigation, left the lad to his brandy and went up on deck.

The sea had an ugly greeny-grey look and the sky was entirely overcast, with all the promise of a thoroughly nasty night. Oakshott lit himself a cigar from a tallow dip that burned under the quarterdeck screen and joined the watch on the wheel. With them was the ship's carpenter, one Henshawe, a Northumberland man, with all a Geordie's bluntness. He touched a forelock to his captain and asked permission to speak on an important matter, this Oakshott granted.

'This ship, sir, she's rotten right through, as far as the timbers are concerned,' announced Henshawe. 'The masts are only fit for hanging washing on, and I wouldn't like to go bail for the state of the keel and scantlings. There's something more, sir – something you should know.' At this point in his discourse, the ship's carpenter looked to left and right with the air of a man who is about to make an announcement of earth-shattering gravity as would strike terror into all who overheard it. Indeed, he had the temerity to lay his hand upon the exalted arm of his captain and guide him a few paces towards the taffrail, well out of hearing of the helmsmen.

'What else should I know?' demanded Oakshott.

'We have the death watch beetle aboard, sir,' breathed the other.

'Yes, I've heard them,' replied Oakshott. 'My family home is likewise infested. You might say that I was brought up with them. But I wonder how they got aboard the *Daisy*.'

The Geordie carpenter tapped the side of his nose, knowingly. 'Ah, sir,' he said, 'it's my guess that they came when she was laid ashore in dry dock in Pompey and certain repairs was made to the transom. I wasn't aboard at the time, but it's my belief that they used infected wood for the purpose. Yes sir – infected wood is what they used. And there are them little devils keeping their death watch upon us all, ticking away like Old Nick's clock that marks off the days of men.'

Oakshott shook his head. 'Like many others, Henshawe,' he said, 'you greatly over-estimate the old death watch. My family home is falling down about our ears, but the old beetle is playing a very inconsiderable part in the process, I'm convinced.'

The ship gave a lurch as a sizable comber slapped against her side; both men clung to the guard rails.

'But it's their ticking as worries me, sir,' said the carpenter. 'My dad, who I was apprenticed to, he told me often that it was Old Nick's clock a-ticking away our hours, and when the ticking stopped, all them in hearing distance would be finished.'

'Not so,' declared Oakshott.

'What then, sir?' asked the other.

'Why, I have it on good authority – and he was a Fellow and Tutor of Trinity College, Cambridge – that the ticking noise made by the death watch beetle is caused by them banging their heads against the woodwork.'

The other looked astonished, then affronted – as if his intelligence had been called into question. Then, remembering his place, he put the civil question: 'For why should they do that, sir?'

'As I understand it, 'tis by way of being a mating call, for to attract death watch beetles of the opposite sex. Good night to you, Henshawe. Thank you for your frank speaking. I shall tend to disregard the beetle, likewise the state of the keel and scantlings, about which we can do nothing. The *Daisy* will last out the war. But I promise you that we'll have new sticks to replace the old as soon as we next get alongside a dockyard wall.'

The carpenter nodded, looked a little relieved, touched his forelock. Oakshott threw the butt of his cigar over the leeward side and went below.

Speaking of mating calls, he thought, as, stripped, he climbed up into his hammock in the packed flat, it would not have come amiss to bang his head against the bulwark to summon the stately former colonial to share his narrow sleeping quarters. Come to think of it, in all his years at sea, from the time he was a midshipman of fourteen and slung hammocks on a score of ships, he had never . . .

(Go to sleep, Oakshott!)

He addressed himself to the task, which was no hardship, for he had had a heavy day, and if the weather continued to worsen, it might well be provident to put into Lisbon. He had an excellent pilot of Lisbon, compiled by an old sailing master - now long gone - who had taught him navigation aboard the *Elephant*. What was his name?

He slept. And was almost immediately awakened by a familiar seagoing sound: the retching of someone tearing out the contents of their stomach against the violent motion of the sea. And it came from behind the sailcloth curtain of the quarter cabin. A low moan followed, and then the sound of tears.

Oakshott swung himself out of his hammock and clambered over his guests' gear to the quarter cabin from which came the sounds.

He drew aside the sailcloth curtain and was immediately assaulted by the acrid stench of vomit.

She ceased her weeping. 'Go away!' she whispered. 'Go away! I don't want anyone to see me in the terrible mess I'm in.'

'You can't lie around like an animal in a cage,' said

Oakshott. 'Get out of there and I'll get you cleaned up. Do you feel better now?' The motion of the ship had somewhat eased.

'Yes, I do - a little.'

'Then - come.'

He reached out his hand into the gloom and found hers, drew her, unresisting, from the cot and guided her into the flat and faint glow of the tallow dip, where by its meagre light he perceived the state she was in.

'Get out of that night shift and throw it in a corner, it can be washed in the morning,' he ordered her.

'But - I - I'm...'

'I've seen a naked woman before. Do as I tell you. I'll go and get water.' He turned his back on her and went on to the upper deck, picking up a bucket on the way. Then, tying a becket upon it, he tossed the bucket into the swollen trough alongside and scooped up three gallons or so of clean salt water, which he then took below.

She was standing by the bulkhead and hiding herself as well as she was able with her hands. In the light of the tallow dip, she put Oakshott in mind of gesticulating nude statuary of Carrara marble that his father had brought back from his grand tour of Italy (in fact it had been his tutor, accompanying the young marquess, who had selected the pieces; Father, eschewing museums and the like, had spent his time in the fleshpots of Rome, Pisa, Florence and Venice), which had been placed in the formal gardens of Sennett Palace - now, alas, no longer formal, but knee high in couch grass and weeds, and the nude nymphs discreetly clothed in bindweed and ivy.

'Come forward to the edge of the screen,' said Oakshott. 'Out here in the open. Don't worry, there's no one on deck save the helmsmen and the look-outs, and they'll not see you.'

She obeyed; shrank a little when he approached her; gave a shuddering intake of breath as, lifting the bucket, he poured a cold libation of Biscay water over her head and down her cringing form. The water ran away into the scarlet-painted scuppers and back from whence it came.

Oakshott rummaged among his washing gear and threw her a towel.

'Dry yourself,' he said. 'The quarter cabin will be cleaned out in the morning. You can sleep the rest of the night in my hammock.'

'But where shall you sleep?'

He shrugged. 'I'll make shift somewhere.'

She had the towel wrapped around her, covering her from armpits to knees, when she essayed to climb into the hammock - a feat which has much hazard for the tyro.

'I can't get up,' she announced.

'You're going the wrong way about it,' he said. 'It's not like getting into bed. Go in face first and turn over when you're in. Grab hold of both edges of the hammock, cock one leg over as if you were mounting a horse, and pull the other leg after you. Simple. You'll soon get the knack.'

She essayed the task, but got stuck half way.

'Damn you, can't you give me a hand?' she said.

This he did, taking her trailing foot in his hand and helping her up, as one would assist a jockey into the saddle. Her foot, small and fine boned, tender as silk, caused him to linger with it a mite longer, perhaps, than was necessary.

She must have thought so too. Established in the hammock, she peered down at him over the edge.

'Tell me truthfully, Captain,' she said. 'Where shall you lie tonight?'

'Here on the deck,' he said. 'Rather this than your fouled bunk in the quarter cabin. And I wouldn't wish to disturb the general's sleep by creeping in alongside him. He needs all his faculties if he's to halt the French Revolution.'

She laughed. Quietly. Throatily.

'There's still room for two in here,' she said. 'Ample room for two, I'd say.'

No man to look a gift horse in the mouth, Oakshott swung himself up without a word. No tyro, he, at getting into a hammock.

On the evening of the next day, after the fickle weather of the

Bay of Biscay had all but becalmed the *Daisy* through most of the afternoon watch, a sharp offshore breeze blew up and with it a following swell. The sloop was making southerly headway at a good point of sail, but with considerable motion. Barbara de Colombe, who was taking the air on deck, began to look distinctly queasy – as Oakshott observed. And the boy general was playing with his toy soldiers down aft.

'Sail on the larboard beam, sir!' This from the masthead. *'A two-decker!'*

Stevens was up in the chains, telescope to eye. 'She's a Frenchie, sir. Battleship. Sixty-four, I shouldn't wonder.'

'Beat to quarters!'

'Aye, aye, sir.'

Marked by Oakshott's watch, the crew of the *Daisy* responded to the summons of the kettledrum and the bosun's mates' pipes. The strict apportioning of duties contingent upon the sighting of the enemy called for every man in the ship to be at his battle post within minutes – seconds – of the call: gunners to their weapons, to prepare them for immediate action; topmen to the sails; fire-parties, signal-men, powder-monkeys, sharpshooters, and the two best quartermasters at the wheel. And with the latter – to be at hand to take over should either, or both, be hit – the ship's bosun, one Alfred Cox.

In view of the drama that followed the sighting of the French battleship, and his own part in it, a brief résumé of Bosun Cox's past naval career would not be inapposite.

Despite his deceptively mild appearance, Cox was an extremely complex character. The senior lower-deck rating aboard the *Daisy*, his early career had revealed little promise of the advancement that he was destined to make in the Service. A pressed man (pressed in similar circumstances to unfortunate Tom Mudge bridegroom of Dartmouth, soon after his wedding, and taken away from a thriving fishing business in Yarmouth, Isle of Wight, to risk his life and neck for King George for a few pence a day with a tot of grog thrown in), the young and choleric Cox had not taken kindly to the reduced circumstances forced upon him by his country's need during the War of the American Revolution, and had expressed his resentment, and exercised his choler by fighting every man on the messdeck who crossed him in any way. This led him to innumerable floggings, and once a near-miss of a hanging, when one of his opponents in a bloody scrimmage fell, hit his head on the carriage of a 12-pounder and never recovered consciousness. Cox was absolved of the charge of murder, but was flogged round the fleet as an example to others.

His attitude to officers, in those days, was understandably hostile to a degree, and it speaks for divine mercy that he was never sufficiently incensed as to strike an officer: a crime which, be the blow ever so light, called for a mandatory hanging of the culprit. By a paradox, it was an officer who - all unwittingly - rescued him from the path of self-destruction, and pointed him towards his present eminence on the lower deck. It happened this way: during a full gale of wind and approaching the mooring buoy in Plymouth Sound, the three-decker in which he was serving was taken aback. During the ensuing chaos, when the men on deck and up aloft fought to bring the ship back to a point of sail - any point of sail - and officers were running hither and thither, giving orders, countermanding them, and contradicting each other's commands, a zealous midshipman, eager to win approval of his divisional officer, leapt to the chains and began to claw his way aloft to lend a hand with a recalcitrant sail, slipped and fell, struck his head on the coaming and plunged overboard, unconscious.

Able Seaman Alfred Cox saw it all. In after years, he was never able to explain to himself what prompted him, upon seeing the slight form of the midshipman lying face downwards in the heavy swell, to leap over the side after him without the slightest hesitation; to grapple the lad, lift his head clear of the water, and fight to keep them both afloat till a line was thrown. And, due to the chaos aboard the wallowing three-decker, a line was not soon thrown.

The midshipman, having been laid down on the deck and pumped out, lived. That evening, Alfred Cox was summoned to the flagship, where he went in his best blues. To his awe and sudden pride, he was received in the admiral's cabin, where none other than Lord Howe commended him upon his gallantry, gave him a glass of brandy and a golden guinea - and changed the character of the trouble-making young AB.

Fifteen years later, with no more crimes to his demerit, with a glowing record of bravery and diligence - and a regard for Lord Howe and his Navy that fell little short of adoration - Alfred Cox was standing on the quarterdeck of HM Sloop-of-War *Daisy*, close by the helmsmen and near to his captain - all unknowingly destined for another encounter with fate.

Oakshott had been watching the French two-decker and had come to a conclusion: 'It's likely she's on passage from Brest or St Nazaire to one of their ports in South Biscay,' he opined. 'It's unlikely they'd attempt to run our blockade of the Gibraltar straits.' He turned to address Barbara de Colombe. 'Would you care to take a squint at our enemy, ma'am? I suppose you've never set eyes on the revolutionary tricolour - well, there's one flying in the wind yonder.'

'Thank you, captain,' said she.

By the contrivance of laying the heavy telescope on Oakshott's broad shoulder and squinting into the eyepiece, and having with some difficulty adjusted the focus, there came into her view what seemed an enormous and most awe-inspiring vessel, of a size that made the *Daisy* look like a toy ship on a pond. The high sides, the towering masts, the ant heap of dark figures scurrying over the broad decks and in the shrouds, the unfamiliar red white and blue ensign fluttering aloft - all conspired to strike her most forceably as a symbol of overwhelming power.

'Are you going to - *fight* them, captain?' she asked, when she had handed him back the telescope and met his eye.

He smiled. 'No, ma'am. It is not within the brief of a sloop-of-war to challenge a line-of-battleship. Nor, by the conventions of naval warfare, will they demean themselves by altering course to try and catch us. As lief would a parish beadle, grown fat and soft with old age and easy living, bestir himself to give chase to a cheeky urchin, knowing full well that, for all the weight of his thick cane, he could never hope to overtake his intended quarry. No, ma'am, since our courses somewhat coincide, I shall shadow him, keeping out of gun range, and report his destination when we reach Gibraltar. Nevertheless, we shall remain at battle quarters till we part company with the enemy.

'The fortunes of war, let alone the vagaries of wind and sea, do not permit one to indulge in comfortable complacency.'

Oakshott never spoke a truer word.

The Royal Navy sloop having without greatly jeopardising its own landfall altered course towards the enemy so as to keep the Frenchman in sight during the coming night, had drawn abreast of the latter by dusk, and was sailing a parallel course just out of gun range.

'Reduce sail, sir?' suggested the master.

'If you please, Mr Quinch,' responded Oakshott.

The hands on deck took in reefs to reduce the spread of canvas and bring the speedy sloop's progress down to that of her slower, unwilling consort. It was this action, which clearly indicated an intent to follow the classic, minor vessel of war's function of shadowing the enemy's movements, that sufficiently incensed the minds of the revolutionaries opposite (who were perhaps not too well schooled in the niceties of naval protocol), to loose off a single shot from one of their lighter, upper deck guns at maximum elevation. This, signalled by a blossoming of white gunsmoke, greatly concentrated the attentions of those on the *Daisy's* topsides; there was much speculation as to how near the ball would fall, and not a little wagering with tots of rum on precise matters of line and distance. The 12-pound sphere of iron, when it splashed into the trough of a steep wave two cables short and out of line by three ships' lengths at least, drew forth the traditional hoot of derision from the Jack Tars. Oakshott's muttered comment was more perceptive: 'I'm greatly obliged to the Frogs for that little demonstration. It shows that, even with their advantage of a following wind and a higher gun platform, they can get no nearer, nor is their aim anything to write home about. Bosun, ensure that we steer at all times no closer to the enemy than this – unless the situation calls for new tactics and I amend the order.'

'Aye, aye, sir,' responded Alfred Cox, respectfully knuckling the brim of his tarred hat.

'Ma'am,' said Oakshott, addressing his fair companion, 'there will not be much more to see, and the weather is not likely to improve. I earnestly advise you to go aft and enjoy what supper the steward has prepared. I would join you, but the situation requires me to remain on deck.'

'I don't feel hungry,' she responded.

'Barbara,' he murmured, so that no one else should hear, 'You'd be well advised to take some ballast on board, I promise you. It's going to be a dirty night, and not one to face on an empty stomach. Be assured that I shall eat my fill.'

'I'm sure you will,' she responded. 'And, Charles, may I take it that, should you be rid of the enemy before dawn, your duties will permit you to call and give me an account of the night's events.'

'Most assuredly,' he replied. 'Goodnight, ma'am.'

'Goodnight, captain.'

Oakshott escorted her to the companion-way and handed her down the ladder. He looked along the gundeck, where the two rows of 16-pounders, attended by their crews, were run out and ready to fire on either broadside, nine a side. Stevens, whose role in battle (until his captain was hit) was that of gunnery officer, assisted by Midshipmen Shacklock and Charteris, ceased his pacing up and down and turned at the sound of Oakshott's voice.

'All well, Mr Stevens?'

'All well, sir,' responded the first lieutenant.

'I think there'll be no call for a gun action this night, Mr Stevens,' opined Oakshott. 'It may be that some of your men will be needed to give aid up top if the weather worsens. At your discretion and when they've supped, let them take some sleep about their guns.'

'Aye, aye, sir.'

★

Oakshott supped alone in the shelter of the quarterdeck screen, close at hand in case of emergency; munching upon the hard tack and ship's biscuit, sucking at the scalding Navy cocoa laced with rum; hanging on to a stanchion with one hand at all times against the kicking of the ship, who was by now taking the sea on her larboard quarter, with a most unhappy effect upon her posture. Somewhere behind him, in the darkness of the quarterdeck lobby that was pierced only by a single tallow dip, the crews of the after battery of six guns were similarly chewing tack and biscuit, gulping down laced cocoa. Beyond them, tucked away in her narrow quarter cabin, the fair American must lie either asleep or awake. Oakshott hoped that she was well, and holding down her supper. It would be pleasant, in the pre-dawn, he thought, when they had perhaps seen the Frenchie safely into harbour and the hands were secured from their quarters, to slip into the quarter cabin and make his report...

'Captain, sir...' It was the master.

'What is it, Mr Quinch?'

'The wind's shifting to the northward, sir, and I'm thinking there's a bad squall on the way.'

'Very well, Mr Quinch.' Oakshott secured the tin mug in a corner, and still holding his last morsel of hard tack climbed up the companion-way on to the quarterdeck. In the few minutes since he had gone below to bolt his supper out of the wet wind, things had changed on the open deck: the two helmsmen and the bosun had taken to oilskins and for the good reason that a constant spindrift of salt water was spuming over the taffrail and sweeping for'ard, drenching all before it, right up to the bows; where, in its turn, the sea was being scooped up over the fo'c's'le and deposited back to meet the libation coming in from abaft.

'Not a mere squall, Mr Quinch,' said Oakshott. 'I would say we were in for a storm.'

'The Frenchman?'

Quinch pointed. Clear, still, and part-silhouetted against the risen moon that fitfully showed itself through scudding clouds, the two-decker sailed grandly on.

'I think we will stand further offshore while we may,' said

Oakshott, 'for I've no fancy to be hove to in a Biscay gale so near to the enemy shore – not with a Frog sixty-four drifting in the vicinity like a bad smell. Take her downwind, Mr Quinch.'

'Downwind it is, sir!' responded the Master.

'Starboard your helm!

'Steer Sou'-sou'-west!'

Aided by Bosun Cox, the quartermasters bore down upon the great double wheel. The hands on deck, crouching in the vestigial shelter they could find, sprang to their sheets that controlled the lay of the sails. The ship turned on a farthing as the saying is, and pointed her elegant bowsprit downwind. The sails burgeoned. An entirely new motion took the *Daisy*, as the passing white horses surged under her counter, and wind and sea bore her further out into the safety of deep water, which is the mariners' only refuge when the furies of heaven blow *à l'outrance*.

Oakshott gnawed on his hard tack and looked back towards the French sixty-four. She, whatever her name, was certainly bound for a south Biscay port, and he could report as much in Gibraltar. Meantime, his responsibility lay to his ship and his passengers. It would have been an elegance to have seen the Frog safely in, and eminently befitting the niggling attention to matters of detail that so often beset him. He swallowed the last of the hard tack, wiped his fingers on the skirt of his old boat cloak, grabbed at the rail as an extra-large wave heaved the *Daisy* on to her nose.

''Tis getting worse, sir,' observed the master.

'Yes,' said Oakshott. 'But if we can hold her on this course for another hour or so, we'll turn about, heave to and wait for the gale to blow itself out.'

'The Froggie – he's turning, sir!' It was Bosun Cox who called, pointing astern.

'Dammit, so he is,' said Oakshott. 'Also aiming to stand further off from the shore before he heaves to. Good ideas are catching.'

'Increase sail, sir?' suggested the master.

'I think we must accept the risk, Mr Quinch,' said Oakshott, 'for I've no taste to go blundering around in the dark, hove to, with a thirty-two gun broadside like to take me, point-blank.'

Orders were passed for the topmen to increase sail, to take the sloop-of-war further ahead of her larger enemy, so that, when the gale increased to such a force that both ships had no recourse but to turn about, face what was coming and ride it out in appalling discomfort but tolerable safety, the *Daisy* would not suffer the dangerously embarrassing proximity of the sixty-four.

The evolution was speedily carried out, despite the appalling conditions of work aloft, where men, hanging on by their toe-ends, and with as much contact with tangible reality as one has in the saddle of a hunter galloping hell-for-leather over stick and stone, let out reef points and freed more salt-caked sailcloth to drive the ship faster along the wind and wave. The increasing speed had an immediate beneficial effect, inasmuch as the ship managed to catch up with the pace of the following waves, and rode for quite some time on an advancing crest with scarcely more motion than if she had been cruising in the Solent on a fine day.

It did not last for long, this eminently desirable state of affairs . . .

With the capricious mathematics enjoyed only by nature, the coming storm, which should have given a gradual increase in its ferocity over the course of, say, five or ten minutes, rumbustiously waxed from one third of its full force to the whole in the space that it takes for a man to draw three breaths. One moment, the *Daisy* was running free on the crest of a wave, the next she was overtaken by a giant comber – the legendary one in fifty – and engulfed from stern to stem, with hundredweights of water cascading down into the gun deck, soaking powder and match, sluicing into the gun muzzles and rendering the charges within them quite useless, sending the crewmen who dozed fitfully about their weapons cartwheeling into bruised and yelling heaps against the fo'c's'le bulkhead.

'Another like that, and we'll be broached to, sir!' shouted

the master against the scream of the wind in the rigging above them.

'We'll turn and stem wind and sea on the crest of the next wave, Mr Quinch!' returned Oakshott, and the other nodded vigorously.

They climbed up out of a deep trough that stood fair to have reached down to Davy Jones's locker. Quinch beckoned to the bosun. The three of them at the wheel bore down. The *Daisy* responded with an unaccustomed sluggishness, suffering, as she was, heaven only knew what unrecorded forces upon her keel in the maelstrom.

The next wave came at her - and it was a monster - before her elegant prow had quite come round.

'Hold fast on everything to hand!' shouted Bosun Cox. 'And may God help us all!'

The wave smote the ship fine on her larboard bow, fine enough to provide the leverage to spin her round as if she had been a duckling in a mill-race. Broached to upon the instant, the *Daisy* reeled and bowed before the onslaught of the immeasurable force that descended upon her plankings, her tall masts, the web of rigging that held one to the other.

Oakshott, who had grabbed the mainmast chains in both hands, had them wrenched from him, and suffered the experience of watching the masts of his ship heel over and touch white water, and a wave sweep right over the upper deck without even breaking in its passage; it is possible that the *Daisy* actually heeled beyond the horizontal at that moment.

After that came a flurry of torturously flapping sails and cordage, as, with a descending cat's cradle of ropes and rigging, the entire main topgallant mast, wrenched from its seating, cracking as it did so, fell like a pencil which, stood upon its blunt end, is knocked over by a passing gust of wind from an open window - point first, and falling till it reached within a few feet of the deck, where it hung there, suspended from its thicker end by the trailing tangle of shrouds, sheets, standing rigging, and maddened sailcloth. And there, poised as it was, the massive spar began to gyrate; slashing from side to side; beating upon the supports of its own parent mast;

returning to do the same to its former cousin the mizzen mast – a blind, malevolent monster intent upon destroying both itself and its family.

'Cut it loose!' shouted Oakshott. 'Get it over the side!' So saying, he was already starting forward, when another wave, striking the crippled *Daisy* fair and square, sent her right over on her beam ends again; her captain, rushing to lend his own elegant hand, his demigod presence, to the brutish and hazardous work of ridding the ship of the blind monster, fell headlong, hit his brow on a support of the quarterdeck balustrade and was for a while relieved of all consciousness of the dire peril in which stood his ship, his crew – not to mention himself and his naval career.

At the extreme of mind-bedazzling danger, particularly when the situation is allied to the most grotesque physical discomfort, as when one's world is turning nigh upon upside down with every breath, there are few who retain the equanimity to stand back and view the odds with a rational detachment (as an illustration: no one would hesitate to walk a plank laid across the surface of a lawn; put this plank fifty feet into the air and you have a predicament that has a greatly unnerving effect upon us all). Oakshott was a man of such rational detachment, but he was unconscious.

There remained, happily for the ship and all who sailed in her, two men in the proximity of the mainmast who shared their captain's rare quality. One of them was the topman Tom Mudge, bridegroom of Dartmouth, sometime posing as barber and the strongest hand aboard the sloop-of-war; his brute courage did not have the same analytical and intellectual basis as that of his captain – but it made shift to the same ends.

The initial problem was to secure the fallen upper end of the topgallant, which was making fair to ripping the sails from both the main and mizzen masts in its wild and unpredictable gyrations, threatening particularly the mainsail, but most particularly the mizzen sail, which, placed the furthest aft and laterally in line with the fore and aft line of the ship like a weather vane, was the *Daisy's* best hope of riding out the storm if she could ever be brought to stem wind and wave. The scope of the deadly pendulum, it should be added, also included Topman Mudge and the two quartermasters at the wheel, who, now that their captain lay unconscious in the scuppers, were the only occupants of the quarterdeck. Every so often, as the ship was pounded and rounded by the enveloping waves, the end of the pendulum careered wildly over their heads, threatening to decapitate them.

And then came Mudge.

He had snatched up a stout length of manilla rope, upon one end of which, in his agonised climb up the companionway, he had already hitched a running bowline - a loop that, when thrown over the neck of a runaway horse, will bring him to a halt on pain of strangulation.

The deadly end of the topgallant was the neck of Mudge's horse.

He approached it at the crouch - a crouch that quickly became a sprawled glissade across the streaming deck, as another comber broke over the wallowing sloop and landed him in the scuppers alongside his captain, with the end of the topgallant striking the air where his head and neck had been a moment before.

Mudge got to his feet with extreme caution, steadying himself against the wild lurching of the ship by grabbing the quarterdeck rail. A whole minute passed, during which Mudge's horse lurked fretfully in his paddock during a lull in the storm; the giant watched and waited, loop and line gathered to throw.

A fitful lurch of the ship; the mad horse snickered and made as if to attack; Mudge stood ready, noose in hand.

Then another of the combers (and there could not be many more such before the *Daisy* must founder, overturn and be lost with all hands) smote the ship's side, setting the deadly pendulum-horse into wild motion; it swung high above the quarterdeck, careered in, missed the ducked heads of the men at the wheel by inches, and - fortuitously-halted for an instant as the *Daisy* stood for that brief length of time on a steady keel (due, providentially, to the tremendous amount of water she had shipped, most of which had found its way down into the bilges and was acting as extra ballast that tended, when it was able, to hold the ship upright, though low in the water).

In that instant Mudge saw his chance.

Two swift paces brought him so close to the deadly head of the mad horse that he could see the fine graining wetly limned on the button capping (when the Navy dressed ship, with sailors manning the masts all over, the bravest and smallest of the crew who dared to stand atop the mainmast with his arms extended, his bare feet implanted on a knobbed finial the size of a dinner plate, was called the 'button boy'). A quick flick of the noose - and it was over the button and drawn taut.

Then began the life or death struggle between man and mad horse, between human flesh, bone and muscle and the fickle and inexorable forces of nature. The next movement of the ship sent the tethered monster swinging wildly out over the coaming; Mudge, having taken a turn round his thick waist, strained against the pull, as in happier times he had set himself as anchor man for Dartmouth tug-o-war team, against the forces of Totnes, Plymouth, Exeter, Crediton, Drewsteignton, Okehampton, Moretonhampstead and the best that mid and south Devon could offer - and mostly to his own team's advantage.

Only - this time his brawn and courage was not directed against six strong Devon lads of his own sort, but counter to the brute forces of nature, as related by Pythagoras, Newton and many others.

The Newtonian principal of gravity hurled him, pinioned as he was, against the rail, where nothing but his own flesh and guts stayed the outward swing of the great spar as it sought the ease of gravity; his flesh and guts held it at the end of its swing - but at terrible cost in pain and effort.

The pain easily overcome, the effort rising like a hawk unleashed as he discerned that the beast could indeed be conquered, Mudge then took the slack of the rope in both massive hands and, bit by bit, assumed control.

Now the fickle spar became no longer a mad horse, but one of the many trout and salmon that he had poached, in the dark hours, in forbidden waters of the Dart and the Teign, the Tamar and all their tributaries throughout his youth. But more like a shark or a whale than trout or salmon; stronger, ineffably stronger - and a killer.

He had it under his command for a while; against the dictates of Newton, he had it against gravity; when it sought to tear once again across the mainsail and add to the rent that it had scored across that widest and tallest spread of canvas on the ship; he held it in check, and from check came mastery. From mastery came direction. Slowly, with effort that made the veins of his brow, neck, chest, arms, stomach, stand out like the lines in a book of anatomy, and his soul scream to be freed of his body, the giant seaman brought the mad monster under his control, defying Newton and all the rest. Slowly, inexorably, working with the pitch of the sea and yielding a little when the advantage was against him, Mudge drew his quarry in, till presently it hovered above his head so that he could reach up and touch it.

'Well done, lad! Make fast! I'll go and slash the other end!' It was Bosun Cox who spoke, and he helped Mudge to take two round turns and innumerable half hitches of the rope, securing the malevolent monster upon a stout cleat.

The task of ridding the *Daisy* of her unwanted main topgallant was but half done. The downward-pointing, button end secured, the upper and by far the heavier end, gaining a purchase from its attachment at the other, took a new and vigorous life upon itself; and up at the level of the main and mizzen topsails where it could wreak incredible harm to the motive power of the sloop. Furthermore, the shifting cat's cradle of assorted cordage that accompanied its every motion, offered any man climbing the tattered shrouds leading up to the main topsail yard (the only place from where it was possible to cut the thing free) a dozen chances of strangulation with every step.

His heart in his mouth, the inspiration of Lord Hood and

his beloved Navy high in his mind, Bosun Alfred Cox clawed his way up the main shrouds, burying his face against them when, with every sickening lurch of the wounded sloop, another gallimaufry of tangled ropes sought to cast a fatal noose over him and hang him in plain view.

Cox had with him a sheathed knife that he had bartered from a sugar-cane cutter in the West Indies many years before. Securing this formidable weapon, called a machete, with a wrist strap, he occupied his passage up to the main topsail yard by slashing at all and every loose piece of cordage that swung within his reach. By the time he reached his goal: panting, blowing, weakened - for he was by no means a young man any more, and half a lifetime of coarse Navy victuals and the seething airlessness of between-decks had played some havoc with his constitution and he was chronically bronchial - the bosun of the *Daisy* could only hang there, head bowed against the tarred rigging, waiting for his strength to return; while all the time, the sloop bowed and submitted to every shattering blow that the beam seas of the storm hurled at her.

The thought of Lord Howe, summoned Cox again to the great effort; rousing himself, he reached out and began to slash at the mass of ropework of all sorts that was either supporting the fallen spar, or had become attached to its proceedings. It was hard and frantic work, what with holding on to the shrouds with one hand and slashing frenziedly with the heavy machete at the thick, tarred cordage. And with every minute that passed, he knew, every shattering blow to the hull and masts of the injured ship might result in a death wound. So, with closing eyes and faltering, fading strength, the bosun of the *Daisy* dragged something from out of his pride of manhood, his integrity as a seaman, his love of country and the image of Lord Howe and his beloved Navy. It is entirely possible that - in the latter stages of his effort, when all but half a dozen strands of thick cordage, only, held the upper part of the spar in place - Bosun Cox was working in a somnambulent state, and only naked will was directing his hand to make the progressively enfeebled - and futile - slashes at the last ropes holding the spar.

And then, through the mists of closing unconsciousness, he felt the warm wetness of a fellow human close about him, and his spirits were roused.

'Thank God,' he said, 'that they've sent somebody up to lend me a hand. Have the rest of the bloody crew been taking a make-and-mend the bloody whiles?'

There being no reply, he inclined his head, squinted in the bad light and the constantly driving spindrift, and saw that it was his captain who shared the slender perch with him: Oakshott, hatless, his sable hair plastered across the brow that was creased with a cruel cut, from which the salty-watered blood was driven in tiny rivulets across his entire face.

'Take a make-and-mend yourself, Bosun,' said Oakshott, 'and give me that cut-and-slasher of yours.'

Cox, heartened, relaxed against the shrouds; watched in great joy, to see his captain expertly sever the last of the ropes which had been beyond the compass of his own strength. And he was still hanging and holding, and rejoicing in his heart, as the *Daisy*, freed of her burden (for the giant Mudge, seeing the top half go free, instantly sliced through the rope holding the button end), with the rent mizzen sail spreading to meet the wind, was swung as neatly as you please to stem wind and sea. Like a lark rising, or a bride leaping to her wedded lover's arms, she pointed her weather vane of her own accord, bearing herself, her crew and her passengers to a long night of bone-jarring discomfort - in comparative safety.

The storm blew itself out with the dawn. Till the dawn, also, Oakshott kept the crew at battle quarters - mindful all through the night that the looming shape of the French two-decker, with its battery of guns that could reduce the *Daisy* to matchwood with one close broadside, could not be far away.

With the dawn, they saw the Frenchman. And a ragged cheer issued across the now glassy waters of Biscay. The once proud two-decker, though still possessing all the puissance of her massive armament, was no more than a floating fortress.

She had been entirely dismasted - fore, main and mizzen,

right down to deck level – in the storm. Oh, and how Oakshott wished and prayed that he might have been in command of a third-rater, or even a big frigate, that he might have closed in and tried the game with that forlorn floating fortress!

Ship's carpenter Henshawe surveyed the damage and opined that the failure of the main topgallant was due to the death watch beetle; producing cuttings from the abutting part of the main topmast which seemed to indicate that the noisy little devils had been boring away up there all unseen.

He was about to state this proposition to his captain in the manner of putting it that would not actually bring him to a flogging at the grating for insolence, but merely to imply the ancient and always intolerable lesson of 'I told you so' – when he caught his captain's eye. And held his peace.

The weather keeping fine, and the tides not being propitious for entering the river Tagus to have a new topgallant fitted by their Portuguese allies, Oakshott sailed on to Gibraltar where the task was carried out exceedingly well. It was also established (to carpenter Henshawe's chagrin and Oakshott's quiet amusement) that the death watch beetle had played no part in the damage.

Next, the *Daisy* sailed for Port Mahon, Minorca, which the British had designated as a base for masking Toulon two hundred sea miles to the south-east. There the *Daisy* was revictualled by their Spanish allies. With some difficulty Oakshott finally prised her away from the overwhelming hospitality of the Minorcans, and was constrained much against his will to pronounce sentences of lashing at the grating for six ratings who had gone adrift in the pursuit of dark-eyed senoritas and had in consequence delayed the ship's departure by a day while they were being found and brought back aboard by a midshipman's shore party, the little sloop-of-war finally made a good landfall slightly to the east and windward of Toulon – a feat of navigation for which Quinch the master had been responsible.

Oakshott had been impatient to make Toulon, partly because he wished to out-race Pell and his Inshore Squadron so that he would be able to exercise his independent command for as long as possible (a British captain, even of a minor ship-of-war, being lord of all he surveys, able to make his own decisions, and answerable only to a court-martial if his judgement leads his ship to disaster), so as to score some triumph for his command before the iron hand of the commodore fell upon him.

There was also the item – which weighed not greatly in the balance, but added its moiety – of the Marquise de Colombe. The fair American and he had enjoyed the mutual delights of the hammock ever since Biscay. In the pillow talk which had usually followed those delights he had elicited that Barbara de Colombe was married to a man who, on their wedding night, had confessed that his predilections did not incline to females, but that he had married her on account of the dowry which she had been able to bring from her prosperous banker father in Boston. She was returning to France, she told Oakshott, because she simply had no other place to go; her father, having laid out the ground bait in support of the financially sagging de Colombe family, and having four more daughters for whom to provide husbands, would not accept her back. Her plan was this: as soon as her young brother-in-law had defeated the revolutionaries before Toulon and advanced towards Paris with his victorious troops, she would be able to rejoin her dubious husband at his château on the Loire, where at least she would have a roof over her head. She declared this plan in doubtful and unenthusiastic tones. Oakshott, mindful of the boy general and his military toys, did not add to her troubles by stating his opinion on the venture, but kept his peace.

All in all, he told himself, it had been a pleasant interlude between him and Barbara de Colombe – but best finished.

'Boat approaching from shore!' The cry came from the

masthead lookout. 'A cutter. Flying a blue flag with white bits on it.'

They were at anchor about a mile from the harbour entrance, Oakshott having decided to give the French till midday before he made his first move. This, clearly, was their first move.

'Pipe all hands, Mr Stevens,' ordered Oakshott. 'Man the side.'

'Aye, aye, sir,' responded the first lieutenant.

'Except those working parties not in the rig of the day, Mr Stevens. Keep them out of sight below. We want to make a good first impression upon the French.'

'Aye, aye, sir!'

Bosun's pipes shrilled out. A patter of bare feet on the upper deck. Bosun's mates yapped shrill orders. The kettle drums took up the rhythm of the running feet. It was soon done. Within two minutes, the crew of the *Daisy* were lining the side, standing to attention, holding hands, each to each, as if in a schottische, against the roll of the ship at anchor in a fair breeze.

Oakshott took a glim through his telescope at the approaching cutter, which was about fifty foot, no more. He could make out only one figure among the small gaggle of half a dozen or so, and he was wearing the white uniform of the royalist French army. The ensign of that now defunct monarchy – white lilies sprinkled upon a blue ground – fluttered from the cutter's gaff.

'Well done, Mr Stevens,' said Oakshott. 'I make it two minutes by my watch. A far cry from Portsmouth, hey?'

The first lieutenant looked pleased with himself. 'Thank you, sir,' he said.

'There's an officer aboard,' said Oakshott. 'No matter what his rank, we'll pipe him over the side.'

'Aye, aye, sir,' acknowledged the other.

In the quite considerable swell, the cutter made no attempt to come alongside (if she had, Oakshott would have warned her off, if only on account of his paintwork), but anchored a couple of cables distant. There a jolly boat was lowered – none too expertly, as the crew of the *Daisy* were quick to observe – and was rowed across, with the white-uniformed figure standing in the stern sheets by the coxswain. It came to neatly enough alongside the sloop, oars were tossed, lines were thrown and taken, and the French officer climbed aboard.

'Pipe the side!' ordered Stevens, and the unmelodic bosun's pipes did the honours as for the captain of a ship.

The Frenchman was tall, cadaverous as to face, but with the broad shoulders of the kind that made his coat look as if the coathanger had been left in. He removed his cocked hat in salute, revealing a none too well-tended white wig that was gathered at the nape in a bow of black silk. And his chin and mouth bore a couple of days' stubble. He was perhaps thirty to thirty-five, decided Oakshott, who doffed his hat also in acknowledgement.

'Commandant de Regle, at your service, Captain,' said the visitor, in pretty tolerable English.

Oakshott introduced himself, and also his passengers, the de Colombes. There followed a rapid exchange of French, in which time Oakshott was able more searchingly to examine de Regle. It puzzled him to see a rent in the other's coat around the area of the heart, a clean hole as might have been made by a bayonet. The white material, moreover, was pinked with blood round the hole, though someone had obviously made some shift to clean it off. The royalist cause must be in bad fettle, thought Oakshott, if even field officers have to take over the uniforms of their dead.

De Colombe broke into his contemplations: 'Commander Oakshott, we will wish you farewell for the present. The commandant has come to take me ashore, there to assume my command of the Toulon garrison. My sister-in-law will accompany me.' He held out his hand with a gesture of condescension that made Oakshott itch to kick him. 'Despite your difficulties, you have striven to make a trying journey as comfortable as possible for us. And now you will remain here, awaiting my orders, until the British fleet arrives, when my orders will be passed to you through your commodore.'

'Aye, aye, sir,' murmured Oakshott, taking the proffered hand, and striving hard to conceal his wild fit of mirth at the thought of Pell receiving orders - let alone obeying them - from this puffed-up young macaroni.

Barbara de Colombe was a different matter. By mutual consent, they avoided each other's eyes, and he bowed to kiss her hand. She murmured a few words of thanks for the services he had provided, to which he gave the conventional response.

After their very considerable luggage had been loaded, they handed her down into the cutter; de Colombe followed after, and the boy general took the opportunity of displaying his seniority by descending last.

Oakshott watched them go, his eyes mostly on the woman seated in the jolly boat's stern sheets as she was rowed back to the waiting cutter.

Stevens was at his elbow. He said: 'Did you remark that boat's crew, sir?'

'Mmmm?' Oakshott was stirred out of his reverie.

'A nasty looking lot, sir.'

'Yes, indeed, but they are Froggies after all,' responded Oakshott. 'They can't help it.'

'Well yes, sir,' persisted the first lieutenant. 'But if that crew of cut-throats, with their whiskers and their greasy hair all done in pigtails fore and aft, their raggedy gear, their scowling expressions - what I mean, sir, is that if they're royalists, what do the revolutionaries look like, those who are chopping the heads off men, women and children alike?'

'We may soon see, Number One,' responded Oakshott, amused. 'In any event, having landed our distinguished passengers, I propose to remain anchored here and await trouble. What I shall not do is to enter Toulon and be obliged to take orders from that young whippersnapper. Call the hands to dinner, Mr Stevens, and join me in my cabin to share an excellent looking bass that the powder monkey who acts as my servant - what's his name?...'

'Stukeley, sir.'

'That young Stukeley caught on a line over the side not ten minutes after we had dropped the hook. Remind me to advance him, Number One.'

'Aye, aye, sir. And thank you for the invitation to

luncheon, which I accept with much pleasure.'

Trouble was not long in presenting itself...

'Sail fine on the port bow. She's a sloop – or mebbe a small frigate. And she's an enemy Froggie, flying the red, white and blue! Coming straight at us downwind.'

In the stern cabin, where the reflected light from the waters outside the wide windows made diamond-shaped patterns on the low deckhead, Lieutenant Stevens leapt to his feet.

'Sit down and finish off your excellent bass, Number One,' said Oakshott. 'If the masthead look-out has only just spotted her, we have time to finish our luncheon, nuts, port and all. You may rely upon the officer-of-the-day to beat to quarters as per my standing orders.'

'Aye, aye, sir,' responded the other dutifully, and readdressed himself to the bass, shovelling it in with a fork assisted by ship's biscuit held in the other hand. Oakshott continued to eat slowly and carefully, savouring every mouthful as if it might be his last, washing it down with a fine, dry white wine from Lisbon.

Above and beyond came the familiar pattering of hurried feet and the sound of pipes and drums. Next came the heavy trundle of wooden wheels as the guns were run in on their tackles to be loaded.

A knock on the cabin door, and the excited face of the officer-of-the-day, one Surtees, was presented.

'Captain, sir – there's...'

'I heard the call, Mr Surtees,' responded Oakshott. He glanced at his half-hunter, which he had laid on the table before him upon hearing the lookout's call. 'Three minutes, as I make it. How are you loaded?'

'Alternate roundshot and chain, sir, like you ordered. Hands ready to make all plain sail. Fo'c's'le party standing by to weigh anchor.'

'And the Froggie?'

'She's a frigate, sir. Twenty-eight guns at a guess. We're out-gunned by ten.' The youthful, unformed face showed no sign of fear, only impatience.

'Then I'm sorry for her,' said Oakshott, remembering the performance of the French frigates on that misty day against the *Simon van Slingelandt*. 'They can't win, for there's none like us.

'Take a glass of port with me, Mr Surtees. And then we'll go and try the game.'

Chapter Six

THE WIND HAD freshened. The enemy frigate was coming on with her sails spread and a considerable creaming at the bows which told that she was making all of seven or eight knots running before the wind.

The *Daisy* weighed anchor, and went off on the larboard tack under plain sail. At that time, the Frenchman was about five cables distant and coming straight at the Briton, with none of her guns able to bear.

'I like it!' observed Oakshott on his quarterdeck, close by the wheel. 'In a single-ship action, the holding of the weather gage can, in certain circumstances, be a positive disadvantage - and I confide, gentlemen (he was addressing the officer of the watch, the master and Midshipman Charteris, who were grouped about him), that this may well be one of those occasions. Mark what follows...'

The *Daisy*, close-hauled and at her best point of sail, had not progressed more than a cable before her starboard battery bore upon the Frenchman, who was still largely heading at her.

'Give fire!' ordered Oakshott. 'Broadside - rigging and hull!'

The starboard battery of nine 16-pounders belched almost in unison: those loaded with roundshot aimed at the enemy's waterline, to pierce her hull, the remainder sending their chain-shot up into her sails and rigging.

When the blinding white gunsmoke cleared away, a cheer

went up from those among the *Daisy*'s crew who were not busily engaged upon reloading.

'We have her foretopmast!'

'And mark how her mainsail is tore about!'

'I did see at least three balls go inboard!'

'Wear ship, master,' said Oakshott, lowering his telescope. 'I perceive that we have caused a certain amount of confusion over there. Now is the time to cross his T and further add to that confusion.'

The *Daisy* was going about as the Frenchman passed her, presenting her unguarded stern, briefly, to whatever the enemy could deliver. He delivered none. With a cat's cradle of foretopmast and rigging descended upon the gun deck, with undoubtedly shots taken inboard, with the concomitant hell of splintered shards of wood and each one a dagger to rend flesh, the Frenchman was otherwise engaged. From across the water, Oakshott could hear the screams of men wounded or dying.

The enemy ship continued its course downwind. Having gone clean about - and as smoothly as you please - the *Daisy* now on the starboard tack, headed straight for the Frenchman's stern, in order to pass her close. Her gunners, trained daily and repeatedly to the task, had already reloaded the starboard battery with double-shotted ball, to maim ships at close quarters.

'Steady as you go,' said Oakshott, when he had determined that he would pass so close under the enemy's counter that he would be able to toss an apple on to his poop. 'And give fire in a rolling volley from fore to aft as your guns bear.'

'Aye, aye, sir.'

There were a few moments when the two ships were obliquely placed, so that the Frenchman might well have slewed his guns and essayed a broadside. No such thing happened. Oakshott's first blow seemed to have almost literally taken the wind out of the sails of his opponent, who wallowed on like a lame duck, sails flapping and largely untended, and, as far as could be seen, nothing but hurried confusion on deck.

Sailing on a broad reach, the *Daisy's* long bowsprit passed the enemy's counter. An instant later, her for'ard gun gave fire, and was almost immediately followed by the next in line. Less than ten seconds it took for the sloop-of-war to 'Cross the T' of the bigger ship; in that time, nine 16-pounders sent their double-shotted loads into the other's counter; smashing through wood and glass windows, punching on and out past light panelling to the gun deck beyond; overturning guns and men in a chaos of splintered wood, flesh, blood, guts and brains.

Oakshott looked behind him as the Frenchman receded astern.

'We'll go about and overtake him,' he said. 'There's not much sailing quality aboard there, nor gunnery either. We'll give him another broadside, ship to ship.'

Midshipman Charteris said: 'We've beaten them, sir. As you often say, there's none like us.'

'They may have neither seamanship nor gunnery, Mr Charteris,' responded Oakshott, 'but those fellows over there didn't overthrow a thousand year-old dynasty and set all Europe on its ear by sitting about on their fat arses - as you will doubtless discover when we board them with cutlass and pistol.'

Charteris swallowed hard and was silent.

'Bring me starboard to him,' said Oakshott. 'A broadside of grape across his upper deck and we'll close to board him. Have grappling irons ready and issue cutlasses and pistols.'

'Aye, aye, sir.'

Death, thought Oakshott as they closed with the wounded Frenchman, was a movable feast in the mind. One did not have any compunction, in one's ardently chosen profession, of inflicting death either upon the King's enemies, or - with prudence dictated by circumstance - upon one's crew. It speaks much for Oakshott's philosophy that he did not bring his own life into the equation.

But all must die, for it is the last thing we do. And all do not perish in the heat of battle, as many might do in the minutes ahead, as the fast moving sloop diminished the distance between her and the wounded Frenchman. There are other ways to die: the way in which his beloved mother had died...

'Grappling irons ready, sir. Cutlasses and pistols provided.'

'Very good,' said Oakshott.

'Shall you require arms, sir?'

Oakshott was no swordsman, but belonged to the cut-and slash school, his formal small sword being no more than a decoration to wear upon the left hip. He was also left-handed.

'Give me a cutlass,' he responded.

A shout from the foredeck: 'They're shooting at us!'

Less than three ships' lengths separated pursuer and pursued. From the poop deck and from the mizzen tree of the Frenchman, bright puffs of white smoke betrayed the presence of marksmen. A musket ball hummed past Oakshott's ear and scored a furrow across the taffrail.

'Close with him,' said Oakshott. 'A whiff of grape - and stand by to board.'

One of the *Daisy*'s sharpshooters - a Plymouth man - using one of the long Kentucky rifles that had done much to cost England her American colonies, fired from the fore chains at the enemy's mizzen tree, and a figure cartwheeled down and fell into the surging wake.

'Well done,' said Oakshott.

Two minutes later, no more, and the sloop's for'ard guns bore on the other's quarter - as indeed did the other's bear on the *Daisy*'s bow, but no activity was to be seen over there, save for ill-devised attempts to clear the tangle of sails and rigging, which, considering the situation, was an irrelevance.

'Give fire!' ordered Oakshott.

Grapeshot - mostly made up of scrap metal from the ship's blacksmith's store, most of it rusty, broken and keen edged - swept across the Frenchman's deck and through the fellows working there, and through those who, seemingly unable to use their cannons, were lining the rails to await the arrival of the Englishmen. It did not make a pretty sight.

'Grapple with him!' ordered Oakshott, and took up his

cutlass. He glanced at the young midshipman by his side, who was similarly armed and with a pistol stuck in his belt. 'Be of good cheer, Mr Charteris,' he said, 'and remember what I told you. This time we will go together. Next time I shall send you on your own.'

'Let's go!'

The thrown grappling irons - six of them - connected with the frigate's bulwarks from bow to stern and were hauled taut. The two ships closed. The froth of water between them narrowed to a leaping distance.

Oakshott leapt, and Charteris went with him; nor were they the first aboard the Frenchman, for those in the waist, where the gap was narrowest, beat them by a whisker. Oakshott got a good hand-hold on the frigate's mizzen chains and was able to cope adequately with a savage-looking fellow who came at him with a long, curved cavalry sabre in the French pattern. He parried the blow: a tinny ring of steel on steel; and then drove his point forward to his opponent's face. The man went down screaming and gushing blood like a poleaxed ox. Very crude. Not for the first time did Oakshott regret his neglect of the lessons that their father had arranged for him and his brother from a French master of the fence, one Monsieur Haquin. But the boring, repetitious drillwork in Sennett's orangery had palled beside the soft delights of fishing for carp in the stew pond, or the fat pony who awaited him in the home paddock...

The Frenchman's deck, thanks to the ministrations of the grapeshot and other benisons that the *Daisy* had laid aboard, was slippery with bright blood, and it was difficult to keep one's feet in the considerable swell enjoyed by two ships caught in an embrace with all sails made and going nowhere. Oakshott looked round for someone else to tackle, and very soon found such an opponent, in the person of a tall, thin fellow in most outrageous costumery of braided coat, tricolour sash and a hat beplumed in red, white and blue, who could only have been the captain of the frigate, though it did not seem to Oakshott that he was of the seamanlike cut of jib - more like a soldier. And he came at

Oakshott in the manner that, to the latter's alarm, put him much in mind of the aforesaid Monsieur Haquin: one foot advanced like a dancing master, the left arm out-thrown to give balance, the point held out and unwavering. In such a manner had he and his brother Jack been taught, in those far off and golden days of youth, to confront one's opponent in the fence. With an unutterable sense of *déjà vu*, and a certainty that he was about to be skewered on the point of the Frenchman's very potent-looking straight sword, Oakshott, taking the Englishman's resolve of being in for a penny in for a pound, took two paces forward, swung wildly with his cutlass to the other's left shoulder, slipped on a puddle of blood and fell flat on his backside.

The Frenchman was on him at the instant, blade drawn back to make a thrust to skewer Oakshott's heart – and this he would have done, had not a pistol ball, driving through the back of his skull and out the front, taking an unbelievable amount of his brains with it and splattering them over the fallen man, put paid to the enterprise.

Midshipman Charteris stood there, smoking pistol in hand, a fine light of fighting fury in his eyes.

'Well done, Mr Charteris,' said Oakshott, wiping warm brains from his face. 'If you do nothing else of note in your naval career, you have probably ensured the succession of the Marquisate of Uffingham and Bow.'

The French put up a good fight, but were out of their element. As Oakshott had surmised, the frigate's crew was mostly made up of young conscript soldiers pressed into sea service, and their late captain a major of artillery. Nonetheless, it took twenty minutes of hard hand-to-hand fighting, plus a lot of jabber in broken French and English, before they were finally constrained to haul down their flag and hand over their side-arms.

'Mr Stevens, you will take sufficient men to sail this ship as a prize back to Port Mahon,' said Oakshott, 'turning her over to Commodore Pell when he arrives there with the inshore squadron. I will land the French prisoners ashore to the royalist forces here. What they do with them is their business. They can do no worse than chop their heads off. Get you gone.'

'Aye, aye, sir.'

'By the way, what is the butcher's bill on this fight?'

'Five killed, sir. And three wounded, one of them like to die.'

'Names?'

'There's Turner and Biggs, Norton, Laney and Swift, all killed.'

'The wounded?'

'Crawford, Norman and young Stukeley, sir. 'Tis the latter who's dying.'

'Young Stukeley - and I never did remember to advance him,' said Oakshott, 'but I will rectify that straight away. Where does he lie?'

'In the orlop, sir.'

Oakshott descended to the lowest deck, where, lit by a single tallow dip, the three wounded lay in charge of the surgeon's mate. Two were unconscious, having, as the surgeon's mate informed his captain, been massively sedated with laudanum. The third - indicating young Stukeley - whose backbone had been quite shot through, was beyond even the aid of laudanum.

Oakshott knelt by the lad, whose pain-filled eyes met his.

'Now see here, Stukeley, I'm making you up to able-bodied seaman as of this day,' said the captain of the *Daisy*.

'Thank you, sir,' whispered the other.

'I would have done it sooner, but it slipped my mind,' said Oakshott.

'Yes sir.'

'How are you feeling - in yourself, like?'

'The pain is very great, sir.'

'Well, it won't last long, lad,' said Oakshott.

Nor did it.

The crew of the *Daisy*, Oakshott not excepted, were greatly elated at the thought of the prize money that would accrue from the capture of the frigate, which, as it transpired, was named *La Vengeance,* but had in happier times been called - oddly, considering the circumstances of her capture - *La Marguerite,* which is French for daisy. Men on the messdecks nightly gathered about such of their fellows who had that little bit more literacy and numeracy to be able to make a reckoning of what a first-class modern frigate might be worth, divided by the number of the crew in proportion of captain, officers and men. All in all, it was generally reckoned that there would be enough prize money for even a humble AB to lay aside enough to purchase an alehouse upon his discharge - the fantasy of seamen, surely, since the days of Jason and the Argonauts. Even Oakshott was not immune to the fever, but covered reams of paper with reckonings of how his prize money might pay for re-roofing Sennett, bringing the tenant farmers' cottages into decent shape, restoring the formal gardens, and so forth.

They had landed the French prisoners and wounded (their dead had been buried over the side, along with Turner, Briggs, Norton, Laney, Swift and Stukeley, in the honourable tradition of the sea) by ship's boats. Oakshott was reluctant to take the *Daisy* into Toulon, preferring, as he put it, to await trouble at anchor in the roads outside.

More trouble came over the horizon less than a week later. It came in the shape of two sixty-fours and a quartette of frigates. And the leading battleship flew the broad pennant of a commodore.

Pell was on the scene!

Chapter Seven

THE INSHORE SQUADRON anchored fairly close by the *Daisy*. From any other commander but Pell, Oakshott might have expected a summons to go aboard the flagship for dinner that evening - no such summons came. In the dog watches, however, there was much coming and going of boats from ship to shore and otherwise, the boats from shore all wearing extravagantly large lily-splattered ensigns of the defunct French monarchy.

And at dusk that evening, surely only minutes before it would have been impossible to have deciphered the message, a string of signal flags rose to the flagship's main, which the duty midshipman, the unappetising Shacklock, deciphered with some difficulty from a copy of Admiral Lord Howe's famous signal book and took aft to his captain.

'Daisy repair aboard Goliath forthwith.'

Oakshott put on a clean shirt, waistcoat, stockings and breeches and called away his boat. Pell, he decided, had - in his own brusque, lower deck way - decided to make amends. It was certain that the arrival of the prize ship *La Vengeance* in Port Mahon had preceded that of the inshore squadron, that Pell had had the pleasure of arriving upon his station enhanced by the news that one of the smallest units under his command had already secured a not inconsiderable victory. Perhaps, said Oakshott, to his reflection in the mirror, he might even forget that I'm the brother of a marquess and treat me like a bloody human being for a change.

As he was rowed towards the *Goliath*, Oakshott had

grudgingly to acknowledge that Pell's flagship was arguably the best turned-out sixty-four he had ever clapped eyes on. The sides had been newly scraped down to the bare wood and repainted with at least six coats of black and umber, for not a line of planking showed. Cordage and rigging was in splendid condition and everything that could be polished was polished. The only thing absent from a truly well-lavished ship - the thing that told of a rich captain who could dig into his own pocket for the small extras - was the notable lack of gold leaf at counter and bows. Not High Church, the *Goliath*, but distinctly Low Church, if not Chapel. Oakshott chuckled to himself at his little jest.

'What boat?' The challenge from *Goliath*'s gangway.

'*Daisy*.' The framing of the question and the answer determined that a ship's captain was being borne. As a ship's captain of His Britannic Majesty's Navy, Oakshott was received aboard the flagship with the due honours of a veritable orchestra of bosun's pipes. And he also had the inestimable pleasure of being saluted by his old friend and shipmate Ned Daventry, greeting him as officer-of-the-day.

'Ned - how very nice to see you.'

'Charlie, you're looking well.' The big man glanced over his shoulder, as if searching out spies. 'Not a word save a word of warning, for the Old Man's awaiting you, and gird yourself about for trouble.'

'Oh, my God, no! What?'

'I dunno, old friend. But from all I hear, you've right set the cat among the pigeons in some regard or other - don't ask me what, for I don't know. Get you aft, Charlie, and I'll see you again before you go over the side, and we'll partake of a drop together before you leave.'

Oakshott nodded, and went aft in a puzzled frame of mind.

What had he done to 'set the cat among the pigeons'? he asked. Had he not safely delivered the boy general and his sister-in-law to the care of the royalist forces in Toulon? (albeit that he had tupped the lady, but the invitation to do so had been freely offered, and frequently, and surely could not possibly be held to his demerit). And he had captured a frigate...

He was saluted by marine sentries at the quarterdeck screen with a fine slap of sidearms; doffed his hat and rapped upon the door of the after cabin.

'Enter!' The sepulchral voice of Pell.

Oakshott entered. The chalk-white face of the most detested commander in the Royal Navy was somewhat set in shadow because he was seated at a table with the glare of the Mediterranean sunset behind him. He was not alone: two officers in the white uniforms of the French royalist army were seated at opposite ends of the table. Both glared at the newcomer as if he had been a gipsy knocking on the door to sell clothes-pegs.

'Good evening, Commodore,' said Oakshott. 'I trust you made a good passage.' It seemed as civilised a manner to start the game as any.

Pell did not reply, nor did he indicate to Oakshott to take the remaining seat at the table. All three men had glasses of drink before them, which, from their levels, the Frenchmen had scarcely touched. It was known throughout the Navy that Pell eschewed the Demon Drink, constantly inveighed against the rum issue, offered only temperance beverages in his quarters; and the famed religious tracts that decorated the bulkheads of his stern cabin bespoke of his intensely puritanical tendencies.

'*Est-ce que c'est le Commander Oakshott*?' demanded one of the Frenchmen, he to Oakshott's left, a man of about fifty, with a curled wig in the old style, and rather more silver braid than his compatriot.

'This is Oakshott,' replied Pell. 'Better known to fame as *Lord* Charles Oakshott.' He grated the words.

The atmosphere in the cabin, thought Oakshott, was distinctly on the chilly side, and Charlie is clearly the recipient of the cold breezes. But why?

He tried another tack: 'Were you in Port Mahon, sir, in time to see the arrival of our prize ship, *Le Vengeance*, formerly *La Marguerite*?'

'That frigate,' said Pell, 'foundered on a lee shore, in a gale off Minorca, and sank with all hands.'

'Oh,' said Oakshott. Poor Stevens and the rest. Poor

Sennett, who will not have her new roof, nor anything else of benefit, this year.

'It is not upon this issue that I have summoned you, Lord Charles,' said Pell, 'but upon the issue of Monsoor the Marquis de Colombe and his sister-in-law the lady Marquise.'

'*C'est incroyable*!' declared the other and presumably senior of the two Frenchmen. '*IN-croyable*!'

'*Vous avez raison, Monsieur le Comte*!' declared his junior, who, as Oakshott speedily discerned, was well into the arse-crawling game.

What is so incredible about tupping a doe at her own request? Oakshott asked himself. And that surely is the only issue upon which these three clowns can be lambasting me.

'Sir, I don't understand,' he said. 'You must enlighten me as to my supposed shortcomings in this matter.'

'I will tell you in short terms,' responded Pell, and Oakshott knew from the way he had not mockingly addressed him by his courtesy title that they were speedily coming to the nub of the matter. 'I will tell you that you have probably - indeed almost certainly - ruined this whole enterprise at Toulon.'

A discreet knock, and Pell's servant entered with a lighted taper, with which he proceeded to illuminate the stern cabin with the half a dozen or so hanging lanterns there.

Better illuminated, Oakshott saw his commodore's face more plainly, and it did not look well: Pell's cheeks had fallen in, the pallor had intensified, the eyes held a different tone that was difficult to interpret. Fantastically, Pell reminded him of his beloved mother upon her deathbed.

But he must not think of that - not think of that...

Pell said: 'I have it from these two Frenchmen that you brought this couple to Toulon on Thursday last and anchored here in the roads.'

'That is so, sir,' replied Oakshott.

'And then?' The question hung heavily in the air - as the saying goes.

'Um - they were taken off by a cutter, sir, which put out from the shore.'

'From Toulon?'

'I did not see the cutter till it was closing. But I would say that it came from the general direction of Toulon. Downwind to us.'

'What ensign - if any - did this cutter fly?'

'The French royalist ensign - white lilies sprinkled on blue.'

'And the officer in command - describe him.'

'Tallish. A mite unshaven. Wore a similar uniform to the gentlemen here. I did not take him to be the commander of the cutter, but an army officer despatched to escort the distinguished passengers ashore.'

'Which he did?'

'Oh, yes.'

'And their gear?'

'And their gear.'

'Describe this gear. Sea chests? Boxes, perhaps?'

'I did not observe it in detail, sir, but there was a considerable amount. Apart from what the general had had stored in my after cabin, it fairly filled the after flat. With respect, may I ask why you are questioning me upon this detail?'

Pell sat back in his chair, and his ice-cold, sick-looking eyes surveyed the standing figure before him.

'You were not aware that a very large part of your passengers' baggage contained gold guineas to the tune of half a million?'

'I had not been apprised of this.'

'Supplied by His Britannic Majesty's Treasury, for the royalist troops in Toulon, who have not been paid since the siege began, in consequence of which the least trustworthy of them, the least disciplined, are on the point of mutiny.'

Oakshott shrugged. 'I would say bully for His Britannic Majesty's Treasury, sir, would you not?'

The sick eyes narrowed. 'Don't bandy words with me, sir,' hissed Pell.

'*IN-croyable*!' interjected the senior Frenchman.

'*Vous avez raison, Monsieur le Comte*,' declared his aide.

'I am not seeking to bandy words with you, Commodore,' said Oakshott, 'but merely to discover by what means I have given offence in this matter. I brought the general and his sister-in-law to Toulon and handed them over - along with their baggage, of whose contents I had not been apprised - to their supporters, with whom they departed without a word of demur or complaint.'

'No sir!' grated Pell.

'But . . .' Oakshott saw - or, rather, sensed - a trap opening up under his feet.

'The gentry to whom you handed over the passengers,' said Pell, 'along with the half million supplied by the Treasury - were revolutionaries. You were gulled, Lord Charles, by a gang of cut-throats with no better credentials than an ensign and a uniform taken from a dead man.

'It is a mistake that, upon your court-martial, is like to cost you your command - and possibly your commission.'

'Oh!' exclaimed Oakshott. And then, as the notion took hold of him, he repeated less forcibly: 'Oh . . .'

There was much more. Many recriminations from the French officers, who, in broken English, told how news of the *Daisy*'s arrival in Port Mahon had been brought to Toulon and widely disseminated on both sides of the lines.

(Comment from Pell: 'While you were enjoying the fleshpots of Minorca, they were cooking up a hell's brew for you here!')

Moreover, the transfer of the half million had been known for months around Toulon and Marseilles, for in their heavy-handed way the Treasury had approached almost every prominent *émigré* in London with a commission to sign for the gold and convey it by fast vessel to Toulon. None of these gentry - save one - had been willing, after escaping from the Revolution, possibly to deliver himself back into the lion's mouth, so to speak. The exception had been young de Colombe, who with awful cynicism on the part of Whitehall, had been offered an entirely spurious command as an incentive to deliver the gold, he who, as Oakshott had discerned, was not fit to command a small mule train. All this had been brought by spies to Paris and thence to Marseilles.

The upshot of it all was that the Toulon garrison had still not been paid, and stood in certain hazard of never being paid till the present unlikely restoration of the monarchy following the quelling of the Revolution. As lief wait for pigs to fly.

And where were the de Colombes? - Oakshott put this question, thinking not so much of the arrogant youth with his toy soldiers as of the beautiful American who had shared his hammock through quite a few rewarding nights.

Ah, they were undoubtedly in the Château de Palmes, which was on the coast between Toulon and Marseilles, one of the enemy strongholds in which they had incarcerated such prominent prisoners of aristocratic birth as would grace the guillotine in the centre of Toulon if and when the city was taken. And, yes, the guillotine had already arrived in its component parts ready to be assembled. With it was one Fauchon, principal assistant to the by now legendary Sanson, despatcher of a king, and diverse persons daily in the great square by the banks of the Seine.

The Frenchmen departed *Goliath* with many hard looks at Oakshott, faced as they were with the likelihood of large scale mutiny and desertion on the part of their forces in Toulon.

Oakshott was left to face the personal wrath of Pell.

Poised to receive the wrath, Oakshott was alarmed when the other was taken by a violent paroxysm of coughing that racked his cadaverous form and reduced him to a crouching, bent, impotent creature in his chair. When it was over and he had dabbed his mouth, Oakshott saw that the handkerchief was speckled with bright blood.

'Is there aught I can get you, sir? A glass of water, perhaps?'

Pell nodded. 'And there are some tablets over there yonder, atop my sea chest. Bring them over, there's a good fellow. I'll take them with the water.'

Oakshott brought the tablets and a glass of water from the carafe. Pell gulped down three, took a long swig and sat back.

'I'm well nigh broached to, Oakshott,' he said, addressing

the other for the first time as man to man, 'and will soon be called aloft.'

'Surely not, sir,' lied Oakshott. 'Why, this fine Mediterranean climate will do wonders for you. The sun. The fine breezes . . .'

Something of the old, cold fire came back into the washed-out eyes. 'Don't gull me, young fellow,' said Pell. 'As to the matter in hand, we may be lucky, for Hood and the main fleet will be here within a week, together with the transports. The redcoats will stiffen the Frogs in Toulon and no doubt hang a few of the likely mutineers. But you, dammit, have not helped by letting that half million slip through our fingers,' he silenced the comment on Oakshott's lips with an imperious wave of his hand and it was not hard to see how this hard man had come up through the hawse-hole. 'And you'll have to face a court-martial, for I couldn't prevent it even if I would' – the vulpine grin of old revealed that the spasm of his fatal illness had passed and that Pell was more or less his hateful self again – 'and I wouldn't, for your brief was to take the marquis fellow to Toulon and not wait out in the roads for some bright cockolorum to snatch him and the gold. And, oh, yes, I know that you were not informed about the gold – and that, Oakshott, will be your best defence at your court-martial.'

'I'll bear that in mind, sir,' said Oakshott.

Pell nodded. 'Touching upon your capture of the frigate, I'll make a favourable report on it to Hood. The action was observed from Toulon and they spoke highly – the Frogs who came aboard – of the way you handled the fight.'

'There was no quality aboard there, sir,' confessed Oakshott. 'Simple tactics defeated them.'

'Maybe so,' said Pell, 'but it's no mean feat for a sloop to take a frigate intact. I'm sorry that you lost her. What was your butcher's bill in all, counting the men who went down with the frigate and those you lost in the action? And you needn't look to me for replacements.'

'Six killed in the action, sir. Twelve topmen and my first lieutenant went down in the frigate as prize crew – I couldn't spare more. Maybe I should have kept the vessel here instead of sending her to Port Mahon...'

'Be in no doubt that you did the right thing, Oakshott,' said Pell. 'An under-manned prize had best be sent to the rear, or she's a temptation to the enemy to recapture her. An enemy ship sunk is better than an enemy ship afloat, prize or no prize.' Pell coughed and dabbed his lips with the blood-splattered handkerchief.

'As to replacements, sir,' said Oakshott, when the other had recovered.

'As to replacements,' said Pell, 'I've no doubt that Hood will be able to supply you from the main fleet when he arrives. I am undermanned and cannot help you.'

'Could you spare one officer, sir?' asked Oakshott, 'to replace my first lieutenant?'

Pell eyed him narrowly. 'You are after something, Oakshott,' he said. 'Out with it - don't bandy words with me.'

'You have a Lieutenant Daventry with you, sir,' said Oakshott. 'He is a former shipmate of mine and I esteem him highly. If you could spare him...'

'Daventry? That great bladder of lard? Take him and with pleasure. A man who cannot rise above midshipman before the age of thirty-five is no use to man nor beast.'

When Oakshott left him, Pell was fighting another paroxysm of coughing. The man who had, in the eighteenth century Navy, clawed his way up through the hawse-hole, was indeed broached to and like soon to be called aloft.

Ned Daventry met him at the gangway.

'Pack your traps, Ned,' said Oakshott. 'You are my newly-appointed first lieutenant. How about that?'

Oakshott woke at the sound of eight bells in his cot in the stern cabin. Some conjunction of fact and fancy made him reach out to take a lissom and complaisant form in his arms, but she was not there. He sat up sharply, hit his head on a beam and swore.

Oh, God, what a head he had! Before leaving the *Goliath*, he and Ned Daventry had split between them a bottle of rum to cement their new relationship, and had fortified the aforesaid by splitting another aboard the *Daisy*.

'Stukeley!' he shouted.

But Stukeley was dead and gone and lying in ten fathoms with a hunk of pig iron around his ankles and a sailor's coffin, which is a bolt of coarse sailcloth. Instead of Stukeley came a frightened looking lad with a decided squint; a lad whom Oakshott vaguely recalled slinging a hammock in the after flat the previous evening.

'You called, sir?'

'Bring me some coffee, please, and a nip of rum. And what's your name?'

'Bantock, sir.'

'Very well, Bantock. To your knowledge, is the first lieutenant awake and about?'

'The new first lieutenant, sir?'

'The very same.'

'Why, sir, the first lieutenant were awake at the end o' the middle watch and did call out all hands to man the side, after that he did call away all boats for to row around the fleet – and the last boat home were made to row around the fleet twice about. Only . . .'

'Only what?' asked Oakshott, pulling on his stockings.

'Why, sir, the first lieutenant did row stroke oar in the boat that came in last, so in a manner o' speaking he did put hisself to punishment.'

We can't lose. England can't lose, said Oakshott to himself, scraping away with his none too sharp razor. Not while we have fellows like Ned.

He cut himself.

'Blast!'

He staunched the flow of blood with a dab of powdered alum, and recalled, through the fumes of alcohol and bonhommie, what he and Ned Daventry meant to do this coming night.

Chapter Eight

'GIVE WAY TOGETHER – but handsomely, mind. There's a rope's end for the man who makes a splash or catches a crab.'

Bosun Cox in the stern sheets of the ship's cutter at Oakshott's elbow gave the order in scarcely more than a whisper. The men plied their muffled oars, and they slid away from the *Daisy*, followed by the second cutter and after that the small jolly boat.

The enterprise was on...

Oakshott and Daventry had, in the cool light of day, examined the plan that they had dreamed of in their cups the night before: they had addressed themselves to the chart of the Marseilles littoral (an exceedingly dubious work, drawn up by a Portuguese naval mission in the early 16th century) and had found that their wild fancy might be made to work after all. The Château de Palmes was clearly marked upon the chart as a prominent feature (not surprisingly, for it had been there since mediaeval times), and stood upon a promontory to the eastward of a small bay almost half way between Toulon and Marseilles. Some soundings were indicated, which suggested that the *Daisy* might enter the bay and lie off at anchor half a mile from the shore. Accordingly, they had slipped away before moonrise and dropped the hook in five fathoms. Oakshott had prudently omitted to inform Pell of the enterprise, referring his conscience to the broad terms of the brief that he had been given him in Plymouth:

'*You will remain in or near the port... giving what aid*

you are able till the main fleet arrives...'

It was a brief that might be interpreted on some occasion – at his court-martial, for instance – as permitting him to make good his shortcoming as regards the de Colombe affair; for to rescue the boy general and his sister-in-law might be taken as a complete vindication of his error in handing over the couple to the enemy. It was scarcely to be supposed that he would also be able to recover the half million in gold, but, as Pell had pointed out, he had not been apprised of the fact that de Colombe had been no more than a dupe to escort the gold. And that would be his defence.

Rescue him.

Rescue – her...

He stared into the darkness ahead. With the eye of faith, one could discern, above the wild and snagged tumbling of the cliff, a formal, man-made shape: a pair of towers dimly silhouetted against the moonless sky; two small pinpoints of light.

'Slow the stroke,' said the bosun at the tiller.

Oakshott looked behind him. Ned Daventry was in the following cutter. Together with the jolly boat bringing up the rear, they mustered thirty men, all armed with cutlasses and a pair of pistols apiece, with reloads to the number of six. Thirty blades, half a thousand rounds, and thirty English hearts held high.

The towers of the castle resolved themselves more clearly. There was a flagpole atop one of them, where a flag of some sort flapped idly in the night airs – a sight which heartened Oakshott, for to the naval mind there is nothing so slack and slovenly as not to lower one's colours at sunset.

Up there, somewhere, he thought, might lie Barbara de Colombe, who had shared his hammock with mutual delight and to whom he owed something – if it was only to prevent her being shortened by her lovely head on some infernal machine.

'Toss oars,' murmured the bosun. Seconds later, the cutter grated on shingle, the bowmen leapt over the side and dragged the craft on to the strand. The rest went ashore dryshod.

'It's a bit of a climb, sir,' opined Daventry, when he had joined his captain.

They both looked up at the towering cliff and the castle ramparts perched on top. In truth, the ascent was steep, but, as Oakshott perceived, there was no scree, the face was jagged with rock and there appeared to be handholds a-plenty. No great feat to climb that - not for a topman who has climbed in a gale to reef a topsail.

'Let's go,' said Oakshott, tending to the priming of his pistols and hitching his cutlass over his backside so as not to be in the way. 'I think we leave three men behind to guard the boats, Mr Daventry.'

'Aye, aye, sir.'

Oakshott went first. To tell the truth, he had to admit to himself that, sailor or no sailor, he had no great head for heights, or for rock climbing; nevertheless, he set his foot upon the cliff, reached for his first handhold, fixed firmly in the forefront of his mind the dogma that had been drilled into him by his topman when first he climbed the mast of a first-rater - *Never look down* - and hauled himself to the next foothold. There he rested for an instant: so far, so good.

It was when he was half way up, and still leading, and he could hear the laboured breathing of the men below him, that - it happened!...

There came a clatter below, a muffled cry, a small fall of rock that ended in a rattle of small stones at the base, and a low moan of something that sounded like despair.

Looking down, he saw, in the moonlight, that one of the men - a straggler, near the last - had obviously had an ill-judged foothold crumble beneath him, and had lost the other. He now hung by his hands only, and even from the distance that separated them, Oakshott could see the terror of despair written in the man's face.

'Hold hard, lad!' came Bosun Cox's hushed whisper, 'an' belay the caterwaulin', or we're all lost. Reach up and take my hand, do.'

Miraculously, the rescue was effected by Cox and another, who hauled up the stricken sailor to firm hand and footholds. Oakshott closed his eyes for a few moments to shut out the image of the sheer wall far below; then readdressed himself to the climb. An age passed - and then, miraculously, they were all crouched together beneath the towering bulk of the castle.

Oakshott nodded to his first lieutenant.

'Grappling iron!' whispered Ned Daventry. Upon which order, one of the men - a young able seaman who had been among the first to reach the top - stood up with a three-pronged grappling hook in his right fist and a coil of light line in his left.

'Hit it first time, lad,' advised Daventry, 'or second at the worst, or we're like to be caught here, after the racket you've made, like rats caught in a bunch of oakum.'

The lad was one of those superior beings who did everything physical in the most nonchalant manner. He hurled the hook on high and paid out the line impeccably - but missed the towering rampart by two feet or more, where it struck against the stonework with a clatter that would have awakened Moses, to fall back with a similar metallic din upon the foot of the wall.

'If they didn't hear that in Marseilles they must all be drunk as rats,' was Oakshott's comment. 'Try again, lad.'

The young seaman addressed himself to his task. As with a keen bowler rolling his wood to the jack, he essayed two or three phantom throws before he committed himself. And threw.

The hook sailed up into the night sky, overtopped the ramparts of the castle, fell a little, lodged itself against the stone parapet.

'Well done,' said Oakshott. 'Up with you, lad.'

The young sailor swarmed up the light rope - no mean feat, this, and ample proof of a spiderish ancestry - bearing a coil of stout hemp over his shoulders. The manner of his ascent was near miraculous, the thin rope affording precious little handhold, but he made great play with his nimble feet, slipping a double loop about his instep with every lift. It was a joy to behold - till he went out of sight in the darkness of the wall.

'He's there,' breathed Ned Daventry at Oakshott's elbow,

and sure enough, the slight figure was etched against the dark skyline on the wall top. Almost immediately after, the hemp scurried down.

'Up with you, Ned,' muttered Oakshott. 'I'll take captain's privilege and go last. You can haul me up, for I have to confess that I never did get the knack of rope climbing.'

It was quiet up on the ramparts: only the light whisper of the wind, the splash of the breakers on the shore below, the hiss of shingle.

They saw again to their primings, hefted their cutlasses.

'The hands will divide into three parties, as arranged,' said Oakshott, addressing Daventry. 'I'll lead the red watch, you the white, and the bosun the blue. We'll keep separate, take what advantages offer themselves and support each other should the need occur. Let's go.'

'Aye, aye, sir.'

'And good luck, Ned.'

'And you, Charlie.'

Their hands met.

Colonel Gaston Lepautre, commander of the Château de Palmes, was not a career soldier, but part of the tide of revolutionary fervour that had been sucked into conflict between monarchy and people. His rapid advancement from the heady days of the storming of the Bastille had not been brought about by his military virtues so much as by his skill in committee work, his ruthless and uncompromising approach to the enemies of the people, coupled with an ability to crawl to his superiors - all of which qualities had raised him to his present eminence, which was not bad for a man who had started life as a butcher's boy in St Antoine.

That evening, he was holding forth to a new arrival at the stronghold: a young captain of artillery who had ridden in shortly after dinner and who had refused all but a morsel of bread and cheese, an apple and a small glass of Muscadet. The newcomer, in his mid-twenties, thin and slight, long and straggling hair, fixed the speaker over the rim of his wine glass with dark and brooding eyes that somewhat disconcerted Lepautre, who was accustomed to being listened to by his subordinates with more accommodating looks, with interjections of: 'You are right, Citizen Colonel', 'How clearly you perceive the situation, Citizen Colonel'; so that he found himself overstating his role of military pundit, as when an actor, uneasily conscious that he does not have the convinced attention of the front rows of the stalls, will declaim more loudly, bring in tricks of gesture, play the full range between charm and stern authority.

'Be assured, Citizen Captain,' he said for the fourth or fifth time, 'that the accursed English will not invest Toulon for long, nor will they seize the fleet - our fleet - though that is their intention. You have ridden far today?' he asked, by way of evoking some attention from the groundlings.

'From the Var,' replied the other, 'from General Dugommier's headquarters. The general and his corps are on their way, and he ordered me to investigate the position outside Toulon and give him a full report upon his arrival. Which I will do.'

Lepautre watched in some fascination as the captain took the last segment of his apple upon the tip of his pointed knife, dipped it into the dregs of the wine and chewed it impassively for a few moments.

It was at this stage of the dialogue that the door of the room was kicked open by a topman of the *Daisy*, and Commander Lord Charles Oakshott stood revealed there: somewhat dishevelled, scuffed by contact with the cliff face, his nankeen breeches ripped at both knees. Pistol in hand.

'Bonsoir, messieurs. Je regrette beaucoup que vous êtes mes prisonniers,' he declaimed in an execrable accent, adding in his own native tongue: 'I'll have both your swords - and then we'll talk business.'

It should not be thought that the progress of Oakshott's red watch to the fortress commander's quarters had been by any means a primrose path.

The position of such quarters, the heart of the stronghold, so it seemed to Oakshott, must lie deep within the central keep - and it was to this middle bastion that he and his men betook themselves; flitting from shadow to moonlight, one by one, well spaced and ducking low.

The door of the keep presented a problem: it was a double, iron-bound monolith of solid oak, with a heavy iron latch that resisted all attempts at movement.

'Locked and latched on the inside,' murmured Oakshott, to the topman crouched beside him.

'And guarded on the inside, too, I shouldn't wonder, sir,' responded the other.

'Undoubtedly,' said Oakshott. 'However, we've no time for idle speculation and must move boldly. I propose to try our luck with what is known in the part of the country I come from as "a little bit of cheeky-soft". Hold your cutlass to the point - and stand ready to thrust.' Whereupon, he knocked, quite deliberately, upon the ancient oak. Three times.

A few moments passed. Then, through the thickness of the door, they heard footfalls approaching. A voice, similarly muffled, growled a challenge:

'*Qui va là*?'

In answer to this, Oakshott uttered a meaningless, portmanteau phrase of sound which, to his English ear, approximated to that of a Frenchman saying something like: 'Enough of the fiddle-faddle, let me in!' It was an utterance that brought a tardy, if not immediate response: there came the sound of bolts being drawn, heavy keys being turned in grating locks, the creak of recalcitrant hinges.

'Stand by!' whispered Oakshott.

The door squealed open an inch, and then another, revealing a thick safety chain swagged between it and its twin. A moment's pause - and in the narrow gap thus exposed there appeared part of a face and an eye.

'*Qui va là*?' the challenge was repeated.

'NOW!' hissed Oakshott.

The topman drove his heavy blade forward with all his considerable muscle behind it. There was a choked cry from beyond. A thin jet of bright blood issued through the crack. It was with difficulty that the topman was able to extricate his cutlass from tissue and bone. The dull thud of a falling body followed.

The killing weapon was next employed to break a way in. This was done by threading the cutlass blade through a link in the safety chain and, using it as a windlass or the spoke of a capstan, with four hands at each end: turning, turning and turning - till, with a clatter, the hasp retaining one end of the chain was wrenched free from the woodwork and the way was open. The seamen burst into the stone-flagged passage that lay beyond - as almost instantaneously, a trio of Frenchmen debouched from an archway to their left.

The latter - clearly on guard duty, but relaxed in shirt-sleeves (one of them even had a hunk of bread in his hand), had been summoned by the clatter of the falling chain, if not by the death cry of their comrade. None of them were armed. They were quickly despatched in silence.

Oakshott and the red had broken into the heart of the fortress.

The passage through the Château de Palmes by Ned Daventry and the white watch was even more impeded. These nine men circled the ramparts till they came to a steep, unbalustraded stairway set against the inner wall and leading down into the pitch darkness of a courtyard far below. On the way, they encountered two sentries, both fast asleep, both raggedly dressed and wearing wooden clogs, their muskets propped up beside them. Sailors' clasp knives drawn deeply across their throats transposed the wretches from sleep to oblivion in silence and with scarcely any pain: no one takes prisoners of sentries, for a live sentry, however indolent, is an encumbrance.

They reached the head of the stairway in time to hear clomping footsteps coming from below. This was followed by a loom of light which resolved itself and its surroundings into a flambeau being carried out of an archway into the courtyard. There were six men, all bearing bayoneted muskets in a most slovenly manner and all dressed after the fashion of the pair who had newly kicked out their lives on the ramparts. They were led by the torch-bearer who greatly aped the appearance of an officer with his grotesquely-plumed bicorne hat, tricolour sash, and a long curved sabre that trailed the ground beside his left hip.

'They're coming up here,' murmured Daventry, 'to change sentries, I've no doubt.'

'Do we pistol them, sir?' asked the leading seaman at his elbow.

'No, we'll take 'em out as quietly as possible,' replied the other. 'Lie low, lads. When I give the signal, follow me roundly down those steps in line ahead keeping close to the wall. In that way, we'll have 'em on a lee shore, broached to and sunk without trace. Lie low - here they come.'

The tramp of wooden clogs grew louder. Peering cautiously over the edge, Daventry perceived that the torch-bearer had ascended nearly half way and that his men were strung out in single file behind him.

'There'll be no room for cutlass work,' said the first lieutenant of the *Daisy*. 'They'll only be an encumbrance, so leave 'em here up top and we'll pick 'em up when the dirty deed is done.

'Have a care, lads! Make ready! And it's to be fists and feet!'

The fancily-garbed torch bearer saw nothing of the pell-mell assault till the bounding figure of Ned Daventry came within the narrow compass of his flambeau's loom, which was no more than a few paces. One instant, he was a bored officer attending to the boring and routine task of placing fresh sentries on the ramparts of a fortress which had never been successfully assaulted since it was built in the middle ages; at the next, he was the first recipient of a string of assailants who were coming at him with dire intent.

He panicked. Dropped his flambeau, which fell over into the abyss, lighting up the courtyard as it went, and he made some attempt to draw his sabre. It was scarecely half way out of its scabbard before Ned Daventry was abreast of him on the wall-side. There was scarcely room for two to pass abreast on the narrow stair.

Nor did they. Not for long...

The Englishmen, hugging the wall, one hand on the wall for guidance in the sudden gloom, simply forged on, kicking and punching.

The fancily-dressed officer was the first to go, elbowed over by the massive Ned Daventry *en passant*. He cried out as he plunged down after his flambeau. Others swiftly followed.

It was soon over...

Seven hollow thwacks and the clatter of side-arms fifty-odd feet below betokened the end of the revolutionaries, all of them having been kicked, punched or elbowed into oblivion. Looking down, the men from the *Daisy* saw their humped forms lying in the flickering, fitful light of the fallen flambeau. Some were still writhing. All were silent.

'Pick up your cutlasses, lads,' said Ned Daventry. 'We move on.'

The party of the blue watch, Bosun Cox leading, progressed by way of a turret staircase that wound down into the ground and subterranean floors of the fortress. There Cox encountered no opposition - though he and his men were witness to the departure of the six men and their officer to their final reckoning at the hands of white watch. Hugging close to the wall, the bosun watched the Frenchmen's departure to their violent deaths - noting that all save the officer had emerged, sleepy-eyed, from an iron-bound doorway before marching off.

Motioning for the others to follow, Cox approached the door, pistol hefted, his other hand outstretched. The latch made a slight clatter, but the door opened quietly enough, and the Englishmen were immediately assailed by the stench that always seems to permeate a compartment that is densely inhabited as a sleeping quarter by men of the lower orders, such as soldiers, seamen and prisoners: a complex mixture of odours dominated by unwashed feet.

A quick look told the bosun that the compartment, which was long, wide and high-ceilinged and had in fact been a communal cell for debtors during the castle's time as a prison under the previous regime, was lined on each side with half a hundred forms sleeping on cots, and was lit by a single lantern hung from the ceiling. To the sound of many snores, the bosun contemplated a silent massacre with knives and cutlasses, or even a decimation by pistol fire - and then his eye lit upon a heavy key stuck into the inside of the lock, where surely it could not have served any useful purpose since the revolutionaries had moved in.

He quietly transferred it to the outside of the lock, closed the door, turned the key - and put the same in the pocket of his breeches.

'Sleep sound, Froggies,' he murmured.

Oakshott had with him a crewman - a Jerseyman - who spoke fluent French, and through him he quizzed the commander of the castle, Lepautre, about his prisoners. Lepautre, sullen, uneasy, perhaps frightened, regressed from his brashness as a grossly over-promoted revolutionary volunteer to the semblance of a St Antoine butcher's lad accused of dipping his hand into his master's cash drawer.

'How many royalist prisoners have you here?'

'I don't know. I have not seen the figures for the day.'

'But - approximately?'

'Twenty - perhaps less.'

'Among them is the Marquis de Colombe?'

'I think so. Yes - we have a person by that former title.'

'And his sister-in-law, Barbara de Colombe? - we will dispense with her title if it hurts you.'

A nod to this.

'And the baggage of the de Colombes?'

This won a sly, evasive street urchin's glance. 'I don't recall any baggage.'

'A considerable amount of baggage was taken ashore in charge of one of your people posing as a royalist officer. Since the de Colombes were brought here, it seems likely that their baggage accompanied them, wouldn't you agree?'

'Perhaps.'

'And is it still here?'

'Perhaps.'

This laborious exchange continued, and the outcome was that Lepautre, driven into divers corners by Oakshott's cross-questioning, finally admitted to eighteen royalist prisoners including two women and a child of seven. And the de Colombes were among them. And their baggage.

Throughout the bilingual interrogation (most expertly interpreted by the Jerseyman), Oakshott was conscious of being keenly watched by the thin-faced young French captain with the straggling hair, whose dark eyes flashed from one to the other of the speakers in the three-part exchange, and always in the end rested upon the tall English naval officer. Oakshott, who suffered a pronounced aversion to cats and who was immediately aware of a member of that species, seen or unseen, as soon as he entered a room containing one, felt something of the same unease in the scrutiny of the slight figure seated opposite him, and who said not a word in contribution to the dialogue, but gave the impression of absorbing and weighing every nuance of it.

It was then that Ned Daventry came in, having been directed there by the sentries that Oakshott had placed in the stairways and corridors leading to the fortress commander's quarters.

'Decks cleared of enemy, sir,' said the first lieutenant of the *Daisy*. 'Them as has not gone aloft is safely below hatches.' Seeing that his captain was in company with the enemy, he drew himself up and touched the brim of his hat in a most exaggerated salute, which Oakshott acknowledged in a like manner.

'We'll now free the royalist prisoners, Number One,' said he, 'and I should like them to be mustered on the beach, ready to be taken aboard the ship. But convey my compliments to the de Colombes, and ask them if they will please attend me here.'

'Aye, aye, sir.'

Lepautre by now had produced keys, and there was a squint-eyed gaoler who had survived the tender ministrations of the *Daisy*'s assault party, who was only too willing to oblige. Without even waiting for a nod of assent from his commander, this fellow scurried off to direct his captors to where they wanted to go. He was labouring to carry in the de Colombes' baggage when the aforesaid pair were ushered with some ceremony, by Ned Daventry, into the presence of his captain and the two Frenchmen, the junior of whom rose to his feet and gave a stiff bow in the direction of the woman; his superior remained seated, glowering.

'How are you, ma'am?' asked Oakshott, taking Barbara de Colombe's proffered hand, observing that she looked tired, that there were dark circles under her unbelievably splendid eyes, that her linen was dirty, her hair untended.

'Well enough, sir,' she replied, avoiding his eye.

'We have been treated most abominably!' screeched her brother-in-law. 'Madame de Colombe has been obliged to suffer the attentions of a loutish gaoler who constantly importuned her, who gloatingly dwelt upon her impending fate on the guillotine. As for the indignities that I have been made to suffer - *I*, a general officer and a nobleman of France . . .'

'Quite so,' said Oakshott. 'And now, sir, if you would be so kind as to confirm that this is indeed your baggage.' He indicated the pile of boxes and trunks which the squint-eyed gaoler had laid in the middle of the floor - and they made an imposing pile.

'Yes, this is it,' said de Colombe. 'Including the two chests which your English *gouvernement* insisted that I bring with me and hand over to the *agent comptable* - what you would call the paymaster - in Toulon. Those two.' He pointed.

'You have keys for these two chests, monsieur?' asked Oakshott.

'I do not, monsieur,' responded the other.

'Ah, well,' said Oakshott. 'We must make what shift we can. Number One, pray have the chests struck open.'

'Aye, aye, sir!' replied Daventry, and turning to Bosun Cox, who stood with him: 'Strike 'em open.'

'Aye, aye, sir,' was the response, and to the seaman at his elbow he said: 'Strike them open, Able Seaman Talbot.'

Able Seaman Talbot was the sort of fellow one meets in life

who is equipped in all parts for all occasions. On this occasion, he had a marlinspike tucked into his belt, a mallet stuck into his bandolier. The spike he probed into the hasp of the padlock that secured the lid of the first chest. The mallet he sharply struck against the spike, causing the hasp, padlock and all, to fly away.

Oakshott opened the lid of the chest. Within were a neatly stacked array of canvas bags tied with string. Slipping the precise reef knot that secured the neck of the bag that he picked up, he tipped it over. A golden hail of English guineas descended.

'Ah, well,' said he. 'We have not entirely wasted our evening, gentlemen.'

A clatter of running feet. A seaman appeared at the door. His eyes were wide.

'Cap'n, sir! . . .'

'Yes, what is it?'

'We've sighted a party o' men marching up the hill and comin' this way, sir. Some of 'em are carrying torches, an' I reckon I counted a hundred heads.'

'I think,' said Oakshott, 'that the time has come for our departure, for we have long overstayed our welcome. Carry the two chests down to the beach. And if you, monsieur and madame, will proceed there also with every haste,' he added, addressing the de Colombes.

The erstwhile boy general stayed his ground, head high, arrogant, defiant. He stared down his long nose at the captain of the *Daisy*.

'Monsieur, I think you have forgotten your duty,' he said.

Resisting the ever-recurring desire to put a boot behind the young jackanapes, Oakshott answered as coolly as he was able: 'Sir, I am well aware of my duty. My first duty is to my ship, which I intend to move out of hazard with despatch. My second is to my shore party and you people. My third is to the contents of those chests. What else have I missed?'

For answer, de Colombe pointed to the two revolutionary officers, one of whom - the senior - cowered in his chair, while the other continued to gaze impassively upon the exchange.

'What, monsieur, are you going to do with that - that *canaille*?' he demanded.

'Well, sir,' replied Oakshott, 'the capacity of my three boats has been further stretched by eighteen persons, together with two large chests - and you may be assured that the chests will be left behind on the beach if I find that I cannot accommodate them. I certainly will have no room for prisoners.'

'Shoot them! Shoot them!' screamed the youth.

Oakshott shook his head.

'You do not know, cannot guess, what these people have done!' cried de Colombe. 'In Marseilles, they have executed children along with their parents. All along the Midi, where there is royalist support they have burned, pillaged, raped, slaughtered...'

'I take your point, sir,' replied Oakshott, and he felt a sudden warmth for this impassioned youth, 'but the Royal Navy does not murder prisoners in cold blood. We may be wrong in this - but I think we are not. And now - let us depart.'

He ushered the de Colombes out of the door. He was the last to leave. He looked back at the two Frenchmen.

'I will lock you in,' he said, 'since my command of your language does not permit me to ask you for your parole. And I don't suppose you understand a word of what I'm saying now.

'Good night to you.'

'Monsieur...'

It was the young captain who spoke.

'Yes?'

'*Comment appellez-vous?* What ees your name, sair?'

'Oakshott. Charles Oakshott, Commander, Royal Navy.' He turned to go, and then paused on the threshold. 'And your name, monsieur?'

'Bonaparte,' replied the other. 'Napoleon Bonaparte, Captain of Artillery.'

Oakshott shrugged his shoulders. Closed the door. Locked it, and left.

*

Lookouts confirmed that the large party of the French were indeed heading along the cliff road up to the castle. The sea was rising, the surf rendering the handling of overladen boats most hazardous.

'Get the people aboard, Number One,' said Oakshott. 'As to the chests . .'

'Yes sir?'

'Open them up, both. Bring the money bags down to the water's edge. And we'll see.'

'Aye, aye, sir.'

The sailors assisted the eighteen released captives into the two cutters, with the bosun carrying a small, frightened girl in his arms.

'There's little enough room, Ned,' murmured Oakshott. 'Some of the hands will have to transfer to the jolly boat and take pot luck that she doesn't capsize.'

'And the money, Charlie?'

'Have the bags broken open and scatter the coins in the bilges of the two cutters. They'll serve as ballast to keep the boats upright.'

'Bloody expensive ballast, Charlie.'

They both laughed.

In the event, cutters and jolly boat left the surf without mishap and headed out, rolling perilously in a steep swell, towards the dark shape of the *Daisy* riding at her anchor. It was a long haul against the wind-driven waves for the three greatly overladen craft, but the question of making two journeys from shore to ship had already been ruled out before they were half way to the sloop-of-war: lights were appearing all over the dark castle, bobbing like fireflies about the ramparts, and the shouts of excited men carried clearly over the water. Oakshott, seated in the stern sheets of the leading cutter, with a fortune in gold coin sliding about his feet with every pitch and roll, reckoned that they had come off with not five minutes to spare.

'What ship?' A hail from the darkened sloop-of-war.

'*Daisy*!' Oakshott himself answered the traditional challenge.

They came alongside, and Oakshott was the first to climb aboard his command. Next came Barbara de Colombe. He handed her up.

'The midshipman will escort you to my stern cabin, ma'am,' he said, 'and will provide you with what comforts you need. I regret that I...'

'Charles...' her hand was on his arm.

'I regret that, under the circumstances, I shall not be able to act as your bath attendant - and that is a pity.'

'Charles. Thank you - for everything.'

He made a formal kiss of her proffered hand. De Colombe was being assisted on to the deck as his sister-in-law was being escorted aft by the midshipman of the day.

'Sir, I am tired,' said the erstwhile boy general. 'I hope that my quarters have been prepared.'

'Indeed they have, sir,' responded Oakshott. 'A hammock has been slung in the after flat alongside me, since the ladies will be occupying my stern cabin. And I wish you a very good night.'

Near dawn...

Oakshott, whose waking habits matched those of a cockerel, was up on deck at first light, boat cloak wrapped about his nakedness, a mug of strong Navy tea at which he sucked, a weevilly ship's biscuit upon which he munched, seated upon the quarterdeck rail.

The inshore squadron took shape in the dawn: Pell's two battleships and the four frigates. Well, he had a fine old surprise to deliver to Pell, and he reckoned that he'd deliver it about eight bells, in full dress, brassbound coat an all. And take Ned Daventry and the bosun, who well deserved a commendation for last night's work. And the gold - less the odd coin or two that had doubtless found its way into a poor seaman's pocket during the row offshore (and what better place for it to be?).

An end to his feud with Pell. The old man had part revealed himself in their last encounter as half way to a human being and a dying man at that. Last night's success would ease a relationship that, in any event, could not last for long...

'Sunrise, sir. Colours!' It was the midshipman of the day.

'Make it so, Mr Charteris,' responded Oakshott formally.

The colour party assembled, the signalman carrying the folded white ensign as if it had been his first-born. Oakshott got to his feet, laying his empty mug upon the deck.

The thin wail of a bugle issued over the slate-grey, glassy sea from the flagship *Goliath*. Colours.

Simultaneously, the ensigns were raised and made fast, *Daisy*'s included.

Oakshott's eyes narrowed as he looked to the other ships, who were bunched together some way off, the *Daisy* having dropped anchor in the dark of a moonless night at a prudent distance from her consorts.

'Number One!' he snapped.

'Sir?'

'Do I see *Goliath*'s colours flying at half mast?'

Telescope to eye, Ned Daventry replied: 'Yes, sir, and so are the other ships in company - all save us.' He lowered his telescope and they met each other's eyes. 'Someone must have died during the night,' he added.

'Pell,' said Oakshott, and knew it with a sudden certainty.

'Lower the colours to half-mast!' ordered Ned Daventry.

Oakshott tapped the capping of the taffrail with the palm of his hand, gazing across at the flagship.

I should have gone over there last night when we dropped the hook, he told himself. I should have given the old devil the good news. Shaken him by the hand before he went.

One never gets it right - quite right - all the time.

Chapter Nine

'WE THEREFORE COMMIT his body to the deep, to be turned into corruption, looking for the resurrection of the body, when the sea shall give up her dead, and the life of the world to come, through our Lord Jesus Christ...'

Sundown on the deck of the *Goliath*, and the captains of the inshore squadron were gathered to pay their last homage to him who had been the most hated and arguably the most professional sea officer in the Royal Navy. Oakshott was there, in full-dress coat like the others. *Goliath* had been sailed out to the deeps off Toulon, and Pell's last plunge was destined to be a hundred fathoms. The fleet chaplain was a true Devonian and he delivered the service of committal in his west country burr ('*turrned* into corruption').

Oakshott shivered and wished he had brought his boat cloak, for the treacherous Mediterranean was showing herself at her worst; with the setting of the sun, the wind had got up from the south, turning the wavetops to spindrift. It would be blowing a gale before *Goliath* returned to the anchorage; he hoped that Ned had thought to veer more cable and was keeping anchor watch – then immediately regretted the imputation.

'... who at His coming shall change our vile body, that it may be like His glorious body...'

In a like manner, and on such a summer's eve, had Oakshott stood at his mother's graveside, and he in his midshipman's short coat, with a light rain falling and the wind getting up.

He shook himself free of the memory . . .

'. . . according to almighty working, whereby He is able to subdue all things to Himself. Amen.'

The Marine guard fired a musket salute as the sailor's coffin of sailcloth was tipped over the side, with Pell's broad commodore's pennant attached to it. They will find a job for you up aloft, thought Oakshott. God forbid that you will be put on the selection board for admission to Paradise. You wouldn't let *me* in.

The *Goliath* was laid on a starboard tack, her sails drawing in the freshening wind. The officers on the quarterdeck gathered together. Snuffboxes were passed round. Someone lit a cigar. Pell's qualities were discussed, and to advantage: it was remembered that he had once swum twice round the fleet for a wager of one penny, and that, in Admiral Rodney's time, he had won his commission in action by serving a gun alone when all the others were dead or dying. A good fellow, Pell, and a fine officer. All else about him forgotten.

'*Sails to southward*!' This from the masthead.

'It's Hood and the main fleet!'

They came out of the gathering dusk: six ships of the line, ten frigates, a cloud of smaller vessels. The far-off, storm-tossed might of England was closing in upon the machinations of revolutionary France. God save the King!

Oakshott, who had accepted a cigar, found it not to his taste and surreptitiously dropped it over the side. No one noticed.

The Irish peer Lord Hood, with a brilliant career of admiralcy in the earlier French wars and in the American Revolutionary War, had been sent to Toulon at the express invitation of the royalist faction there, whose intent was to surrender their quite considerable fleet, along with the town, its forts and batteries to the English, to be held in trust for Louis XVII, son of the guillotined monarch.

Upon Hood's arrival in the port, he landed a body of soldiers and marines, who took over the town and the forts.

By the next day, the admiral was in possession of the best French harbour in the Mediterranean, a sizable fleet, together with stores and ammunition. It was the simplest capture ever known in the annals of the Royal Navy - but there was a snag, and Hood was wise enough to discern it: his own slender forces, and the loyal Toulon garrison (though fortified by the half million in gold coin that Oakshott had recovered) could not possibly hold it indefinitely against the overwhelming might of revolutionary France. He appealed for help. Help came. The Spaniards sent ships and three thousand men. The Queen of Naples, sister to the tragic Marie Antoinette, engineered the despatch of ships and men. More vessels arrived from England.

The situation took on a distinct look of improvement for the defenders of Toulon. Six hundred English and Spanish marines assaulted a revolutionary outpost, bringing away cannon, ammunition, standards. General O'Hara arrived from Gibraltar with two regiments on foot, along with artillery and took command of the land forces. But the equation still did not make sense: how to defend Toulon with about twelve thousand men against something like forty thousand? Moreover, the French were constantly being reinforced: by General Doppet from the Rhone, by General Dugommier from the Var. It was the latter who had had the prescience to send on ahead the young captain of artillery, Bonaparte, knowing him to be an officer who was destined for advancement (though even the prescient Dugommier could have had no inkling of the extent of this advancement!), to make an appreciation of the situation. Bonaparte's summation was simple: 'All you have to do is to send away the English fleet,' he said. 'And to do that you have only to sweep the harbour and roadstead with your batteries. Drive off the ships and the troops will go with them. Take the promontory of La Grasse, which commands both the inner and outer harbour, and Toulon will be yours in a couple of days, *mon general.*' It was the advice of an artilleryman - and incidentally of a military genius.

Bonaparte's advice was taken. The revolutionary forces assaulted the promontory, upon which stood two forts,

L'Aiguillette and Balaquier. There followed some bitter and bloody fighting, in which O'Hara was wounded and taken prisoner and Bonaparte was stuck in the backside by a bayonet thrust from a marine and had to be carried off the field. La Balaquier was taken. Within the hour, its guns were firing upon the ships in the inner harbour.

Lord Hood called a council of war.

Oakshott was summoned aboard the flagship well after midnight, and in no good humour. By a newly arrived frigate had come mail from home, and with it three letters for him. From his brother came a ten-line bleat that his new wife had left him and returned to London, concluding with the words: 'I have not been permitted to share her pillow, let alone tumble her. I hold you responsible, Charlie, for BLOCKING MY CHANCES. But for that PRIM AND PRISSY BAGGAGE, I could get me to London, buy me a decent coat or two, a new wig from Fox's, reside at the club and seek me out a COMPLAISANT FILLY to marry...'

The missive from Harriet being brief may be quoted in full:

Dear Charles,

To put it bluntly, your brother is not what he had seemed on first acquaintance. Almost from the start, his manner, his very person, has revolted me beyond bearing. As I warned you in my last letter, I am retracing my steps, back to the life where, at least, I could keep my self-respect.

And she signed herself, simply, 'Harriet'.

The news that his closely-reasoned scheme to provide an heir for the marquisate had finally foundered through his brother's total repulsiveness depressed Oakshott intolerably, and the feeling was only lightened by a long letter from Irene Chancellor, in which, without the slightest hint of intimacy and endearment, she gave him the latest news of the county and a few gobbets of scandal from London society in which the Prince of Wales and his circle figured most prominently. She ended with best wishes for his health and safety. Oakshott stuffed all three letters into his tail-coat pocket and had himself rowed over to the flagship.

He was received by the officer of the watch and immediately conveyed to an after cabin where sat Hood's flag captain, one Captain Dancey, under whom Oakshott had once served as midshipman, and with some mutual liking and respect.

They shook hands and talked of old ships for a while. Presently the sound of concerted musket fire brought them to the realities of the moment.

'Our forward patrols are out tonight,' said Dancey, 'in the hope of spiking the guns up at the fort, but by the sound of it they have run into an ambuscade, poor fellows. You did well at the Château de Palmes, Oakshott, and in taking that frigate - pity she foundered. Pell, before he died, penned a most favourable report on you to his lordship.'

'That was generous of him,' said Oakshott soberly.

'More generous that I would have believed possible,' said Dancey. They had both known the Pell of old.

'What now, sir?' asked Oakshott. 'What followed the deliberations of the council of war? - if one may ask.'

Dancey shuffled the papers on the desk before him and cocked a shrewd eye at the other man. The flag captain was a short, fast-moving, swift-thinking man, often likened to a fox or a ferret.

'One may ask, Oakshott,' he replied, 'but one will not necessarily be told the whole truth and nothing but the truth. However, this stricture does not apply to ships' captains - though they are required to keep the information secret from even their own officers. Understood?'

Oakshott nodded. 'Aye, aye, sir.'

'In short terms,' said Dancey, 'the allied fleet is going to abandon Toulon to the revolutionaries. Now, what do you think of that, hey?'

'I see no alternative,' responded Oakshott. 'Now that the French have taken the heights, we are sitting pigeons. Tomorrow at dawn we'll have to move out to the roadstead - as we've done every day this week - or be shot to pieces, piecemeal. And if the revolutionaries take the other forts - which is obviously their intent, and we don't have the numbers to stop 'em – the situation is going to deteriorate even further.'

Dancey gave him an appraising glance. 'You have a head on your shoulders, Oakshott,' he said. 'Your summation is shared by his lordship and his staff, also by the army. I would add that it took the allied council of war eight hours to agree to that summation – but we were somewhat encumbered by the Spaniards and the Piedmontese, not to mention the Neapolitans. I would further add that the Neapolitans, who hold the fort at Cape Lebrun and the other at Cape Lesset, declared quite absolutely that they would surrender upon the approach of the enemy, and are resolved to remove their ships and men at the earliest opportunity – commencing tomorrow.'

'And the French royalists, sir, what is their view upon the matter?'

The flag captain cracked the knuckles of his right hand with the unhurried deliberation of a man shelling walnuts. 'They have not been informed that the allies are to abandon Toulon,' he said at length. 'To do so would be to cause a panic in the town and port. There would be wholesale desertions, looting, drunkenness – you know the kind of thing.'

Oakshott said: 'And when we have gone – what then will happen to the people we came to help?'

'There will undoubtedly be widespread and indiscriminate massacres,' said Dancey. 'The revolutionaries are rather adept at that. In the course of a few days, however, government dignitaries will arrive from Marseilles, along with the guillotine, and the slaughter will be resumed in a – tidier manner.' The watchful, shrewd eyes were upon Oakshott, gauging his reaction.

'We will surely save such of those poor wretches as we are able, sir,' was his reaction.

Dancey nodded approval. 'That we shall, that we shall,' he said. 'We will bring off from shore all who present themselves for evacuation and transport them to Port Mahon. What's more, we shall not leave till we have blown up all the powder magazines and arsenals, stores, and any of the French fleet that cannot be removed. And that, Oakshott, will be your task.

'Tomorrow, you will place yourself under the command of Sir Sidney Smith, who has arrived with a flotilla of light vessels.

'Save and destroy – that will be our motto in the next few days, Oakshott. And the devil take the hindmost!'

At first light, Bonaparte's battery in La Balaquier fort opened fire upon the English fleet anchored right under their noses in the harbour; but the fleet was already under way and heading out for the relative safety of the roadstead, with all the manoeuvrability of open sea, plus the opportunities to close from time to time and lob round shot at maximum range and elevation up at the fort – and take a certain amount of punishment from the fort in return. It was a routine that part of the fleet had been following for a week and more: closing into the harbour at dusk to land troops and victuals, taking aboard the wounded, delivering and collecting despatches, and then retiring at dawn.

'Anchor aweigh, sir!' This from the fo'c'sle.

Oakshott was about to give the order to make sail and follow as tail-end Charlie of the fleet when, in the growing light, he perceived something: a conjunction of position and angularity that put an idea into his head.

'Call away all boats, Number One,' he ordered. 'Keep the sails furled. Prepare to tow the ship to the shore.'

Puzzled, Ned Daventry touched the cock of his hat and murmured acknowledgement. Pipes shrilled. Ropes sang in blocks. The *Daisy*'s boats gently hit the water, fully manned. Minutes later, the cutters and the jolly boat were pulling their mother ship across the glassy waters of the harbour.

Oakshott took sight, through a circle made by his thumb and forefinger, upon the fort, which was clouded with white gunsmoke in the growing dawn and accented by rippling sparkles of orange flame. They were firing upon the retiring fleet – but not upon him. No violent eruption of water told that anyone had eyes for the small ship crawling slowly across the harbour in the deceptive half light with tell-tale white sails closely gathered in. It was like playing that childhood game where one quietly crept up upon one's opponent's back and must never be caught in the act of moving when he turned and challenged.

There was a short length of quay immediately in front of his bows, long enough to take the sloop and perhaps one other, no more, and it was backed by tall, wooden-built dockside warehouses. As they drew closer, and Oakshott continued to gauge the angle of the fort through looped finger and thumb, he was confirmed in his first opinion: the promontory upon which the fort stood was slowly being obscured by the roofs of the warehouses.

'Have them lay her alongside the quay, Number One,' he said.

'Aye, aye, sir.'

It was neatly done. The jolly boat's crew took ashore headrope and sternrope, and the *Daisy* was pulled alongside. And in the process of her so doing, the upperworks of the fort disappeared from Oakshott's view. When they were made fast, he reckoned that nothing but the *Daisy*'s topmasts would be visible to the French up there – and that they would scarce be noticed among the forest of masts, fishing vessels and the like, scattered about the complex of harbour walls.

The best place to hide the branch of a tree is in a forest.

He and Ned Daventry breakfasted together in the stern cabin: salt beef, ship's biscuit, small beer and lime juice.

They munched in silence. The guns of the fort kept up their fire, joined in a duet with rolling salvos from the fleet in the roadstead, and the rattle of musketry in the heights above the town was continuous.

Ned Daventry picked his teeth and said: 'Out with it, Charlie. What's in your mind? You didn't bring her alongside to watch the grass grow. I know you better than that.'

Oakshott drained his beer mug. 'I've in mind to make a bit of a clatter while we're here, Ned,' he replied.

'Such as?'

'Such as take a couple of guns ashore, set 'em up somewhere close to the fort and give the Frogs something to think about.'

The big man shook his head. 'Charlie, Charlie, as sure as hell you're going to get yourself court-martialed one of these days,' he said. 'You ache for it as a bridegroom lusts for his bride. And you were ever thus. When do we leave?'

'Straight after the hands have finished breakfast,' said Oakshott. 'We'll land numbers five and six starboard guns from the waist. Twenty men a gun should suffice to drag 'em. As to my court-martial - well, you know the score: if we succeed, my brief to remain in or near the port, giving what aid I am able till the main fleet arrives, will be deemed to have been slightly extended. If we fail ...'

He shrugged. They both knew the score. The tremendous latitude allowed to a ship's captain in the exercising of his initiative was the mainstay of the Georgian Navy's vitality, but the principle hung upon success or failure; there were no second prizes handed out for a brave try. Furthermore, as both men were aware, while Oakshott, when operating alone, carried all the power of the King, both Houses of Parliament Assembled and the Admiralty, he was now seconded to Lord Hood and, more nearly, to Captain Sir Sidney Smith.

'Smith's a stormy petrel,' observed Ned Daventry. 'One such as yourself, Charlie. He'll want to scrape some glory and advancement from this enterprise, and he'll not thank you for stealing his thunder.'

'Damn Smith,' said Oakshott without heat. 'Call all hands to haul out those two guns, Ned. We'll stand or fall together on this trick.'

'As we have done many times before, Charlie,' responded the other. He gazed down to the swillage at the bottom of his mug. 'You know, this beer, the cask was broached last Thursday and laid aside to settle, I would not feed to the ship's cat.'

★

The landing of the two 16-pounder cannons on to the quay was an evolution that was carried out with the swiftness and dexterity that attended the launching of the cutters. Twenty men per gun assembled with stout hemp tow ropes which were attached to the run-out rings. Another party commandeered a horse and wagon from a none too co-operative fish merchant on the quay and loaded round shot, grape shot and powder aboard it. The entire operation was completed in fifteen minutes by Oakshott's watch. He nodded to Ned Daventry.

'Well done, Number One,' he said. 'Let's go.'

Leaving the senior lieutenant aboard the *Daisy*, with specific orders relating to every contingency, but all directed to the safety of the ship, the shore party set off. If Oakshott had any cause for repining at all, it was that either he or Ned Daventry should have remained aboard; but he had no intention of missing what was, for a seaman, the heady experience of directing gun against gun with the despised soldiery, and he knew that Daventry felt the same.

The road up from the quay was steep and cobbled, and took all the sweat of the sailors to pull the two 16-pounders up it, the small wheels, meant only for running in and out across the gun deck, clattering their noisy protest all the way, and bringing folks to doors and windows to regard their passing with awe and some fear. How many of these, thought Oakshott, will survive the indiscriminate slaughter and the guillotine after we have gone?

'Roundly, lads, roundly!' he barked, to relieve his feelings as much as anything. 'We haven't all day to stand about and gather buttercups along the way.' This sally won him a round of laughter and some raucous retort, which he ignored, save to exchange a wink with Daventry. The lads were in good spirit.

The road stopped being a road, became steep steps, up which the gun haulers had to manhandle their intractable charges with considerable difficulty, with curses phrased in the intonations and dialects of Devon and East Anglia, of Kent and Stratford-atte-Bow on the London river, of West Wales, and many else.

Presently, they brought the guns to the top. Oakshott snapped open his telescope, took a look, and passed it to Ned Daventry.

'What do you think, Number One?' he asked.

'Call it a half mile, or bit less, sir,' responded the other. 'Lord Hood would give his eye teeth, or his bollocks, to be here with his full weight of gunnery where we are. Do we open fire now, straightway?'

'I think we first make some shift of shelter and concealment,' said Oakshott. He pointed. 'We'll knock a couple of holes in yonder stone wall as will give some protection from the enemy balls when, inept though they may well be, they must certainly divine our position and our range. See to it, Number One.'

'Aye, aye, sir.'

The position was at the top of a steep valley, at the other side of which the gaunt bulk of the fort La Balaquier dominated the harbour and roadstead, and whose guns continued to fire - not like foxhounds well in hand, controlled, but more like lapdogs let loose, slovenly - upon the English fleet cruising to and fro out in the roads, themselves returning fire at extreme range and elevation and scoring perhaps one random hit out of every other broadside against the granite walls of the citadel. As soon, thought Oakshott, send a lad with a pea-shooter.

There was a low stone wall bounding the grass paddock to where they had brought the guns, and in obedience to Oakshott's order, the sailors were hacking out mortar with their marlinspikes and wrenching out the granite blocks. Soon there were two holes large enough to take the barrels of 16-pounders and allow for training and elevation.

'Your orders, sir?' asked Ned Daventry.

'Load with round shot and commence continuous fire upon their gun ports, Number One.'

'Aye, aye, sir! Load your pieces, prime your pieces, and report when ready!'

Powder ladles were filled, and the bores having been searched, the crusty black propellant was eased into the muzzles. Good priming powder was dribbled into the touch-holes, and the gun captains blew upon their smouldering slow matches – coarse rope soaked in saltpetre. The guns were trained. The long barrels were elevated by wedges so as to direct the shots upon the ramparts of the fortress from whence the enemy pieces were desultorily firing down upon the English fleet in the roads.

'Starboard five ready, sir!'

'Starboard six ready, sir!'

'Give fire, Starboard five!' shouted Ned Daventry.

The gun captain of Starboard five addressed his linstock, at the end of which smouldered the pinpoint of spluttering flame, to his touch-hole.Instantly, an eruption of white smoke and orange fire flashed from the hole like a fountain, and was instantly followed by the detonation of the charge within the barrel.

From where Oakshott was standing – immediately behind the gun – his forward view was totally eclipsed by the cloud of white smoke that was almost immediately dispersed by the wind, upon which he was able to see the progress of the ball as it rose to its apogee and descended towards the granite ramparts at the far side of the valley.

It struck some ten feet or so immediately below an embrasure, and the servers of both guns murmured approval.

'That'll wake 'em up and teach 'em that war ain't all beer and skittles,' said Ned Daventry, 'nor frogs and brandy-wine. Give fire, Starboard six!'

Oakshott similarily observed the progress of their second ranging shot: it cleared the ramparts by about ten feet.

'Over!' he called.

'Right lads,' said Ned Daventry. 'Enough of fiddle-faddle. Imagine to yourselves that your mother-in-law is sitting atop there. Starboard five will elevate by a shade, six will depress by a shade. See to your wedges. And continue rapid fire. I want three rounds a minute from each gun. Carry on!'

He strolled over to where Oakshott was standing. 'That wasn't bad,' said the captain of the *Daisy*. 'I don't know who's in command over there, but if it was me I'd be greatly concerned to be bracketed by two shots right out of the blue.

By the way, I presume that you arranged for victuals to be brought?'

'Hard tack and salt pork for all, sir,' responded the other. 'And a bottle of claret for the wardroom.'

'Good. We'll take luncheon at one of the clock, Ned,' said Oakshott.

The guns thundered out in unison, again and again. They were now striking the fortress's parapet.

'I think we must soon expect return visits,' said Oakshott, 'however ineptly delivered. What, pray, is the vintage of the claret?'

'Seventy-nine. I secured it down in the town, from a widow lady, in exchange for a small sack of potatoes.'

'Not a bad year. I hope the bottle has not been greatly shaken up, Ned, during our passage up here?' he added anxiously.

'I carried it myself, Charlie, as I would have carried my first-born, had I had one.'

'Ned, I can always rely upon you for the essentials,' declared Oakshott.

By their fourth salvo, the *Daisy*'s guns had searched out the enemy parapet and had put out one of their pieces: a ball having gone clean through the embrasure, striking the cannon and setting it back on its carriage so that the barrel pointed up vertically - and since no attempt was made to set it to rights, one assumed that the gun's crew had either taken fright and fled, or had been so heavily mauled as to be incapable of action.

Oakshott weighed up the odds. On the fortress wall that broadly faced their position, there now remained four guns, possibly five, that might be trained to fire upon them. Call it five to two - and the enemy also had the advantage of seventy-five to a hundred feet of height.

'Take them out one by one, Ned,' he said, 'starting with the nearest, which is the fellow on the left.'

Daventry nodded acknowledgement, his words being obscured by the discharge of Starboard five. It was only seconds after that there came what Oakshott had lightly referred to as 'return visits'.

The return fire from the fortress was signalled by a single gun seeking out the range of its assailants. The first ball fell lamentably short and called forth howls of derision from the men of *Daisy*, indeed, one of them climbed up on to the wall and waved his neckerchief to the French. Their second ball took him square amidships and the severed halves of his body were carried close past where Oakshott was standing, splattering him with bright blood as they went.

'Enough of the tomfoolery,' growled Ned Daventry. 'There's quality up there, after all, and unless 'twas a pure fluke, the man who aimed that shot knows his trade well. Continue firing.'

'Monsieur...'

Oakshott turned to see that he was addressed by a French royalist officer in white regimentals, who had prudently been brought to their captain's presence by two scowling and suspicious seamen, part of the musket guard posted around the position. Oakshott dismissed the latter with a nod. He then introduced himself to the newcomer.

'Capitaine de Courcy,' said the other as they shook hands, 'of the *Régiment de Guyenne*.' His white coat had long since been grey, the gold lace hung in tatters, he had perhaps one button left out of five. But he had the bearing of an aristocrat, a soldier, a man. He pointed away to the left of the *Daisy*'s guns. 'My company is in that knoll, among the trees. To your right' - pointing - 'is a detachment of your own marines. You have done well to knock out one gun already, Commander. When do you leave Toulon?'

'Leave?' Oakshott stared at his questioner, observing his eyes, which, if young, were world-weary, and his smile had a gentle cynicism. Not a man with whom to dissemble overmuch, but dissemble he must. 'Why should we leave?'

'Monsieur, it is clear that the revolutionaries' policy of capturing the forts will eventually render the port inhabitable for your fleet,' said de Courcy. 'I cannot see that it is in England's interest to support the French royalist cause, which in any event is a forlorn hope. Your only interest is to take away such of the Toulon fleet as you can get away, and the rest you will sink or burn. Correct? I repeat my question: when do you leave?'

Oakshott shrugged. 'I don't know,' he said in all honesty.

'But soon?'

'It's possible.'

'Our Neapolitan friends are leaving already,' said de Courcy, 'at least, I hear that the officers are loading aboard their wines from the forts, which is as good an indication as any. I should think they will be gone from here by dawn, and the forts will be occupied by the *sans culottes* soon after.'

A lively cheer following the discharge of Starboard six drew the two officers' attention to the enemy fort, where a shower of broken masonry revealed that the shot had smashed into the edge of an embrasure and knocked the gun out of sight. Down by the wall, Ned Daventry raised his thumb and forefinger.

'Two, sir!' he shouted.

But the incoming shots were taking their toll. The stone wall was being well pounded, two men had been hurt, one badly. With a curious feeling of detachment, Oakshott saw a ball - a large one, a 32-pounder or thereabouts - hit the turf ten feet from where he stood, tear an earth furrow in the greenery, and roll to a gentle halt at the far end of the meadow, for all like a wood closing upon the jack in a village bowls match back in rural England.

'I think it might be prudent, monsieur, if we took cover behind the wall,' said *Daisy*'s captain.

By then, both opposing batteries having found range, the firing was fast, furious, and accurate, and though no enemy shot had entered the English sailors' rough-hewn gun-ports, the wall was heavily pummelled and soon likely to fall; while the men working the pieces were constantly being showered by hunks of stone as incoming balls carried away the capping of their makeshift rampart.

There was a thunderous detonation from the citadel: a cloud of white smoke that almost entirely encompassed its upperworks.

'Well done, lads, we've hit a powder cask,' said Ned

Daventry. He grinned across at Oakshott. 'That will slow 'em down somewhat.'

'It's not that I blame you for deserting Toulon, monsieur,' murmured de Courcy. 'Militarily speaking, I would do the same in your place. But, you see – and this is why I have come to speak to you today – I have a mother and three young sisters living down in the town.'

Suddenly, his eyes were not world-weary any more, nor his smile cynical.

'*Look to your front*!' shouted one of the gun captains. '*They're coming out*!'

'It's a sally!' cried Ned Daventry.

From an iron door at the foot of the citadel, and immediately opposite their position, there issued forth twenty-thirty-forty musketeers in the motley rig of the revolution, who strung themselves out in three columns with quite commendable expertise and proceeded to descend into the valley in the direction of the English position.

'Number One,' said Oakshott, snapping close his telescope.

'Sir?'

'Do you please load with grape, Number One. Triple-shotted. And a double charge of powder.'

'Aye, *aye*, sir!' The big man grinned broadly.

'And give fire upon my command.'

Ned Daventry touched the cock of his hat and saw to it.

Oakshott trained his telescope again upon the advancing musketeers, who were by now beginning the slow ascent of the valley towards the English guns. 'Poor bastards,' he said. 'Why do you fellows always advance in column? I had this from a cousin of mine who fought in Canada and in America. While the Briton is always happier in extended line – what we are pleased to call the Thin Red Line – your soldiers will advance in columns, and even against guns. Is this a national characteristic, or am I taking the argument too far into the metaphysical? Stop me if I bore you.'

'They will not reach here,' said de Courcy. It was not a question.

'We shall murder them,' said Oakshott.

'Let them die – murderers all!' De Courcy bowed his head.
Cicadas were singing in the long grass. A pigeon hooted in the copse to their left. The guns had all fallen silent. Save for a distant rattle of musketry in the lower part of the town, it seemed to Oakshott like one of the Indian summer days at Sennett when Mama was alive: picnic in the home park, with lemonade and China tea, thin cucumber sandwiches, relish plastered upon Bath Oliver biscuits, water ices, plum cake, seed cake, plump peaches that washed your face at one bite, tart green apples whose taste was a memory as tangible as if it had only just happened.

The Frenchmen were plodding steadily up the slope in three columns, bayoneted muskets ported high. A hundred and fifty yards away, give or take a couple of yards.

'Sir?' It was a question from Ned Daventry.

'Not yet, Number One. We don't want to put 'em off.'

Leading the centre column was an officer in the fancy dress rig that the revolutionary leaders affected: cockaded, sashed and befeathered in red, white and blue. He could not have been more than twenty years of age. Oakshott concentrated upon him; waited for the moment that he opened his mouth.

'Sir!' Another call from Daventry, more urgent still.

'Hold your fire, Number One,' said Oakshott.

Another twenty paces and the moment came that Oakshott had been waiting for. The young officer shouted an order, upon which his men broke into a run and began to fan out from their columns to charge the wall.

'Give fire, Number One!' yelled Oakshott.

'Give fire both guns!'

The instants of slaughter were mercifully hidden from the Englishmen by the choking clouds of gunsmoke; when it cleared, the wing columns of the enemy were lying in humped heaps, some still, some writhing. The centre column was decimated. The young officer, staring down at the stump of what had been his sword arm, sank to his knees with an expression of tortured agony. The rest of his men, numbering about six or seven, turned and fled down the slope, shedding their muskets as they went.

Oakshott took the arm of de Courcy and led him away. 'Walk with me a while,' he said. 'Touching upon the matter of your mother and sisters, you must send a messenger down to the town with instructions for them to repair aboard my ship the *Daisy* before nightfall - I stress before nightfall - for certain ships of the fleet will come back into harbour under cover of darkness and I shall then be entirely at the beck and call of my superior.'

The Frenchman pressed Oakshott's hands and, to his intense embarrassment, kissed him on both cheeks. 'Monsieur, I shall never be able to repay you,' he said, 'but be sure that your reward will await you in Paradise.'

'That will be most gratifying,' said Oakshott, disentangling himself. 'And now, if you will excuse me, we will resume the bombardment. Perhaps you will do us the honour of joining us for luncheon, which - the enemy permitting - my first lieutenant and I are taking at one of the clock. Coarse ship's fare, I'm afraid, but we have a bottle of claret which may not be intolerable...'

Chapter Ten

THAT EVENING, to no one's surprise, the Neapolitans abandoned their two forts at Cap Lebrun and Cap Lesset and moved their ships and men out of the harbour, and to hell with everyone else. At about the same time, when it was dark enough, Captain Sir Sidney Smith – he whom Ned Daventry had described as a 'stormy petrel', and with some justification – brought his force of light vessels into the inner harbour. This flotilla comprised the sloop *Alert*, the *Swallow* tender, three gun-boats, a Spanish mortar-boat, and the fire-ship *Vulcan*. Their dark shapes were coming to anchor as Oakshott and the shore party descended to the quay, with the two guns' iron-shod wheels making an almighty clatter on the cobblestones.

Oakshott was greeted on the gangway by the senior lieutenant, who was in a fine tizz. 'Sir, sir,' he bleated, 'I hope I have done right in this matter, for the ladies did say that the orders came directly from you.'

'Take a hold upon yourself, Mr Jobling,' said Oakshott. 'Take a couple of deep breaths, and then tell me what you have done.'

'I can best show you, sir,' replied the other.

'Then do so, Mr Jobling, and with all despatch.'

Jobling led him to the end of the quarterdeck, where, by the rail, they were able to look down on to the gun deck. The unhappy man did not need to point: it was all too apparent.

'Oh, my God!' breathed Oakshott.

'That's what I mean, sir,' said the other. 'Did I do right?

Was - er - this your intent?'

'Oh, my God!' repeated Oakshott. And said it yet again for good measure.

By the faint moonlight, he could discern, in the gun deck below, a sea of faces turned upwards to regard him: mostly women and children, but there were some men - and all were standing, for there was no room for them to sit. And they watched him in an awesome silence.

'How many are there, Mr Jobling?' asked Oakshott presently.

'Eight - eight hundred and five, sir,' faltered the other. 'All heads were counted as they came aboard.'

'I had not thought that Captain de Courcy had so many relations, friends, and neighbours,' said Oakshott.

'Sir?'

'Let it pass. I would not have believed that a sloop-of-war could take so much top hamper without sinking, nor did I chance to observe the line of flotation when I came aboard. Where does it stand, pray?'

Jobling swallowed hard and said: 'Well above the boot topping, sir, and within a foot - perhaps less - of the lower edge of the gun ports.'

'Then it were better that no one were taken of a violent sneezing fit,' said Oakshott, 'or we shall all settle quietly down into the hogwash. And there are the guns to be brought back inboard. And there's no room for 'em. You had better clear the spaces and send some people into my stern cabin flat or into the fo'c's'le.'

'The - the stern cabin flat is already occupied by the people, sir,' responded Jobling, 'likewise the fo'c's'le.'

'Ah, well,' said Oakshott, 'we must all make our small sacrifices in these hard times. Usher as many as you need into my stern cabin. And I shall have to count my silver spoons before they depart. I speak in jest, of course. Why do you look so doleful, man?'

The senior lieutenant shuffled from one foot to the other. 'Sir, your stern cabin is already filled to suffocation,' he said.

Very deliberately, Oakshott selected a four figure number at random in his mind, calculated its square root, and said quietly: 'Well then, Mr Jobling, you had best shift as many people on to the quarterdeck as will accommodate the guns. And when you have done that, you will please call away the jolly boat to convey me to the *Alert*, so that I may learn from Sir Sidney's own lips what further alarms and excursions await me this night.'

The flotilla leader *Alert* was a modern sloop-of-war, new-built at Buckler's Hard, as made the old *Daisy* look like something that had sailed against the Spanish Armada. Oakshott was brought straight to her captain, who was sitting alone with a chart spread out before him and the detritus of a meal scattered about.

'Oakshott, sir. *Daisy*.'

'Ah, Oakshott. I sent one of my mids ashore to contact you earlier. That was a smart move of yours to hug that sheltered quay. I gather that you have been away causing some mischief at the top of the town. What luck with the game?'

'We knocked out three guns and routed a sally-party, sir,' said Oakshott.

'Well done.'

'And incidentally collected French royalist refugees, mostly women and children, to the number of eight hundred and five, who are at present aboard.'

'Did you now? Well, that must be placing some strain upon your commissariat, not to mention your sanitary arrangements. The tender will go alongside you forthwith and take them out to the transports which lie in the roads. That will be *Swallow*'s task this night: ferrying the wretched royalists. Would you like to take a glass of brandy-wine? I won't go bail on its antecedents.'

Oakshott made assent, studying his superior, of whom he had heard quite a lot. Sir Sidney Smith was some few years older than he and built on what the more flowery of novel writers would have described as 'the heroic mould': tall, even when seated, a thick thatch of hair, nose like an eagle, watchful eyes, yet a curiously gentle voice. He wore a post captain's epaulettes with his undress coat, yet his stock was not tied formally, but in a loose knot like that of a vagabond or gipsy. The lower limbs that were thrust out before him were encased in Hessian boots which were boned and polished to gleaming perfection.

'Your very good health, Oakshott.'

'And yours, sir.'

'Yes, the *Swallow* will deal with the refugees, of whom I fear there will be many, and the more the better. The rest of us, Oakshott, the remainder of the flotilla, will concern ourselves, this night, with cutting out and destroying. See here' - and he pointed to the chart - 'in the larger basin, there is a great galley upon which are several hundred revolutionary prisoners in chains. We will have that galley, Oakshott. There is a great powder ship in the inner harbour - here - which I have ordered the Spaniards to board and sink, since I have no great feeling for a hundred tons of powder floating round in a battle. There are more ships in the inner basin - here - which the Spaniards will burn. Here in the inner harbour are two seventy-fours which are filled with more revolutionary prisoners. Those ships we will have if we can. And it must all be done before first light.'

'We abandon Toulon at first light?' asked Oakshott.

Smith nodded. 'The enemy will have all the forts by dawn, and you may be sure that they will have over-run the royalist positions above the town. Our own soldiers will retire throughout the night and be taken off in small boats to the transports out in the roads, piecemeal.'

'And what are your orders for me, sir?' asked Oakshott.

Smith tapped the chart. 'I know I can rely upon you, Oakshott. There's much to be done. I think you will clear those two seventy-fours, put prize crews aboard and have them sailed out to join the fleet in the roadstead. Or else burn 'em!'

Smith was as good as his word. By the time Oakshott had finished his drink, shaken hands with his superior and taken to the jolly boat, the tender *Swallow* had upped anchor and was slinking towards the quay on headsails and mizzen. The transfer of the refugees from the *Daisy* was well under way by the time Oakshott arrived back aboard; with hard-bitten tars assisting terrified women and children - and some passably terrified men - over the side, and with all the tenderness of nursemaids.

By this time, all hell was being let loose in the town above, most of which seemed to be afire, while the crash of gunfire was heavy and continuous.

'It's going to be a hot night, Ned,' said Oakshott. He wrinkled his nose. 'God, the stench of that smoke. What's burning up there?'

'People, perhaps,' ventured Daventry. 'They tell me that the revolutionaries have broken through and are everywhere, and that some of the so-called royalists have mutinied and are rampaging round the town, drunk as hell and up to any mischief that offers itself.' He pointed to a detachment of marines, some hatless, some wounded, bandaged and unbandaged, who were forming up on the quayside nearby under the glare of a sergeant, for all the world as if they were back on their parade ground in Chatham. 'The sergeant was telling me that they went in as a company and, as can be seen, they've come out a platoon.

'What's our task this night, Charlie?'

'Once we're rid of the refugees, Ned, I want you to muster a shore party - take a score of the steadiest veteran hands we have - and secure two French seventy-fours lying alongside in the inner harbour yonder. They are presumably still crewed by royalists, who have been using them as prison ships, for my information is that they're loaded with captured revolutionaries. Persuade, if you can, whoever's in command over there to land the prisoners - preferably without first cutting their throats, though that really isn't our affair any longer - and sail out into the roads to join the fleet.'

'And if they refuse - or if the crews have already deserted?'

'Clear the ships and burn 'em.'

'Aye, aye, sir.'

The transfer of the refugees completed, the *Swallow* cast off, and Oakshott watched her go, fretting at his own inactivity, since, as captain, his primary responsibility lay to his ship, while he would have rejoiced at the opportunity of going ashore like Ned Daventry, who was assembling a party of hands on the quay: twenty mature men, armed with cutlasses and pistols.

'Mr Jobling!' shouted Oakshott, with more acerbity than was necessary.

The senior lieutenant came running and touched his hat. 'Sir?'

'Muster another shore-party. A midshipman and six. Have them search those warehouses opposite for anything worth taking away in the line of stores, paying particular attention to explosives, for we don't want to blow ourselves up along with Toulon - and then have them set fire to the whole lot.'

Jobling acknowledged the order and ducked away to carry it out.

The sound of firing increased and grew ever nearer. Away in the larger basin astern of the *Daisy*, a big ship was blazing at anchor, redly lighting a scene of small boats plying to and from the shore. The illumination prompted the fortress guns to open fire upon them, their discharges adding to the hellish din, their round shot kicking up waterspouts all about the boats. Oakshott saw one of them struck fair and square, immediately to sink, spilling its occupants - British soldiers most likely - into the water.

'What happened to the midshipman's party, Mr Jobling?' snapped Oakshott.

'Mustered and ready to go ashore, sir,' replied the other.

Really, thought Jobling, one had never seen the old man so snappy. Still, knowing him, he wants to be doing other than pacing his own quarterdeck alongside the wall. And the way things are developing in this hell-hole, he may well have the opportunity. As may all of us!

All that night, the allied troops continued to file through the narrow streets to the wasting boats, and though they were for the most part under fire from the fortress guns, the withdrawal was to be broadly successful. The Spanish admiral, one Langara, was remiss in many regards. The great powder-ship which Lord Hood had ordered him to sink he instead caused to be set on fire - and it was this same ship which Oakshott had observed in the larger basin astern. It is difficult to fathom why an experienced senior naval officer should have done such a thing, unless he had a maniacal addiction to fireworks - in which case his mania was well satisfied that night in Toulon. After blazing comfortably for an hour or so, the powder-ship blew up with a shock that shook the very foundations of the harbour and town. One of Smith's gun-boats and a ship's cutter were sunk by falling timbers, but miraculously only one officer and three men were killed. Langara then proceeded to pile Pelion on Ossa by neglecting to burn the ships in the far basin, giving as his excuse that there was a boom across the entrance; the real reason was that the jacobins had secured a gun battery commanding the basin, and the going was far too hot for Langara.

And still the withdrawal continued: confused, informed by conflicting orders, by misinformation, by cowardice and gallantry, by luck good and ill, and by plain stupidity - just like so many battles.

The midshipman's shore party, comprising the youngest bucks of the *Daisy*'s crew, led by the Devonian lawyer's son, the unprepossessing Midshipman Shacklock, enthusiastically ransacked the warehouses opposite, bringing off enough casks of salt beef, pork and tobacco to provision the sloop for a sixmonth; finally, finding no explosives there, setting fire to the wooden buildings with glee - they all being hotheads and somewhat inclined to destruction for the sheer hell of it.

And what, thought Oakshott, is Ned Daventry doing?

'Mr Jobling!' he called above the din and clatter.

'Sir?'

'Send a runner along the quay to the two seventy-fours in the inner harbour. My compliments to the first lieutenant, and is he going to take out the two ships or burn them? And, in any event, what is occupying him all this time?'

It was at this moment that they came...

They came like the first flurried wave on a sea-shore that presages a storm, and kept coming: a tormented mob of frightened people, most clutching treasured possessions, some of pathetic fancy: one woman had a flowering geranium in a plantpot; others carried silverware, pictures, small furniture, clothing; many bore screaming children in their arms; they came out of the night that was ablaze and deafening with sound.

'Oh, my God!' said Oakshott. 'Stand by to receive boarders!'

There was no stopping the influx: they saw a ship alongside the wall and they streamed aboard it; handing up their silverware, their pictures, their children and all the rest; while the press-ganged, flogged, ill-victualled, foul-mouthed, underpaid and sentimental British tars took them. In less time than it would take to tell, the *Daisy* was sunk yet again to the lower level of her gun ports, and the wild-eyed, panic-stricken people were still piling inboard, pushing their way to imagined safety, elbowing aside cockaded and epauletted Commander Lord Charles Oakshott on his own quarterdeck. There was no end to them that could be seen: they stretched up the steep street into the smoke and flames.

'Mr Jobling!'

'Sir?'

'Have the ship cast adrift. Cut the shore lines if you must, before she sinks under the sheer weight of flesh. Sail her out into the roads. Transfer these people to one of the transports and return here – but not alongside: anchor close offshore within hailing distance. Give me your sword. I left mine below and all hell is let loose down there.' He grinned. 'I should be surprised if all my silver spoons haven't been pocketed already. What was I saying?'

'That – that I was to anchor close offshore, sir.'

'Make it so, Mr Jobling.'

'What are you going to do, sir – if I may make so bold as to ask?'

'I'm going to see what aid I can render to the first

lieutenant,' said Oakshott, hefting Jobling's sword, which was none of your winkle-pickers to wear on the hip on ceremonial occasions, but a stout, curved blade with a heavy stirrup hilt and guard for balance. 'Tell off a dozen hands to come with me. But quickly - quickly!' - he glanced sidelong at the irresistible tide of panic-stricken folk who continued to pile aboard - 'before the *Daisy* settles down on the putty for ever.'

A dozen tars, led by their captain, elbowed their way through the throng and on to the quay. Headrope, stern rope and springs were sliced through with cutlasses. The *Daisy*, borne by the gentle offshore breeze, drifted away from the wall, sails unfurling as she went, watched with wailing anguish by the wretched people crowded there, and with more of them descending the steep street from the upper town, like lemmings hell-bent for self-destruction.

'Follow me, lads,' said Oakshott, setting off at a smart trot down the quay.

The state of affairs in Toulon, that night, had reached a stage where all plans were awry, all well-meant intentions gone adrift. The burden of advantage clearly lay with the revolutionaries, who, having taken all the forts dominating the harbour, would be dictating the issue at first light; but still in the dark hours between, the Royal Navy, by its presence, had some advantage to - in Sir Sidney Smith's phrase - rescue and destroy.

Oakshott and his party had no difficulty in locating the two French seventy-fours that Ned Daventry and his men had been despatched to deal with. The ships were still afloat and tied abreast alongside the wall, though to Oakshott's eye, the inner ship lay significantly low in the water. To his very great relief, the bulky figure of his old shipmate and present first lieutenant was on the quay nearby - along with his party.

'What kept you, Number One?' demanded Oakshott. 'The order was to cut out or burn, plain as you please. And the damned things are still here!'

Daventry took off his hat and wiped his brow with the sleeve of his forearm. 'Sir, you have arrived just in time for the last act of the drama,' he said. And then in a resounding shout: 'GIVE FIRE!'

'Aye, aye, sir!' This from the for'ard end of the inboard ship.

There was a dying splutter of flame. A muffled curse. A stronger burst of flame. And then – a deluge of fire that immediately engulfed the fo'c's'le of the inboard ship, spread aft with the speed of thinking, rose aloft, consuming yards, sails, masts, rigging with the breath of light. Instants later, the ship's consort was similarly aflame. The draught of air sucked into the conflagration whipped off Oakshott's second best hat and bore it off to feed the inferno.

He and Ned Daventry backed away to the far wall of the quay, so great was the heat and the fury.

'That's a hell of a good fire, Ned,' said Oakshott. 'And two damned fine ships that might have been saved to sail with the Navy.'

''Twas never possible, Charlie,' said the other. 'The so-called royalists had deserted before we came, and had opened the sea-cocks of both seventy-fours, so that they were settled on the bottom with – I think our rough count was nine hundred-odd prisoners aboard, all in irons or roped with their hands in a strangle-knot behind their necks. We freed 'em all, and a fine old time it took, I tell you.'

'What of the freed prisoners, where did they go?'

'Up into the town, Charlie, all nine hundred of 'em. And I tell you that I wasn't glad to see 'em go. It's my opinion that it would have been a happy chance for us if them two ships had settled a couple of feet further down on the putty, instead of leaving the prisoners with the water only up to their chests.'

'They were belligerent?' asked Oakshott. 'Even after you'd freed them?'

'That ain't half the word for it,' responded Daventry. 'Pirouet the Jerseyman, here, he said that they were calling to each other as they sped away that they'd find weapons and be back to settle the score. Shall we go back to the ship, sir?'

'We don't have a ship, Number One. Not as of this moment.' And Oakshott explained what had happened.

It was while he was doing this that the freed prisoners returned: all nine hundred of them, most of them armed with some blunt instrument or other and a few with firearms. Leading them was a wild-eyed fellow with an unkempt beard; upon sighting the British seamen in the shocking glow of the blazing ships, he pointed to his followers and screamed an order.

'Stand by to repel boarders, lads,' said Oakshott, bringing his sword to the 'on guard' position and wishing for the umpteenth time in his fighting career that he had applied himself with more assiduity to the lessons of M. Haquin in the orangery at Sennett. 'Number One, I think that our best option is assault. There's no quality over there, and a determined charge may send them packing like a flock of frightened sheep.'

'I'm of the same opinion, sir,' conceded the other. 'They're only a rabble, and in my opinion a rabble is moved only by fury or by fear. Let us put some fear into 'em.' He cocked his pistol. 'Ready when you are, Charlie!' he whispered.

'CHARGE!' shouted the captain of the sloop-of-war *Daisy*.

The assurance that comes from being one of a body of nine hundred-odd men does not long survive the sight of a dozen or so trained fighters coming in at the rush, blades extended, pistols firing, emitting the practised sort of shouts that a seaman learns to give to his fellows high up in the rigging in a full gale. Those at the rear of the nine hundred-odd were in the privileged position of being able coolly to reckon the odds and to discern that the British charge was no more than desperate bravado – so does the observer see more of the game than the player. Those at the front were in a very dissimilar position: they were the unhappy recipients of the charge's full force. The bearded leader received a pistol ball in the forehead, directed there by Ned Daventry; he fell forward on his face with a look of slight amazement. Others of his followers who carried firearms loosed off their shots wildly and scored nothing. The men from the *Daisy* came on, cutlasses swinging. There is something about the separation of a head from its trunk that is particularly discouraging to the uninitiated observer – particularly when he is next in line for a dose of similar medicine. The front rank of the freed revolutionaries broke and ran with all the fervour of a man in a hurry to drag a rapist off his mother. They had nowhere to go save through their comrades to the rear; in attempting so to do, they were hacked down by the sailors. The second rank, persuaded by the screams of their comrades and drenched by their spurting blood, were similarly inspired to flight. Those further to the rear suffered a similar fate: the men of the *Daisy* leapt over their fallen adversaries and continued on, blooded blades cutting and thrusting.

It could be argued that, in that steep and narrow street leading down to the jetty, it was the nine hundred-odd untrained, untried revolutionaries who were the agents of their own defeat. As the gunpowder trail of panic scorched on, so that even those far to the rear (who knew that all they needed to do was to stand fast) gave way before the argument of *sauve-qui-peut*, the chaos rapidly escalated: men were trodden underfoot by their own sort, to escape the swinging cutlasses they struck out indiscriminately to win a way through.

The massive tide facing the men of the *Daisy* baulked, turned, fled.

Breathless, wondering, Oakshott watched them go, dripping sword held low.

'I never would have believed it, Ned. Never!' he breathed.

'Nor I, Charlie. Nor I,' said Daventry.

That was the height of the shore party's triumph; everything after that was disaster. Descending again to the quay, they heard the tramp-tramp-tramp of disciplined infantry on the march. Thinking the newcomers to be British redcoats, the sailors let out a cheer and ran down to greet them.

The coats were not red, but blue – and fifty or so in number. Their officer wore a tricolour sash and plumes, and all sported hat cockades of the same colours. These were a different sort of soldier from the rag-tailed mobs that the men of the *Daisy* had been accustomed to tumble in Toulon.

The French detachment drew up in two ranks facing the sailors. The officer gave a sharp order and the front rank knelt. Another command brought muskets to the present. Before Oakshott could collect himself, the shots rang out. A ball tore a scarlet furrow across his brow, and he fell on top of Ned Daventry.

That night, thanks to Sir Sidney Smith's flotilla, something like fifteen thousand men, women and children were brought out from shore, escaping the fury of the Jacobins. The English destroyed eleven ships in the harbour and carried away about twenty (but for the dereliction of duty by the Spanish Admiral Langara, a further fourteen ships of the line and five frigates might have been destroyed).

Dawn brought scenes of unsurpassable horror to the port. The Jacobin troops, local citizens, and released prisoners from the hulks ran amok. Royalists, those who had supported the royalists, those who simply, by their manner and bearing and by their dress looked as if they might have sympathy with the old regime, were slaughtered out of hand. Even the common workmen who had been employed by the British to improve the defences of the port did not escape the vengeful fury, but were rounded up by the hundreds, set up against walls and mown down by cannon loaded with grapeshot.

However, by noon on the following day, a certain civility descended upon Toulon in the personages of three senior functionaries from Paris: the brother of the rising star Robespierre, one Barras, and one Freron. With them also came the expert Fauchon, assistant to Sanson, executioner of Louis XVI, along with a brand new guillotine.

In the elegant phrase of Lord Hood's flag captain, the slaughter was to be resumed in a tidier manner.

Oakshott became conscious at daylight and promptly vomited. He found himself to be lying on a quite pretty tiled floor. The ceiling was painted in the Italian manner, in fresco, with a scene representing the apotheosis of someone or other. Squinting sidelong, he saw a youngish fellow in the white uniform of the former regime. He lay in a pool of dried blood and was palpably dead.

When he tried to raise himself up, he found that his movement was circumscribed by a weight across his lower extremities: a weight that revealed itself to be Ned Daventry. Daventry was alive and breathing, but some of the whistling breath was being inhaled and exhaled from a blood-bubbling wound in his massive chest.

Gently easing himself from under the giant's weight, he laid his old friend and shipmate more comfortably, stripping off his own coat, bundling it up and laying it under his head; in the act of so doing he roused Daventry, whose bland eyes opened.

'Charlie. It's you. I'd thought that when I awoke in Heaven, the first face I'd see would be yours.'

'You ain't in Heaven, you old beanpole,' growled Oakshott, 'nor like to be. They're stoking the fires down there for you in t'other place.'

Daventry laughed, causing an emission of blood from the corner of his mouth. 'You were ever the humorist, Charlie,' he said at length.

'And you talk too damned much,' said Oakshott. 'Rest yourself Number One. Take a make-and-mend.'

'I mind the time,' said Daventry, 'it was in the old *Spartiate*, seventy-four, and you were senior mid of the gun-room. The master's mate as instructed us . . .'

'Rest yourself, Ned,' interposed Oakshott. 'Somehow we've got to get out of this bloody place, and with you not fit to knock a parrot off its perch how'm I to do it on my own?'

The big man grinned and nodded. 'And where are we, Charlie?' he asked.

'Well, we're in some kind of municipal building at a guess,' replied Oakshott. 'What they call the *mairie*, I'd suppose. With us in this chamber is about' – he looked round – 'a couple of hundred fellows, all French by the cut of their jibs and by such uniforms as they wear.'

'None of our fellows, Charlie - none of the shore party?'

'I don't see any, Ned. I think they must all have been taken out in that musket volley - all save you and me.'

The giant lay still and silent for a while, and then he said: 'What was it the master's mate asked us that day, and to which you responded so humorously?'

'Damned if I remember,' replied Oakshott.

'It were damned funny, in any event.'

'I shouldn't wonder.'

'Something touching upon Greek - or it may have been mathematics.'

'It must have been mathematics,' said Oakshott. 'By the time I joined the Navy, my Greek was all dried up, along with the Latin. Why don't you shut up and get some rest?' He looked away, out of the window that gave a view on to a cobbled courtyard, and ashamedly found that he was weeping like a baby.

'Anyhow,' said Ned, 'it were most humorous and had the whole gun-room laughing for a week.' He coughed painfully.

'Some people,' said Oakshott, 'will laugh at any bloody thing. Will wager upon the colour of a tavern serving-wench's drawers and laugh when they have lost.'

At midday, the prisoners were given dry bread and water. With this repast came a porcine individual garbed in all the finery and ostentation that the egalitarian republic of the new France bequeathed upon her officers. He took the names of all the prisoners present. Oakshott supplied his own and that of Ned Daventry, who had slipped back into merciful unconsciousness.

Oakshott's wound did not pain him a lot. The dried blood that entirely encompassed his face and head cracked, crazed and fell away every time he changed expression, or opened his mouth to bite upon bread or sip at a pannikin of water.

When he had satisfied his hunger and thirst, he fell back, but was presently disturbed by a sound outside the window. Puzzled, he drew himself up and, supporting himself against the sill, looked out. The other captives – those who were not gravely hurt – similarly went to the windows.

Out there, two men pushed a cart upon which rested two long shafts of wood, highly polished. A third had a carpenter's workbox, which, having laid on the cobblestones of the courtyard, he opened and produced from it a hammer, screwdriver, set square and a spirit level; meanwhile his assistants (younger and by their deferential manner clearly in awe of their master), lifted down their burdens, went back to wherever they had come from and presently returned with more bolts of wood. With a decided sense of unease, Oakshott followed the motions of the principal actor in the sunlit afternoon charade; how, with unhurried care, he laid two planks of wood as a base, checking their truth with his spirit level and instructing his assistants to place small wedges here and there, till he was satisfied that he had a flat surface – a perfectionist, he. Next, directing his assistants to perform the manual task, he caused to be erected two uprights connected to the centre with stout bolts; and every bold tested for tightness. Next, the assistants brought two tall poles fashioned of varnished wood, both deeply grooved, which they proceeded to set up at each side of the central block of the construction. Oakshott knew then what he had surmised: *they were erecting a guillotine!*

'The main structure having been set up,' said a voice at his elbow, 'they are now attaching the few and simple mechanical parts of the machine. The windlass that raises the knife...'

Oakshott turned to see that he was being addressed by de Courcy, captain of the *Régiment de Guyenne*, his late companion at the quite successful foray against the fort on the heights.

'... the rope hoist, the catch which is tripped by a jerk of the cord – so uncomplicated is the device. I thank you, monsieur, for saving my mother and sisters from – that.'

'I am sorry that we shall not similarly be spared,' said Oakshott. 'Or so I suppose.'

'Oh, yes,' said the other. 'They will execute us tomorrow, for we are the first of a long *tranche* as will keep Citizen

Fauchon busy for the rest of this year.'

A little later, Ned Daventry choked and would have drowned in his own blood had not Oakshott turned him on his side. The big man grinned up at his captain.

'I remember now how it was you answered the master's mate aboard the *Spartiate*, Charlie,' he whispered. 'And his name was Widmerpool.'

'That's it,' said Oakshott. 'Widmerpool. You've a good memory, Ned.'

'Aye, but you'll have to refresh it in some details. I mind that Widmerpool put the general question to the class as to how many cables in a nautical mile, and you said that, newly joined the Navy, you didn't know, but, being a country-bred lad, you could tell him how many square yards in an acre.'

'Ah, yes, I remember that one,' said Oakshott.

'Tell it me, Charlie,' said the first lieutenant of the *Daisy*. 'Tell for old time's sake.'

'Well, these four fellows came into a tavern and ordered the finest wine and victuals that could be provided,' said Oakshott, 'after which they strolled out casually, one by one, as if to the heads. Only they didn't come back.

'And so - four ate for naught.

'4840 - the number of square yards to an acre.

'It isn't that damned funny, Ned.'

And then he saw that, even though the bland blue eyes were still fixed upon him and there was a smile on the good-humoured face, Ned Daventry was beyond the compass of his voice.

At dusk (and the guillotine was now erected and in full view of any of its prospective victims as chose to look out of the windows on the courtyard side), the porcine functionary came back in again and read out a list of names of those who were to meet their end on the grim machine on the morrow. With the mincing bureaucracy of a despotism, they were in alphabetical order.

'... Cuvier, Armand - Dampier, Jean-Phillippe - Damrosch, Hugo - Dancourt, Jacques - Daniélou, Pierre... Daventry, Edvard...' He had some difficulty in pronouncing that.

'He's dead,' said Oakshott. *'Il est mort.'*

'Ah, merci - er - monsieur,' responded the other, crossed out the name and resumed:

'De Courcy, Hyacinthe...'

Oakshott met the eye of the royalist captain; the latter shrugged.

And - later - 'Oakshott, Charles.'

At an order from the functionary, two ill-garbed soldiers came and took up Ned Daventry's body, elbows and ankles, to carry it out. They scowled when Oakshott blocked their path for a moment to tear off one of the buttons from his late shipmate's uniform coat, for he knew that Ned had a sister living in Kent. On second thoughts, he tore away one for himself also - the gilt button with the fouled anchor encircled by a wreath of oak leaves - slender enough mementoes for the sister in Kent and himself, always supposing that a miracle occurred, such as Sir Sidney Smith and his flotilla briefly re-occupying the port before dawn and taking off more prisoners. The thought cheered him immensely. He laid himself down and was soon asleep, with half an ear cocked for the sounds of activity.

It was in the early hours before dawn that the double doors into the chamber were opened and a party of three men strode in, one of them carrying a lantern.

'Commandaire Oakshott!' It was a summons.

Oh, my God, thought Oakshott, am I to be guillotined by moonlight?

He sat up. 'Yes?'

'Come with us.'

All three carried pistols. There were not many options open to him. Shrugging into his coat, he went with them. A few frightened faces, pale in the loom of the lantern and in the moonlight from the window, faces of men sleepless upon the fate that awaited them at dawn, looked up and watched them go.

Outside, they crossed the yard, close by the engine of death, and under an archway leading out into the street. A bored sentry watched them go.

'Where are you taking me?' asked Oakshott of the man who had demonstrated that he possessed a little English.

No reply.

They were descending to the quay, booted feet clattering on the cobbles and the sound echoing around the dark-walled warehouses. Everywhere there was the stench of burning. Some musket fire - sporadic - from the distance. A dog barked close at hand.

They came to the quay, which was high above the water at that point. Out at sea, beyond the breakwater, Oakshott could pick out the riding lights of the allied fleet at anchor; they seemed a very long way off.

His captors halted by a steep flight of steps leading down to the water, where, tethered to a ring bolt in the wall, a small whale-boat bobbed and jinked in the lapping wavelets.

Oakshott turned to the English speaker, puzzled.

'Well - what now?' he demanded.

The other pointed down to the whaler.

'Go!'

'Killed while trying to escape' - Oakshott was familiar with the phrase, a euphemism beloved of tyrannical regimes since pre-history. And yet, why bother to act out this charade when the keen blade of the guillotine awaited at the dawn?

'I don't understand,' he said.

'Go! Now! There is not much time!'

Oakshott needed no third bidding, but went down the steps in some haste, fully expecting to feel a pistol bullet hit him in the back of the neck on the way down. None came.

There was a pair of oars in the whaler. Oakshott shipped them and cast off from the ring bolt; gave way with vigour and did not look up to the jetty again till he had the boat well on the move and pointing towards the breakwater.

No longer three, but four figures watched him go. The newcomer was slightly built, with a high-cocked hat. By the light of the lantern, Oakshott discerned the starveling's face and the straggling hair of the young captain of artillery whose life, it could be argued, he had saved from the petulant fury of the boy 'general' de Colombe. And as he watched, plying upon his oars, the captain raised his hat in salute to him.

(What was the fellow's name? Something odd. Hardly likely that one's paths will ever cross again. And he never did give me the opportunity to thank him for settling his score with me.)

It was a long haul out to the roads, with the wind-borne waves against him all the way. And dawn was coming up on his right by the time he identified his own command and brought himself to her.

'What boat?' The challenge came smartly from the gangway.

'*Daisy*!'

He was home again. They piped the side for him, and Oakshott turned back to look up into the heights of the town, where, in the dawn light, they would be bringing out the condemned to the infernal machine in the courtyard of the *mairie*.

Chapter Eleven

THE LAST TIME he had crossed Whitehall had been in the fair promise of Spring; now he had to bow his head against the sleet and biting winds of February. He made his way up the Strand, pushed his way through the door of Mogg's Diversions, shook the white shards and crystals from his boat cloak and looked about him.

Harriet had written that she was going back whence she came; this was as likely a place as any where he might find her.

There was no sign of his quarry amongst the promenaders, or with the folk sitting at tables before the stage. Oakshott had ordered himself a glass of brandy and hot water, when, with a slight prickling at the back of his neck, he heard – and recognised – a small, but nicely-pitched voice coming from behind him, from the stage:

Come cheer up, my lads, 'tis to Glory we steer,
To add one thing more to this wonderful year.
'Tis to Honour we call you, nor press you like slaves,
For who are so free as the sons of the waves?...

He turned. It was she. Looking curiously more at ease with herself than when he had first seen her: there was a smiling assurance to her demeanour, a complete lack of the defensiveness that she had formerly displayed to the world. The experience of being a marchioness and chatelaine of a stately home – albeit such as Sennett – must have resolved something within her. Perhaps it was the relinquishing of all that – poor Jack included – which had revealed to her her inner strength.

And now everyone was joining in the chorus, he, Oakshott, included:

Heart of oak are our ships,
Heart of oak are our men,
We always are ready;
Steady, boys, steady!
We'll fight –
And we'll conquer again and again!

More interminable verses, more choruses, during which the tall officer in the boat cloak was repeatedly pledged. Harriet's attention having been drawn to him as a centre of attraction, she came straight to where he stood as soon as her song was finished.

'Charles, how nice,' she said. And kissed him on the cheek.

'You're looking very fine, Harriet,' responded Oakshott.

They found a seat at table, and he took stock of her again. Yes, she had quite changed. It was a pity – such a pity. A woman like her, with her intelligence, her new-found assurance, perhaps with a certain ruthlessness in her make-up (after all, she had dived into matrimony with poor Jack, and surely for no other reason than advancement for herself and her family – and would probably have stuck it out save for Jack's total and irremediable awfulness) would have set Sennett back on its feet. And with an heir to follow poor Jack...

'Where's Mr Daventry?' she asked him. 'Where's Ned, Charles? I gathered that he had joined your ship. Is he with you tonight?'

Oakshott shook his head.

'He's – gone?'

He nodded. She began to weep quietly.

'We got a bloody nose at Toulon,' said Oakshott, 'but we gave as good as we received. Saved a lot of folk from those murderous devils, along with ships – good ships – that we either took or burned. And lost a lot of good men.'

'Like Ned.'

'Like Ned.'

Her head bowed upon his shoulder and he comforted her.

'I – I'm sorry about Jack, Sennett and all,' she said. 'If only it could have been you, Charles. If only you could have been the older brother.'

He squeezed her hand. To his surprise, it was uncommonly small and soft, and the eyes that looked up at him were full of warm promise: a far cry from the cold grey ocean of winter, the blizzard blowing down Whitehall outside.

'Are you living far from here?' he asked.

'I've lodgings in a basement in Pimlico,' she said. 'It's very cosy.'

'I'll go and get a cab,' he said.

In October of that year, Harriet, Marchioness of Uffingham & Bow was brought to bed of an heir to the marquisate: a baby boy of ten pounds, with the lungs of a bosun's mate, a thriving thatch of raven-dark hair, the promise of his ancestoress's vari-coloured eyes, and the Oakshott family looks written all over him.

The sixth marquess, seated in a comfortable chair near the carved and gilded font in the private chapel of Sennett Palace, his gout-ridden and copiously bandaged foot stuck out before him, took nips from a brandy flask while viewing the proceedings.

Harriet had unexpectedly returned to him in February, and that was a blessing, for he had unaccountably missed her. Through the miasma of brandy, port and claret in which he now spent his waking life from morn till night, he seemed to have no recollection of coupling with her a-plenty since her return – indeed, he could not call to mind a single occasion; but the living proof was there, screaming as it was dipped wholesale into the font water: the Reverend Mr Clarence Hardcourt-ffinch, hunting parson and three-bottle man, was also a staunch supporter of cold baths to quench Old Adam in the young male.

The marquess's eyelids drooped. It was unfortunate that he no longer had the capacity – nor, indeed, much desire – to take his spear to the lists of Hymen (to quote grandfather's colourful phrase), but at least let it be said that one had fulfilled one's obligations to the family succession; to great-great-great-grandma Eulalia's memory; to poor, cuckolded Alexander, first of the title.

The marquess momentarily roused himself and caught the eye of his brother Charlie, who was standing as godfather to the baby along with Squire Horrocks of Mondisfield Hall, and that toothsome Irene Chancellor, who, as godmother, had taken the half-drowned heir of Uffingham & Bow from the zealous parson.

They smiled at each other, Charlie and he. And then the older brother fell asleep, missing the rest of the proceedings, including the three hour sermon upon the blessings of family life, interspersed with anecdotes of the hunting field and allied topics.

Charles Oakshott was experiencing a great sense of relief – as well he might have. The succession – in the form of the robust, screaming, raven-headed young monster whom Hardcourt-ffinch had come near to consigning to Davy Jones's locker had it not been for the swift intervention of Irene Chancellor, who was now handing it to its mother – was safe.

His future in the Royal Navy was assured, also: a letter from the Board lay in his coat-tail pocket, and was the object of his present rejoicing.

But – let it be said that the sweet curve of Irene Chancellor's eyebrow was more immediate, this day, than the desert of grey ocean and the far-off, storm-tossed ships that held the line for England.